THE CIPHER

THE
CIPHER

Genni Gunn

Signature
EDITIONS

Cover design by Doowah Design.
Photo of Genni Gunn by Tom Hawkins.

This book was printed on Ancient Forest Friendly paper.
Printed and bound in Canada by Hignell Book Printing Inc.

Library and Archives Canada Cataloguing in Publication

Title: The cipher / Genni Gunn.
Names: Gunn, Genni, 1949- author
Identifiers: Canadiana 20240417968
| ISBN 9781773241425 (softcover)
Subjects: LCSH: World War, 1939-1945—Italy—Fiction. | LCGFT: Historical fiction. | LCGFT: Novels.
Classification: LCC PS8563.U572 C57 2024 | DDC C813/.54—dc23

We acknowledge the support of the Canada Council for the Arts the Manitoba Arts Council, and the Manitoba Government for our publishing program.

Canada Council   Conseil des arts   MANITOBA   CONSEIL DES ARTS   Manitoba
for the Arts   du Canada   ARTS COUNCIL DU MANITOBA

Signature Editions
P.O. Box 206, RPO Corydon, Winnipeg, Manitoba, R3M 3S7
www.signature-editions.com

In loving memory
of my father

Leo Donati
(1919 – 1972)

The struggle for liberty is clearly not over. Far from it. The threat to liberty is greater than it was forty years ago, because of the fanatical passions searing the hundreds of millions who are abandoning traditional ways of life and looking for a better future.

Most states today are ruled by dictatorships, some old, many new. It is easy for people in free countries to talk about uprisings and revolutions, to relax while waiting for popular agitation to express itself and overthrow dictatorships. The twentieth-century experience shows that within a country ruled by dictators, a few may feel the moral duty of standing for liberty; but that the work of conspirators rarely achieves its aim unless those who live freely in free countries give a helping hand.

Massimo Salvadori
from *The Labour and the Wounds*, 1958

INTERMISSION

Pozzecco, Italy, 2010

It begins with a lawyer's letter: my father is in hospital in Trieste.
I have not spoken to him in years, not since he moved back to Italy seventeen years ago. After my mother died, I gouged him out of my life, certain he had been the cause of her anguish. In that charged, desperate time, I didn't write to tell him of her death. Let him discover it for himself. Each new resentment added to the rest, like gauze wound tightly against grief.

Memory is unpredictable and unstable. Sometimes, I can transform my happy childhood incidents into betrayals; see familiar faces as strangers, curious looks as critical ones, half-smiles as sneers, laughing eyes as ridicule. Everything shifting. Sometimes, my memories feel like impulsive choices, re-envisionings, erasures. Is my father really the monster I've created?

Unrecognizable at the hospital, his face is a mesh of crisscrossing tubes, eye sockets swollen, cheeks bruised and scraped, forehead bandaged. "A week ago, he tripped on the street," the attendant says. "A fall." I recreate the father of my youth, proud, tall on the pedestal we put him on. *A fall.* He lies in an induced coma. What do I know of him, really, his life compressed into secret sediments I'd like to excavate. He was a series of entrances and exits. Running towards and away from us.

I return to my father's home in Pozzecco, and prowl dank, darkened rooms for clues, tiptoe past six identical bedrooms, their doors ajar, their walls alive with the austere portraits of the dead, whose remains lie in the cemetery nearby, whose youthful faces stare from photos encased in glass on the tombstones. Now, no one is left to remember them; they have become droplets of rain, sinking underground, fragments of lives, cryptic and impenetrable.

My heart flutters in my chest, my stomach churns in anxiety. How odd to be back, so far from my Vancouver home, in this old house, among strange sounds and childhood nocturnal fears. My father grew up here, motherless, fatherless, raised by his aunt Isabella. And years ago, he returned, like a sea turtle drawn back to his birthplace, only he came not to nest, but to die.

The seventh bedroom belongs to my father — an unmade bed, an open wardrobe, three hanging suits, black boots and suede lace-up oxfords neatly lined up below them, white shirts folded on a shelf, grey cardigan hung on a hook. A room awaiting his return.

In the wardrobe to one side are stacked banker's boxes.

One by one, I open each and plough through a barrage of bills, articles clipped from newspapers, old magazines, theatre tickets, wedding invitations, the archeology of a life compressed. One box contains the letters and postcards I sent him, wrapped in tissue paper, a blue ribbon around them — letters written to him in my child's hand when I was four, five, six, eight, ten. I'm afraid to open them, terrified of my raw childhood yearning — evidence I can't sanitize or demonize. Tears come unbidden, and I wipe them away impatiently.

I've been trained to look with a dispassionate eye, to observe and document. I am an archivist at the Vancouver Archives, a custodian of society's memory. I scan through data, teasing out details, connections, retaining relationships between records, trying to understand their chronology and significance. For years, I've been curating the past and present, deciding what to preserve to mark this present time. Sometimes, I make copies of mysterious documents and take them home to solve them, as if they were cold cases. A letter addressed to an unknown lover; a birth certificate of an unnamed child; photographs of a house long demolished. I pore over these items, underlining words and phrases, searching for the subtexts that link one file to another, one narrative to another.

Right now, I stare at the letters in my hand, the evidence of loneliness and longing. I should have stayed home, safe, where I couldn't be undone by my childhood, where I couldn't be so easily dropped from one fold of memory to the next.

I turn back to the banker's boxes. The last one is older than the rest, its yellowed cardboard water-damaged and smudged, its lid affixed with packing tape. Pandora's box. I pull a nail file from my bag and cut the tape.

Inside are his treasures: a postcard from his uncle Claudio, a wooden Masai Kenyan mask, a small straw basket, a terracotta *fischietto* — the whistle, good-luck charm from Puglia — an embroidered handkerchief, a photo of Mount Etna, an Omega military watch, and an 1898 Bible with gilt-edged pages, beneath which lies a small book, with lettering declaring it to be a *Soldier's Service and Paybook*. I open it. My father's youthful face stares back, above someone else's name — Nardo Cassar — then below, "Enlisted into the British army March 18, 1942."

There must be some mistake. My father's name is Nino. He is Italian. How could he have been in the British army? I flash through our short lives together: the silences, the absences, the tension, the unspoken strife between my parents, the echo of their tones — a dissonant symphony on replay, the heart attack my father suffered in his forties, my leaving home, my father's desertion, my mother's death.

It all begins anew when an oval photograph of a lovely young woman falls from the book's interior, edges darkened and uneven, as if once it had been inside a frame. I turn it over. *Olivia, my love.*

I catch my breath, press the paybook and photograph against my chest, to divine their secrets, thinking *evidence*, trying to position the clues within the folder of my father's life.

"You mustn't upset him," my mother always said. "His heart is damaged."

Damage of the heart. Loss, loneliness, love.

Part 1

BEFORE

1

London, 1939 / 1940

On the day Great Britain and France declared war on Germany, Olivia Baldini sat in her Fourth Form history class, carefully aligning the edges of her notes, so they formed a uniform pile.

"War," Mr. Chambers said, "is filled not only with glorious wins but with heroic defeats." His students sat up a little straighter. They all considered Mr. Chambers slightly odd. Things came out of his mouth they didn't expect. He quoted obscure passages from plays and poetry they hadn't studied, as if they could understand their meaning. *"By these arms the monster of Nemea lies crushed; upon this neck I upheld the sky!"* he said now. Olivia shifted in her seat, thinking of Ovid in the *Metamorphoses*. She knew the quote came from there, because Ovid belonged to her Italian heritage. She had been taking Italian language and literature classes since she was six. Even though she'd never been to Italy, her father was born there, and he wanted her to preserve a connection to the old country, though he himself had left close to twenty years before. Even his father had left, only instead of coming to Britain, he'd settled in France. Olivia hadn't been to France, either. One day, she wanted to travel and see how the world measured up to the one depicted in books. While Mr. Chambers continued his lecture, she quietly took pens and pencils out of her school bag, and slowly lined them up on her desk, until the left edge formed a perfect line. The ensuing pattern pleased her, the way the straight edge contrasted the jagged right-hand side. She realigned the pens and pencils, put the longest one at the bottom, so they formed a kind of triangle.

"Jack Cornwell," Mr. Chambers said, "was no older than you lot. Yet he fought in a war and earned a Victoria Cross." He frowned at Olivia, and she stopped fiddling with the pens while he delivered a familiar monologue of battles fought in WWI, of death and heroics. General this and General that, Olivia heard, thinking history was full of men hailed as heroes, leaving out the women who were as brave and daring. Surely, he'd read all those Greek and Roman myths, populated by heroines. To this end, she had been searching the library and discovering a multitude of women who were indispensable during various wartimes, like Epipole of Carystus, one of the first women to have disguised herself as a man to fight in a war; or Fu Hao, who in the 13th century led numerous military campaigns; or Zenobia, who led armies into battle against the Roman Empire. The more Olivia had read, the longer the list grew. She had brought these lists to class, but Mr. Chambers had dismissed them.

Olivia squirmed in her seat. She was fifteen, a pale, slender girl, with shoulder-length hair swept off her face with a ribbon headband. She felt restless and impatient, as if something were about to happen.

"We must be wary in the coming months," Mr. Chambers said. "We exist in a delicate balance," though he didn't say with what exactly. Olivia imagined the entire island of Britain rising out of the sea, poised on the peak of a seamount. She picked up a pencil and balanced it on the back of her middle finger, trying to hold it perfectly still. Mr. Chambers spoke of race laws, invasions — signposts to an inevitable war. Olivia listened, but instead of fear, she felt anger at Britain's inaction.

"Three years ago," Mr. Chambers said, "when in October, Nazi Germany and Fascist Italy signed a treaty of cooperation…"

Years scrolled back like a ticker tape and stopped at 1936, months spiralled and settled on October, focused on the weeks — fifty-two circles of sevens, then onto the U-shape of the twenty-fifth — all happening in a split second. *October 25, 1936. A cloudy, rainy evening. I'm with my brother Aldo, my parents, and my younger brother Mick on a train platform in Victoria Station. A train headlight bores through the fog, and I hear the thunderous weight of steel on steel, the prolonged screech of brakes. The doors open and men and women spill out, their faces searching for loved ones. Their faces imprint into the Rolodex in my brain. Aldo moves towards one of the doors and we follow. He is wearing his long brown winter coat. He hugs Mamma and Papa, then Mick, then turns to me. I can smell the tobacco on his coat. He wraps me in his arms, murmuring reassuring words while I cry. Then he boards. The train slides out of the station, and I run alongside for a final look. Aldo's arm waves from a train window. Papa catches up and holds me back, while I memorize everything: the shouts, the laughter, the warning whistle of an oncoming train, the rain pelting the metal roof, Mamma's soft sobs, Papa's reassuring words, my own heavy heart beating. What if he never comes back? We walk through a throng of people, who are all returning, meeting loved ones. Ours is gone. Back home, I run upstairs and write in my diary every detail I can remember of those last few minutes. I vow to never forget.*

"Olivia," Mr. Chambers said sharply, and she looked up. "Are you daydreaming?"

"Sorry." Olivia sat up straighter, trying to focus on the present. The word "October" had triggered her, sending her back in time, to that particular day when her hyper-remembering began. She wasn't sure how or why it happened, exactly, but she could recall every single moment of her life since then, in extreme detail, and re-experience all the original emotions as if they were occurring in the present. It exhausted her, her mind a film reel on which the past constantly assailed the present, dates or the naming of events activating her mental calendar. While Mr. Chambers talked of Germany's aggression, of Italy's invasion of Albania, Olivia thought about her older brother, Aldo, at the train station to "visit the grandparents" in Italy, as her father would say, though Olivia sensed he had gone there to *do* something. She was sure of it. He was with the partisans, or the communists, or some other similar organization. She would love to join him.

Aldo. *His arm waves from the train window.* A lump began at the back of her throat, and Olivia swallowed, trying once again to focus on the present. Let it go. Let it go.

An alarm sounded unexpectadly, calling all students to an assembly.

"Britain has declared war on Germany," the Headmaster said.

Some of the boys whooped, as if this news were good, but one of the schoolmasters cuffed them, and they became silent. They returned to their classrooms, somewhat glum, confused, not knowing how this event would personally affect them. War. Olivia wasn't sure what to think. If Britain had declared war on Germany, and Italy had aligned with Germany, didn't that mean Britain was at war with Italy? She didn't want to ask anyone, and when Mr. Chambers dismissed his students, she waited by her locker for her friend, Barbara, who would surely know.

Before Barbara had moved to the neighborhood, Olivia had felt as if she were living in a world in which everyone had amnesia. A tall, gangly French girl, Barbara was a straight-A student, who had an echoic memory. Fluent in French, German, Spanish and Italian, Barbara recalled sounds the way Olivia recalled moments of her life. The girls had bonded over their unusual gifts, and Olivia finally felt she had found a kindred spirit.

Where was Barbara now? Olivia closed her locker and waited. They always met at the end of the school day. Students streamed past her and out the doors, their voices mingled with the scuffs of their shoes, their heavy footsteps. When twenty minutes had passed and most students had left, Olivia walked to the end of the hall and stared at the low grey clouds, the rain. Ten more minutes passed, and still no Barbara. Olivia glanced at the hands of the large clock set in the wall a few metres away. She'd wait another ten minutes, and then leave. The hands shifted methodically every minute, and Olivia imagined she could hear the complex whirring of gears. Finally, when she was about to give up, Barbara came hurrying down the hallway, loaded with bags, which she dropped in front of Olivia.

"Sorry I'm late. I had to clear out my locker." She knelt next to the bags, and upended them so books, notebooks, papers, pens, pencils, food wrappers, a scarf, a sweater, and mittens, all spilled out.

"But why?" Olivia asked, bewildered.

"I'll be going away," Barbara said. "My parents have already made arrangements for me to go to stay with my cousin in Cornwall."

She sighed. "They've been ready for this for a while." She began to sort and pack the items back into the bags.

"Why didn't you tell me?" Olivia said, expressing her dismay.

"It wouldn't have made any difference," Barbara said. "I was hoping this would never happen."

"But why must you go?" Olivia said. "If Britain's at war, doesn't that mean everywhere will be unsafe?"

"Maybe," Barbara said, "but no one's going to bother bombing some little country village. Or at least, they're less likely to." She frowned. "They'll be bombing strategically, like military zones, ship-building, ports, that kind of stuff."

Olivia said nothing, staring at her friend. She memorized the way Barbara's blonde hair swirled around her face, how she bit her lip while thinking; she memorized Barbara's black-and-white checked skirt, her white sweater. . .*I'll be going away...*

"Hey," Barbara said, "it's not like I'm dying." She smiled. "I'll be back as soon as it's safe."

"Sure," Olivia said, unconvinced.

"I'll write to you as soon as I get there," Barbara said.

"Sure," Olivia said again.

"One sec," Barbara said, rooting in her bag. "Mum gave me the address just in case..." She withdrew a small notebook and found the right page. "Copy this down. If anything should happen, this is where I'll be." She stood up and embraced Olivia. "It's just temporary, you'll see."

They left together, then after another hug, each turned towards home. Olivia walked slowly, perturbed by Barbara's news.

A group of schoolboys stood on a corner, Jerry among them. She made herself walk past them calmly, avoiding the cracks in the sidewalk as she went.

"Fascist!" one of the boys said.

She turned, startled. "What?"

"You're Eyetalian, aren't you?" One of the boys sneered.

"What's wrong with you?" she said. "I'm as British as you are." She was born here, lived in the same neighbourhood. They *knew* her. She looked at Jerry, but he avoided her eyes. A wave of panic broke over her. *Jerry. July 16. A hot, muggy day. The end-of-term school dance. I'm helping at the coat check, when Jerry walks towards me. My cheeks are burning, my breath pounds. He stops in front of me and asks me to dance.* In a split second, Olivia relived every look, every step, the walk home, the near kiss, glued to the flow of those sweet moments, before turning away, and hurrying past the boys, whose laughter followed her down the street.

After that, having the Italian surname Baldini was not easy for Olivia. She was already judged as a little weird, partly because students considered her obsessively meticulous, and partly because she could recall dates and events in such detail. While before they simply called her *weirdo*, now their vocabulary included *fascist* and *wop*. She looked up the meaning of *wop* and its etymology made no sense to her. 1912. American English slang. The word came from the Italian dialect *guappo*, meaning a swaggering, boisterous man from Naples, possibly connected to the Camorra mafia. What had this to do with her? She asked her father why they were calling her this slur. Wasn't she British? She'd never even been to Italy, and had spent her entire life so far in Britain. "They're ignorant," her father said. "Don't listen to them."

The following week, the form tutor issued gas masks to all students, and each day, the students practised putting them on, huddling under their desks, using their flashlights. At night, Olivia and her parents gathered around the radio, listening to the news bulletins, fearful of air-raid reports. Papa dug a large hole in the small yard behind their house, in which he fit a government-issued Anderson air-raid shelter. Mamma stocked the shelter with woollen blankets, canned goods, and bottles of water, which Olivia rearranged by item and size. The government strictly enforced blackouts, and at night, the family stumbled about the house using flashlights and candles. On the street, cars were black silhouettes, their headlights masked into the slits of wolf eyes.

In early November, snow began to fall, and frost sheathed the limbs of trees. Teardrops gathered at the edge of branches, fell, melted, then froze into treacherous ice ponds — the most severe winter in Great Britain since 1895. The extreme shortages of basic goods made matters worse.

The government began to evacuate 400,000 children, as well as women with infants, from cities to rural areas. Rampant fear consumed the population. However, when by February no bombs had fallen, half of the evacuated children returned home.

Olivia's brother Mick began speaking of wanting to enlist. "I can't stay here and do nothing!" he said. He was seventeen, not old enough yet, working in their parents' café downstairs, and for the past few months, after closing, he had hosted meetings of socialist activists.

"We need you here," Papa said. He'd heard that Aldo had joined the Italian Communist Party and was constantly in danger, and he could not bear the idea of sending another son to war before his time.

"I have to do something!" Mick said. All spring, at night, they listened to the broadcasts: the Soviet Union invaded Poland; Warsaw surrendered and the Polish government fled; Germany and the Soviet Union divided Poland between them; the Soviet Union invaded Finland; Germany invaded Denmark and Norway, France, the Netherlands, Belgium, surging through Europe, surrounding British, Belgian, and French troops on the beaches of Dunkirk, where a fleet of 800 vessels rescued 300,000 men; France signed an armistice agreement with the Germans, who occupied the northern half of the country and the Atlantic coastline. The Germans seemed unstoppable.

A week later, Mick quietly slipped away, lied about his age, and enlisted in the Merchant Navy, leaving only a note.

Mamma was frantic. Two sons gone.

A few weeks after Mick's departure, on June 10, 1940, Italy entered the war and invaded southern France.

That night, a fierce knocking at the door of the house awakened Olivia. Her bedside clock read a quarter to three a.m. She scrambled up, wrapped a dressing gown over her pajamas, and followed her father and mother down the stairs.

"Open up!" the voices shouted.

Papa unlocked the door. Two officers stood on the sill. "Carlo Baldini?" one said, flashing his Special Branch identification.

"What's wrong?" Papa said, alarmed. "What's happened? Is it my son?"

The officer shook his head impatiently. "You're under arrest," he said. "Get dressed quickly and pack one bag."

Olivia's mother put her arm around Olivia's waist and pulled her close.

Papa frowned, bewildered. "But on what charge?" he said.

"Orders. We're rounding up all Italian-born citizens," the officer said, looking past Papa. "Where are your sons?" He strode across the room and yanked two photographs in their frames from the wall: one of Vittorio Emmanuele III, the King of Italy, and the other of Il Duce, Benito Mussolini. "Fascists!" he hissed. One of the frames slipped from his hand, and glass shattered across the floor.

"But we are British citizens," Papa said. Olivia and her mother now stood behind him, holding their dressing gowns tight across their bodies. "I've been here more than twenty years." He ran a hand through his hair. "My family," and here he waved his arm to include the two women, "are all British born. We are not fascists. I am a simple café owner."

The officer consulted his notebook. "Where are your sons?" he asked again, shifting from foot to foot.

Papa shook his head. "One is in the British Navy and the other is in Italy visiting his grandparents."

The officer sneered at the word "Italy" as if the word substantiated Papa's arrest. He scribbled something in the notebook, then waved his hand in front of Papa's face. "Hurry now. Get dressed and pack a few things. We have no time to lose."

"Where are you taking my husband? What has he done?" Mamma asked, stepping forward.

The two officers ignored her.

"But when is Papa coming back?" Olivia said, her voice tremulous.

The officers stared her up and down, shook their heads, but said nothing. While Papa and Mamma went upstairs to do the men's bidding, Olivia cowered by the stairs, wondering why they were detaining her father, who was the gentlest of men. *Coming back, coming back.* The words began repeating in her head, a mantra, a premonition.

The whole exchange lasted less than twenty minutes. Mamma packed toiletries, a change of clothes and underwear. Papa dressed, and then gathered his heavy winter coat and folded it over his arm. Olivia's arms encircled his neck, unwilling to let go. He kissed her, then embraced Mamma. "Can you tell me where I'm going?" he said, but the two officers ushered him out without another word.

When the door clicked shut, Mamma collapsed in a kitchen chair, sobbing, while Olivia rubbed her shoulder. "It's those fascists!" Mamma said. "Their arms can reach even here!" She wiped her tears angrily, got up, and retrieved the Mussolini photograph. She spit on it, before ripping it to shreds. She had never wanted it on the wall, but Papa had insisted they keep it there, lest someone betray their anti-fascist sentiments to the Italian Consulate. He feared Aldo's fate back in Italy. Mamma switched on the radio and turned the dial, trying in vain to find some explanation. "Clean up that shattered glass," she said.

Olivia got out the broom and dustpan. She began with the largest shards and made piles of glass according to size. *Shattered*, she thought, hearing the word rebound in her head. Her own tears began, though she'd been trying to hold them back. "What are we to do now?"

Mamma stopped twisting the radio dials and drew herself up. She took the broom out of Olivia's hand and swept all the glass into one large pile, which she pushed into the dustpan. "We will open the café as usual," she said. "We will hold our heads high." She pulled Olivia into an embrace, patting her back.

"Let's get some rest now," she said, and the two of them went upstairs.

At the door of her bedroom, Mamma turned and kissed Olivia, murmuring, "Tomorrow, I'll make inquiries. This is all a mistake. It'll be all right, you'll see."

Olivia went to her own room and lay down, her head filled with questions and fear. *Fascists!* The word circled in her head until it settled into a sign she'd seen long ago in the Italian Consul offices. THE ITALIAN FASCIST CLUB. *December 12, 1936, snow, an ice storm. Mamma does not want to go, and Papa is yelling that he has to be a member in order to pay taxes on property he owns in Italy. Does she want him to forfeit his land? Mamma frowns but says nothing. She's London-born, of Italian-British parents who have been in Britain for several generations. Why should she care about a plot of land she's never seen in a village in northern Italy? She met Papa here in London twenty-one years ago, when he came to look for work. I know she hates being forced to attend these "meetings." I hate it, too, because we have nothing to do with fascists. Papa says they're more social gatherings, featuring dances and card games, rather than politics, but his voice is not convincing. We arrive after dark, slipping and sliding on the icy roads. The Consul gives a speech about Italy's ongoing war with Abyssinia. He doesn't say "invasion" though I know that's what it is. He asks the married women in the room to remove their wedding bands and put them in a basket as a gift to Il Duce, to help the war effort. Mamma looks at Papa, her eyes stricken. The audience applauds. She follows the women up to the front and deposits her wedding band in the basket. In exchange, she receives a steel band with the inscription "Oro alla Patria 12.12.36," Gold for the Fatherland. Mamma sobs quietly on the way home, and Papa keeps his arm around her shoulders, his eyes shiny with tears. "La fede," she whispers when they're back home. "Faith," the Italian name for a wedding band. She twirls the steel band round and round her finger. "What kind of man takes a woman's wedding band to use for blood money?"*

After that night, her parents never returned to the club, though possibly her father had paid his property tax there. Olivia now wished she'd been more alert, more attuned to her father's motives. And now he had been arrested for no reason and taken who knows where.

In the morning, a radio broadcast reported that a special branch of the government had rounded up several thousand men of Italian origin as enemy aliens and had taken them away for internment at an undisclosed location. As well, anyone of Italian origin over sixteen years of age was forbidden to ride a bicycle, drive a car, a sea-going vessel or aircraft without police permission. Mamma abruptly turned off the radio. "Come on," she said to Olivia, who hovered over her, unsure what to do. "We're going down to open the café."

Downstairs, the café remained empty after they opened, and none of their regular customers turned up. The streets were strangely deserted. Slowly, a sound emerged, muffled at first, like a radio left on in another room, then as it neared, more audible. Olivia and her mother heard men's agitated voices, a commotion. Olivia rushed to the doorway and watched a crowd slowly advancing, chanting, throwing stones through windows of other Italian establishments. "Mamma," she said, panicked. "We must lock up and go upstairs. Quickly!" She and her mother fled as the crowd advanced.

From behind the curtain of an upstairs window, they watched a mob of several hundred men push carts filled with stones and hurl them through windows until the street became a corridor of broken glass shimmering in the daylight sun. When they heard shouts below them, Olivia and Mamma flattened themselves against the sides of the window, terrified to think of those men downstairs, smashing everything, looting. Olivia recognized some of the men, men who only yesterday were drinking coffee, standing at the bar, chatting with Papa. How had they become enemies in a single night?

They remained upstairs as the mob moved on, until an eerie silence fell over the street. Gingerly, they tiptoed downstairs to find shattered glass, upended tables and chairs, jagged china bits on the floor, mangled espresso machines, and display cases fractured and crushed. The open door hung on one hinge, its wooden front split and splintered. They pushed it shut as best they could, and placed a table against it to hold it together. Then, they went back upstairs.

Mamma sat down and made a list of what they'd need. She was a different person, calm and in control. She went downstairs, pulled a light jacket from the coat hook by the door and slipped into it.

"I'm going to Uncle James's to see what we can do," she said. "Lock the door behind me, then go upstairs and stay there till I get back."

Olivia nodded, kissed her mother, and did as her mother asked. She watched Mamma cross the street and head towards Uncle James's house. He had connections. Surely he would have news of Papa and know what to do. She tried to settle down, thinking Barbara was right to leave. It wasn't safe here. No bombs were falling; the enemy was their own neighbours, their own countrymen. In her bedroom, she browsed her bookcase. Reading calmed her, removed her from the present, and immersed her in others' lives, lives less frightening than hers felt right now. She took down *Rebecca*. She'd read it when it was published a couple of years before. *December 25, 1938, dry bitterly cold day, snow flurries. Christmas morning. Mamma, Papa, and Mick sit around the tree, awaiting my reaction. How happy they look! How happy we all are!* Her brain skimmed the intro of the book, and stopped at the passage where the narrator recalls the room without its inhabitants: *"The little heap of library books marked ready to return, and the discarded copy of* The Times. *Ashtrays, with the stub of a cigarette; cushions, with the imprint of our heads upon them, lolling in the chairs.*" She felt this absence now, her family abruptly split apart. What if officers from the special branch took her mother away and she never returned? Olivia scanned the shelves to make sure the books were in alphabetical order, though no one, other than her, had entered her room, then she tapped each title on the spine. She took a deep breath, and sat down, the book open on her lap. Presently, she began to read, and the anxiety in her chest abated.

Several hours later, in early afternoon, Mamma returned with two workers bearing sheets of plywood to cover the windows, and new hinges and brackets to mount at the sides of the door, along with a wooden bar slid across it to keep them safe. "We'll brazen this out," she said. "I refuse to be intimidated in my own country."

The week passed slowly, each day a silent reminder that Papa was gone, and they knew not where. At night, they listened to the broadcasts, looked at the newspapers, but could find nothing. In the daytime, Olivia began work at a shipping office — a job Uncle James had found for her, knowing their circumstances. Olivia was grateful she could contribute financially now that Papa was gone and the café was in shambles.

One night, when Olivia arrived home, Mamma took her hand, and bade her sit down. "You know I love you, Olivia," Mamma began, "but I don't feel it's safe for you to be here, not until we hear something from Papa." She paused. "I've had a letter from Kent."

Olivia closed her eyes. She concentrated on the sound of paper rustling in Mamma's hand. Letters always brought bad news: death, illness, loss of jobs, heartbreak, or banishment.

"Grandma and Grandpa have kindly invited you to go and stay with them for a while." Mamma put up her hand to still Olivia's objections. "Just until things settle." She took a deep breath and let it out slowly. "I intend to go with Uncle James to see what I can find out about Papa. It would be best if I didn't have to worry about you here alone."

"What about my job?" Olivia said.

"You can keep working and commute to Kent." Mamma sighed. "It's the best solution," she said. "You'll be safe at work during the day, and safe at night with your grandparents."

The following week, Olivia, Mamma and Uncle James stood on a platform of the Victoria train station…*the doors open and men and women spill out*…where after a few tight embraces, Olivia boarded, as they waved goodbye. She stared after them as the train left the station, memorizing every detail of their faces, their clothes, their outstretched hands, all superimposed on the time when Aldo left, only now her arm waved from the open window, as she watched the small girl she once was receding into the distance.

The days passed slowly with no news. Olivia made herself concentrate on her training at work. Mamma had closed up the house, and entrusted the café to Uncle James. Olivia had no way of reaching her. The uncertainty made her anxious. Finally, two weeks later, a letter arrived from Mamma. Olivia's father had been contacted by the Italian Ambassador and offered two possibilities: to be deported to Italy or to go to Canada to an internment camp. Italy had seemed the best solution. She and Papa had had to make a difficult decision: "I couldn't let him go alone," Mamma wrote. "And we tried to decide whether it would be possible for you to join us, but in the end, Papa felt you are much safer there with your grandparents. They're British, so no one will bother them. My dear Olivia, this is the safest place for you…"

Olivia sat motionless, the letter in her hand. How could her parents have left without her? She set the letter down beside her and moved her knife and fork so they formed two sides of a square outside her plate, then added a spoon across the top. She thought about the last full day with her mother, and began to cry as a sudden replay began… *June 11, mild cloudy day. Mamma and I frantically lock down the café, run upstairs, then watch those men, those familiar faces who only yesterday joked with Papa and spoke politely to Mamma, They advance with their cart of rocks, as if we were the enemy. But we have done nothing. Now they are here, below us, frenzied with hatred I don't understand. Mamma's and my hands are joined tightly. Mamma is mouthing a prayer, "Dear God help us!" Below, men hurl stones through the windows. I wince at each shatter, each blow, and close my eyes…* Grandma covered Olivia's hand with her own. "They'll be all right," she said, squeezing Olivia's hand. "I promise. Things will be okay."

Olivia had nodded, though she didn't believe they'd be all right at all. They were headed into a war.

2

Abyssinia, 1941

Nino Fabris crouched at the entrance of a shallow cave in Abyssinia, tense and vigilant.

A high-pitched whistle pierced the night. Nino half-stood, reaching for his revolver, fear reverberating through him.

"Bird," one of the men said, motioning him back down. "A nightjar."

Nino nodded, unconvinced. The local tribesmen were expert mimics of bird whistles. He listened carefully to the rhythmic call, waiting for the sound of footsteps, the white robes and truncheons.

He was one of eight Italians scattered in caverns and under rock ledges, soldiers belonging to different units, without orders, each fleeing into an inevitable trap. What irony, he thought, to rely on these soldiers, many of whom were fascist sympathizers, who a generation ago might have tried to kill his entire family. He was no more a communist than his father or uncle had been, but he was staunchly opposed to Mussolini's regime. Not that any of this mattered right now, when he, like the others, was merely trying to survive. Addis Ababa had already surrendered to the British, and any Italian soldiers who were still free had fled or were fleeing to the mountain fortress of Amba Alagi where 4,000 Italians were mounting a last stand.

All day, they'd trudged across a desert plateau of sandstone canyons, through dry gravel riverbeds and burning salt flats. The chilled night wind howled through him. He tightened his jacket, still unaccustomed to the vast temperature changes: in the day he choked on hot dusty air, the temperature over forty degrees, yet at night his teeth chattered.

"We're all going to die," his friend Elio said, his voice raspy with phlegm. He lowered his head into his hands. A reedy nineteen-year-old, unfit for battle, he leaned over and spat on the ground. He didn't belong here any more than Nino did. It seemed so long ago that they were radio operators on a merchant ship, dreaming of exotic travel. But the war had changed all that, their ship requisitioned to replenish forces, arms, ammunition and medical supplies in Italian East Africa. They'd been on shore duty when their ship was attacked in Massawa and lucky to have escaped, Nino thought. And luckier still to have found a convoy of soldiers and motor vehicles, the remnants of an army headed to Amba Alagi. Yet that convoy, too, had been attacked, and again, Nino and Elio had survived, along with six soldiers.

"We're not going to die," Nino said, though he, too, felt doomed by the senseless trek uphill to evade capture, to a destination that would render them easy targets for British planes.

Every sound unnerved him: strangled cries, groans of wounded soldiers, squeals and grunts, spine-tingling whoops, mocking laughter. *Hyenas.* He forced himself to remain sitting, focusing on the night sky that extended to eternity in a scaffolding of stars. He wondered if Aunt Isabella was watching these same stars, whether her skies flared with explosions. He hadn't heard from her in months.

In early dawn, he spotted the black shape before he heard the rumble of a biplane overhead flying low, machine-gunning.

The men flattened themselves against outcrops. Gunners fired at the airplane with such fury, it flashed, hovered in mid-air, then burst into flames and nosedived towards them in a high-pitched squeal, exploding as it hit the ground.

Nino watched the pilot's slow descent, his parachute open, his easy capture.

The men broke camp, ready to resume their advance. One called Nino and thrust the British pilot at him. "Take him away and shoot him," he said.

The pilot was a pale boy, twenty, twenty-one, his uniform ripped, and one side of his face swollen and bloodied. Nino's heart pounded in his ears. He prodded the boy forward with his gun, until they were behind a craggy cliff. The pilot turned, arms up, palms open in surrender. For a brief moment, in the pilot's face Nino saw his cousin, the one living in Britain.

He raised his rifle, and while the boy flinched, he shot into the air. "Go now, run," he said, motioning the pilot away. "*Run.*"

The pilot stared at him, confused. He began to run. Stopped. Turned.

What is he waiting for? Nino thought.

He hesitated a moment longer, then ran towards Nino and, crying, hugged him. He slid his watch off his wrist and pressed it into Nino's hands. Then he sprinted away, and dissolved like a mirage swallowed by the clefts and hollows of the steep red canyon walls.

Nino clutched the watch against his heart, mouthing a silent prayer for the pilot, for them all, no different except for their place of birth, their national politics and policies. He hurried back to the others, who were already scrambling up the brown scorched earth.

Three hours into their trek, Elio began coughing. "Hold on a minute," he gasped.

"Are you okay?" Nino asked, and Elio nodded, though clearly, he wasn't. "Let's sit for a moment and rest." He lifted Elio's rucksack from his back, and set it on the ground, then pulled out his water flask and encouraged him to drink.

Elio was ashen, sickly. "Oh, what's the use?" he said.

Nino sat quietly for a moment, thinking Elio was right. They were on a suicide mission. Along the road, they'd met deserters who told stories of countless troops surrendering; of massacres of Italian civilians in the town of Dire Dawa; of the Italian viceroy's negotiation with the British, his surrender of Addis Ababa without a fight, of the governor's subsequent suicide. Nothing made sense. Death and destruction. Folly upon folly.

"Ready?" Nino said, after a quarter hour. In the distance, soldiers and vehicles wavered in the heat like a mirage. He and

Elio were on their own now. *On their own.* He'd spent much of his life in this state, not by choice but by circumstance, although he sometimes wondered whether he created some of this circumstance. Not now, though, not here, with Elio. He raised his binoculars and scanned the horizon. A small file of women came into view, draped in colourful sashes and shawls sheltering them from the sun.

Elio scrambled to his feet, but he was unsteady. For the past week, he had been sniffling and coughing, his legs plodding. He struggled to put on the rucksack.

"Let me help," Nino said, wishing he could carry it, though he was already weighed down with his own rucksack. "There'll be a field hospital up there."

"It's just a cold," Elio said, unconvincingly.

They set off slowly and travelled in the shadow of mountains covered with pink puffs of mimosa and the balloon shapes of candelabra trees, whose milky sap was extremely poisonous. Clouds blanketed the sky, and a driving rain began, all at once. Still, they plodded on against a howling wind, negotiating the damaged tunnel, the roadblocks and blown-up bridges until they found a cave under a crag and settled there for the night. Nino built a small fire, and they ate what was left of their provisions. Elio's cough was worse. He spat brownish phlegm. Nino settled him against the driest part of the cave.

"There it is," Elio said, though he didn't sound enthusiastic.

Nino nodded, staring at the imposing peak of Amba Alagi, shrouded in mist like a malevolent castle in a fairy tale. It truly was a place of evil, of bad luck. Years before, during the first Italian invasion, African troops up there had persisted for nine months, before succumbing to the Italians' mustard gas attack. And before that, in the late 1800s, a force of 3,000 Italian soldiers was surrounded and massacred by Abyssinian troops. Nino shuddered, wondering if they were next, despite the fortifications — dugouts and shelters carved into the rockface, scattered outposts to cover gun positions — all added to the natural spokes and ridges that radiated in all directions. But what good would these be if the British bombed them from above? "We'll be trapped up there," he said.

"Maybe not," Elio said. "We should be optimistic," though his face betrayed his real feelings. He tugged a handkerchief from his pocket and blew his nose.

"Maybe," Nino said, to reassure him.

From the inside pocket of his jacket, Nino withdrew and reread Bianca's letter, in which she told him that having not heard from him, she had gone to Pozzecco and introduced herself to his aunt. *She is lovely and was very welcoming*, Bianca wrote. *We are awaiting your return.* Nino sighed. It was true he hadn't written to Bianca for several months, unsure of his feelings. And now she had gone to his aunt, as if they were engaged. Were they engaged? Neither of them had mouthed the words; he hadn't asked for her hand in marriage. Her parents might well refuse him. Yet, even as he thought this, he knew she had reason to believe they might be engaged. Betrothed. Though he had made no promise, he had made love to her. In the envelope was a small photograph. Bianca stared back at him, lips slightly turned up in a smile. She was small and slender, with wavy black hair swept to one side and held there by a barrette covered in tiny pearls.

"Is that your wife?" Elio asked, reaching for the photo.

Nino shook his head. "No, not wife." He handed the photo to Elio. "*Fidanzata*," uttering the promise he wasn't sure he believed in.

Elio stared at it, then at Nino, before handing it back. "She's very beautiful."

Nino shrugged and gazed at the photograph anew. He'd met Bianca four years before, at the house of his friend Lorenzo, while in Pistoia studying for his International Radio Telegraph certificate. Lorenzo had introduced him to a group of anarchists, who had been fighting against fascism since the start of Mussolini's reign, when two of their friends had been murdered. Bianca was sixteen, a quiet, intense girl. Over several visits, he began to speak to her, bewitched by her beauty, her bright eyes and welcoming smile, and her sincere allegiance to the group. At these sessions — because they were more than parties and less than meetings — Nino and Bianca sat together, witnesses to the stories of violence and resistance. Nino, too, had a similar story his uncle Claudio had told him when, at seventeen, Nino had spent a summer with him in London, learning English, which he needed for entrance into the International Radio Telegraph school. Awakened in the dark by loud knocking and shouting, Uncle Claudio had told him, he had tiptoed to the bedroom window. Their home was secluded, several kilometres outside Udine in northern Italy. Below, a group of armed men shouted, "Communists!" and banged on the door, their lanterns casting sinister elongated shadows across the ground. They'd been drinking and were now intent on entering. Uncle Claudio knew who they were — *squadristi*, fascists who roamed the countryside, intimidating dissenters. "Your grandfather was a union man," Uncle Claudio had told Nino, "and therefore, considered a socialist at a time when Mussolini was rising to power."

"Communists!" the voices yelled, then one of the *squadristi* fired a shot at the door.

Uncle Claudio had hastily dressed, motioned the women and children into an upstairs closet, then he, his father, and brother had gone down, their guns loaded and firing. In the end, Nino's father and grandfather were dead and the house set ablaze. If Nino closed his eyes, he could almost hear loud cracks, his mother's screams, his aunt's wails, his father's cry, then the hiss and bursts of flames that had engulfed his mother. Two of the *squadristi* had died, and the others had run away, after a parting shot that broke Uncle Claudio's femur. The men were never caught, and Uncle Claudio, Aunt Lucia and their two chidren had emigrated to Britain.

His story was no more, no less violent than those of the others.

He thought of those times now, inside the cave in Abyssinia, wondering whether Lorenzo and the group had been conscripted into a war they opposed. Or whether they were involved in some type of armed resistance. He imagined Bianca with them, fierce and faithful, ready to sacrifice herself for them.

When Nino left Pistoia, Bianca had pressed her address into his hand, and he had secretly returned to see her time and time again. Her parents, however, had their sights on a lawyer from Torino, who had already approached Bianca's father with a marriage proposal. Although Bianca had categorically refused this man's advances, her father was hoping she'd change her mind. Though she could frequent friends, her father would not allow her to spend time alone with a man. Bianca, however, was resourceful. In the evening, after everyone was asleep, she would sneak out and meet Nino in the narrow street at the back of her house, between the glow of streetlamps. The first time he went, he parked his motorcycle several blocks away and walked to the street where she met him, arms out, and he felt his heart would burst.

He had never been in love before, and was afraid of the intense emotions he experienced in her arms. Yet away from her, he felt relief, as if he had escaped. He was young, not ready for long-term commitments, his life spread before him as an endless highway of possibilities.

"Will you marry her when the war is over?" Elio asked. "If we make it out alive, I mean."

"I don't know," Nino said. "I'm not even sure I want to live in Italy anymore."

Elio frowned. "It's our home."

Nino remained silent, unwilling to explain how on that teenage visit to his uncle Claudio in Britain, he had understood that outside Italy, there were countries where he could live without concealing his beliefs, and that since then, the word "home" was tinged with violence.

"This war will be over soon," Elio said, then launched into a convulsive coughing burst.

"There'll be a medic up the hill," Nino said again, replacing the photo and letter in the envelope, then the envelope in his pocket. "He'll have something to help that cough."

They huddled together for warmth. Though it was dangerous, they had to travel in daylight, because the terrain was too treacherous. Nino stared into the darkness, wondering what good fleeing to the top of a mountain would do. Maybe he should have surrendered in Massawa and been done with it. Up here, it was unlikely the Italian forces would be able to withstand an assault from the British and their allies. They would probably be killed. He turned on the radio. *In Abyssinia, 30,000 brave Italian troops are holding back British invaders*, Radio Roma broadcast.

"How can that be?" Elio said, his face hopeful.

"Propaganda," Nino said, disgusted by the constant lies perpetrated by the fascists. He turned off the broadcast and closed his eyes. Mussolini believed Italians were not cruel enough, not ready to kill, and he had made it his aim to overhaul them into killing machines. Six years before, in 1935, Mussolini had sent to Africa Rudolfo Graziani, one of the most ruthless military officers, called "the butcher of Fezzan" when he was in Libya, because of his brutal treatment of the people. Graziani built concentration camps in Abyssinia and after an assassination attempt on his life, ordered three days of brutal retribution against the Abyssinians, resulting in the massacre of 20,000 civilians.

Nino tried not to think about all this, the injustice. He envied the deserters and wished himself far away. But where could one go to escape the dark — these scenes etched inside his lids? In his jacket, in a pouch against his heart, he carried the watch of the unknown pilot. A redemption. He wondered if he'd meet the pilot again, if he'd even survived. He yearned for a story in which he would return the watch and nurture a friendship. He yearned for a desertion of the self.

Long after Elio slept, Nino lay awake, recalling a story Aunt Isabella had told him about a cousin who had hidden in the attic of their family home for the duration of the First World War. He could hardly imagine four years of seclusion, the claustrophobia, the fear. He wished he'd met this cousin; he wished he could have asked him how he'd stayed alive, whether he'd made the choice to hide, whether he regretted it, whether he'd found a good life in Argentina, where many Italians had relocated at the end of that war. Perhaps, Nino thought, if he managed to survive, he'd go and see for himself. He daydreamed awhile, imagining Argentina covered in silver filigree. *Argento.* Silver.

He finally fell asleep, and the ground beneath him ruptured into a widening chasm, a cauldron of fire. He couldn't move, straddling the blaze, flinching at each explosion, each flare onto his wrists, his legs. Women wailed, men shouted, flames singed his hair. He was trapped. *Mamma*, he called, but saw only smoke.

"Wake up," Elio said, shaking his shoulder.

Nino opened his eyes: against the dawn light, the cave's interiors were jagged threatening shapes, and beyond, rock formations suddenly came alive as if they were an army come to destroy them. He shook himself awake, broke camp, then half-carried, half-dragged Elio, weaving along knife-edge ridges to ledges, ducking into nooks and crannies sculpted into stone, while bombs fell, exploding, reverberating across the gorges. Adrenalin kept him moving, through the sulphurous air, his mind blank, his only goal to reach the top.

At Fort Toselli, they found the remnants of an air attack — lorries, their chassis burned and jagged, an arm protruding from an open window, doors agape, corpses splayed on the ground, curled as if to evade the shelling, a leg, a torso, blood everywhere. Elio was near unconscious. Nino set him down, then moved like a ghost among the dead, sidestepping doubts and grief, and searched the lorries for provisions, topped up their rucksacks with cans of tuna and prosciutto, packs of *panne duro*, and sweet biscotti, guilty to be profiting from others' misery.

He urged Elio up and continued until, past sundown, he scaled the last ridge, and a soldier helped him carry Elio to a makeshift hospital, where dozens of wounded men lay on dirty cots, awaiting the solitary medic, who leaned down over each of them, deciding what could be done, who could be operated on, who could be bandaged, and who could only be consoled. Soldiers lifted the dead onto stretchers and carried them out. Elio collapsed in a coughing fit, on a blanket on the ground. The air was thick with smoke and dust.

Up here, in the daytime, Nino existed amid the groans and wails of the wounded, in a slow-motion blur of bombshells, grenades, and explosions. Emboldened by the Allies' fierce siege, local tribesmen now emerged to join the fighting, their white robes incongruous in the rain and mud, armed with truncheons and rifles. They beat Italian soldiers, then pushed them over the cliffs to their deaths. A few feet away from Nino, one raised his rifle, but Nino was quicker. There was no choice: you killed or were killed. Nino scrambled from one hidden crevice to another — screams ringing in his ears — sometimes barely a little ahead or a little behind, using the bombing as cover, focusing only on survival.

At night, he closed his eyes and collapsed in dreamless sleep. There was no time for life reflection, for nostalgia and regrets, no time to lie in the darkness and let memory wash over him.

When possible, he climbed to the field hospital to visit Elio, whose coughing and fevers persisted. The medic told him unless Elio was evacuated to a hospital in the city, there was nothing more he could do. Casualties were high, and the relentless attacks didn't allow for the retrieval or evacuation of the dead or wounded from the flanks of the mountain.

Finally, in mid-May, a shell hit a fuel dump and contaminated their only source of drinking water. The Duke of Aosta negotiated an agreement and surrendered to the British.

The next morning, the Italians, exhausted after days and nights of continuous bombardment, trickled down from their redoubts, trenches and grottos, like runnels of rain that gathered into one single human river of disheartened men. Nino walked behind Elio's stretcher. The generals and high-ranking officers in the lead, they marched past their victors, 5,000 men journeying into captivity.

3

London, 1942

From her desk in the office of the shipping company, Olivia imagined flashes of explosions, underwater missiles racing to their targets. The war had disrupted shipping lanes, and the government had armed merchant ships, which now travelled in convoys. Crews were on board for days and weeks, and the ships were often torpedoed. She searched for news of her brother Mick's ship, dreading the discovery that it had been hit; she had stopped befriending the seamen, who like her brother, could so easily disappear. In the past year, over 700 ships had sunk and along with them half the crews. Thousands of men were dead or missing. As far as she knew, Mick was still alive, as, she hoped, were her parents. She hadn't heard from them in over a year, not since they'd arrived in Italy. Fortunately, they had the house Papa had inherited in the Italian village of Musadino. Within two weeks, Papa had been conscripted and sent to Dalmatia. Mamma was desperate and alone in the austere hundreds-year-old house, with three floors but no inner stairs. She had electricity, but no running water. Olivia tried to imagine her mother fetching water in buckets from an outdoor public fountain and carrying it up all those stairs. They had lived comfortably in London, with a modern bathroom, a washing machine, and a Hoover vacuum cleaner. Worse still, other than a few words, Mamma could not speak Italian, and could barely understand her grandfather's dialect, never mind decipher a whole new one. Despite all these hardships, Mamma had written, thank goodness Papa had continued paying the taxes on this property. She could not imagine where she would be otherwise.

Beyond that, Olivia had no news of when Papa would return, or whether Mamma had heard of or seen Aldo. That day on the train platform — could it really be six years ago? She hadn't expected Mamma to write about him, having seen the VERIFICATO PER CENSURA — PASSED BY CENSOR — in large letters across the bottom of the envelopes.

She stood up to get her jacket. Her co-worker Philip turned towards her.

"Is it that time already?" he said. He was a tall ruddy young man, a telegraphist, whose job had kept him from being drafted. He smiled. "April 16."

Instantly, she replied, "Cloudy, light rain. The *Caspia* tanker, torpedoed in the Mediterranean, off the coast of Lebanon. Twenty-seven perished out of thirty-eight. Survivors rescued by Royal Navy HMML-1023 and HMML-1032." She smiled. "You were wearing brown trousers, a tan knitted jumper over a white shirt, and a brown jacket." This party trick she could do with dates had become one of their daily jokes.

"What about me?" one of the other co-workers said.

She shook her head. "You were probably not even here that day," she said lightly, though she could easily see him on that reel in her head, in a light blue suit. They often teased her in the office, both awed and perplexed by her memory, though some of it wasn't predictable. Although she could recall entire books, when it came to recounting days with detailed accuracy, she could do so only if she had experienced them. Every moment of her own life was as vivid as if it were occurring in the present.

"I'll take your word for it," Philip said. He winked at her.

A flush rose in her cheeks. She turned her head away, busying herself organizing the contents of her purse — lipstick, comb, and hair clips on one side; wallet on the other, tissues on the bottom. For the past couple of months, she had been experiencing alarming waves of heat when she spoke to Philip. She had not had time for dating — most single men her age had gone to war, and anyway, Grandma thought she was too young to tie herself down.

"See you tomorrow," she said. Seventeen now, Olivia was one of several girls working in the shipping company office, alongside young men who were doing essential work, or were too young to be conscripted, or who had returned from Dunkirk and were not fit to fight, or women whose husbands were fighting, so they had to work. She'd been lucky in that she had shown an interest in wireless telegraphy, was given instruction, and within eight months was working as a radio technician. The job was interesting, offered the possibility of news of Mick, but was also frustrating, because many of the ships had obsolete equipment, so she wasn't always able to receive broadcasts.

"Olivia!" Philip called from the doorway, and she turned.

He was still wearing his headset, his face concerned. "I'm sorry," he said.

"What's happened?" She hurried back inside with him. "Is it *The Empire Arnold*?"

He nodded. "Torpedoed and sunk at 10°45′N 52°30′W by U-155 Kriegsmarine." He turned to her. "Oh, Olivia. I'm so sorry."

"And the crew?" Olivia asked. She collapsed into a chair. Mick, she thought, and closed her eyes. *February 12, 1940. Intermittent rain beats on the café windows. Mick froths milk for a cappuccino, his face dark and unhappy. Last night his girlfriend broke up with him during a meeting, and he has been surly ever since. I don't like her much, because she believes violence is the only way to defeat the fascists. I don't like the idea of violence, of Mick being involved in something that could land him in jail. There is enough violence right now, without adding to it. I say this to Mick after school, when I get him alone, but he waves me away, as if I don't understand. He is becoming more and more like Aldo and I'm afraid we will lose him too.*

"Nothing yet." Philip leaned over and touched her arm. "Are you all right?" he said, looking anxiously at her.

She nodded, though she didn't feel all right. The words "torpedoed and sunk" circled in her brain. She knew this moment would be with her always. *August 4, 1942, at 15:15.* She set her purse down and took off her jacket. "I'll wait till we hear more," she said, though she knew it was irrational.

Philip shook his head. "You know there won't be anything more for days or weeks."

She sat motionless, willing herself to stand up, take the train, give Grandma and Grandpa the news, and then what? She had to reach her parents. *Torpedoed and sunk.* She wanted to go home, but where was that? Home had become a shifting target. *Torpedoed and sunk.* Cousins had moved into her London house and were running the café there, as if nothing had happened; her father was fighting a war in Dalmatia; her mother was trying to survive in an Italian village under fascist control; Aldo she imagined was ensconced in some dangerous partisan hideout; Mick she could only visualize submerged in the Atlantic waters, neither dead nor alive; and she was in a strange city with relatives, who could not replace her parents and brothers. *Torpedoed and sunk.*

Philip touched her shoulder and she looked up. "If you can wait fifteen minutes, I'll walk you to the station." He had asked her out to a movie once, and she had declined, not because she didn't like him, but because Grandpa wouldn't allow her to stay late in the city and take the train home alone at night. She'd been embarrassed to tell him this, as if it made her sound too childish, and he hadn't asked her again.

She nodded and leaned back in the chair. She should consider herself lucky to be working here. She closed her eyes and, unbidden, a fast-forward replay of last year began... *Red Cross job training, my team searching for survivors after an air raid... sporadic bombing, casualties... women's caesareans deliver dead babies... long exhausting hours... TB patients lie on heavy rubber sheets outside the hospital grounds... mental patients wander aimlessly impervious to the shrapnel raining down... I dodge them all, then board a train, often delayed, to return to Kent.* A lump rose in her throat, her eyes filled with tears, as if she were returning home now, mourning the early deaths, the illnesses and wounds. She sighed and opened her eyes.

Philip smiled and held up his finger. "Almost done."

To relieve her and Mamma's distress, her uncle had pulled a few strings and gotten her the job at the shipping company. She knew she was fortunate and shouldn't be complaining, but what she wanted was to be with her parents. If they were still alive, they'd be in dire straits, with a scarcity of food, Italy under international sanctions.

"Ready?" Philip asked.

She let the word "ready" now circle in her brain. *Rea-dy, read-y, read-y, red-y.* The word began to lose its meaning the more she repeated it inside her head. *Red, red,* she thought, her brother's blood seeping into the sea. Was he ready for death? Was she? She shook her head, and Philip touched her arm.

"Come on," he said, picking up her jacket, urging her up.

She followed him into the warm August day, where they skirted mounds of rocks and bricks on the way to the train station, an awkward silence between them. Earlier this year, an undetonated bomb had exploded and demolished a block of houses and stores. Though the sirens had stopped for now, Olivia was vigilant. She could imagine the air filled with the cries of women and children, with the shouts of men searching through the rubble for survivors. And how could she know there weren't other perils awaiting?

"Listen," Philip said as they neared the station. "If there's anything I can do…"

She shook her head. "Thank you."

"Are you sure you're all right?"

No, she wanted to say, I'm not all right. She wanted to go home, to be with her mother and father and brothers. She wanted life to return to an earlier time, when she had not realized how happy she was, how much she loved them all, how they would soon be separated, how every day following would be filled with uncertainty. Instead, she said, "I'll be fine."

He pulled her to him, and she slipped her arms around his neck. His lips brushed her hair. Then, the train arrived, and she boarded, then with a smile and a wave, she departed.

"I have to go to Italy," she told Barbara the following Saturday. The two girls had reconnected when Olivia began working in London and met on their days off — a small respite in a life of worry and exhaustion. "I need to speak to my parents." She held out a government letter. Nine crew members had been killed in the torpedoing of the *Empire Arnold*, its captain taken prisoner, and while most of the surviving crew had been rescued by a Norwegian ship and taken to British Guiana, Mick was among those missing in action.

"Try to be positive," Barbara said. "Mick could be just fine, rescued and not accounted for yet. He's not dead. He's only missing."

Missing, Olivia thought, only *missing*. She tried to calm herself. Surely, he would be found, and she would hear he was alive on the other side of the world. She shook out her napkin while her brain replayed *February 12, 1940. ... Mick is becoming more and more like Aldo and I fear we will lose him too.* "I have to tell my parents, I have to—"

Barbara reached out to still her hands. "What about your job? You need to be patient and wait out the war."

Olivia waved her hand, impatiently. "I can't wait."

Barbara studied her for a moment. "There might be a way," she said. "If you're interested in different work."

"What do you mean 'different work'?" Olivia said, frowning.

"To help the war effort," Barbara said. "Government work."

In late September, Olivia received a formal letter requesting her to go to the War Office. Her first thought was *Mick*. Surely bad news would be delivered face to face. Good news would come in a letter. She thought in these terms: if he was *missing*, he could be *found*. The letter, however, was an invitation for an interview.

She arrived at Whitehall at the appointed hour and was shown into a small bare room in the War Office basement, where a Mr. Potter asked her a series of innocuous questions meant, she assumed, to help him decide whether or not she would be suitable for a government job. He asked about her nurse training with the Red Cross. "I understand you speak Italian," he said. "We train people here," he said, "and we send them to the country of their origin, or if they speak a foreign language well, we send them to that country, where they can use it and be useful to the war effort."

Olivia nodded, silently thanking Barbara.

Mr. Potter shuffled a series of papers on his desk and stopped at one particular page, which he slowly read, then he studied her for a moment. "What can you tell me about April 7, 1939?"

Olivia frowned, startled, but instantly the day appeared before her. *"A cool day — 48 degrees F."* She scanned her school day, the afternoon chat with Barbara, a couple of hours of helping in the coffee shop, aware this government official was looking for something other than her personal life. She continued her fast-forward scan until her family was seated around the radio that night, leaning forward. "*Disgraziato!*" Papa had said and they all knew he was referring to Mussolini. "It's the day Italy invaded and annexed Albania," she said to Mr. Potter. "General Guzzoni attacked all the ports simultaneously, and although the Albanians tried to fend off the attack, they were betrayed by Italian agents who sabotaged the artillery and removed the ammunition," she said, repeating the announcer's exact words.

Mr. Potter stared at her, half-frowning, half-smiling. "Good." He stood up. "Now come with me, and I'll take you to sign the Official Secrets Act," he said, without telling her what she was to keep secret. "After this, there will be a background check, and if all goes well, I'll explain more."

Afterwards, out in the sunshine, Olivia walked a bit to make sense of her interview. She wanted to ask Barbara what this work would entail, excited at the prospect of being sent to Italy. She would find her parents, she would find Aldo, and they would all be reunited.

"What's going on?" Philip asked, when she returned to work

"I had an appointment," she said, vaguely, without looking at him, hoping he would ask no more questions.

"Are you all right?" he asked.

She turned and looked at him. "I'm fine," she said, then turned back to her desk.

His eyes bored into her, questioning. She'd have to create a story, something to easily explain these absences.

"Olivia," he said, and she turned to him, "Would you like to see a film with me?" He continued quickly, before she could answer. "There's a comedy playing, *Breach of Promise*, something light to take your mind off the war…We could go to an early showing…"

"I can't tonight," she said, without explaining.

He stared at her for a moment, as if to assess whether to pursue the offer, then shrugged.

"I can go another night," Olivia said, a blush rising up her cheeks. "But I'll have to get permission from my grandfather."

Philip smiled, visibly relaxed. "You tell him I'll come on the train home with you afterwards, so you'll be safe. Just name the day."

Before heading home, she took the Tube to her old neighbourhood. Much of it had been destroyed and rebuilt. She had not been to their house and coffee shop since leaving it two years before, afraid someone would arrest her, though this was absurd, because she was not guilty of anything. Grandma and Grandpa had dissuaded her, in case, they said, someone was watching their house. Olivia frowned. They were not a political family. Was her father's membership in the Italian Fascist Club enough to judge and suspect them of evil?

As she approached the coffee shop, she realized it had become a deli with a different name. She pushed open the door, and a bell rang. Her cousin Alba stood behind a counter, and when Olivia approached, she leaned forward and whispered, "Go away. We don't want any trouble." She turned to help a customer.

Olivia stood perfectly still, shocked. This was her family's property. *London. September 14, 1940…"DP," a girl yells in the hallway at school. Displaced Person. Is this what I am? The girl is with my cousin Alba and must not be aware of her Italian origin. I am no more displaced than she is. I wait for Alba to defend me, but she walks on without looking back…a sound emerges, muffled at first, like a radio left on in another room… men's agitated voices… a crowd slowly advancing, chanting, throwing stones through windows of other Italian establishments.* Alba now came around the counter and pushed a hand into Olivia's back, propelling her forward out the door. "It's not safe," she whispered. "You'll be the ruin of us all." Then she shut the door firmly behind her.

In her second interview at Whitehall, a tall young man led her into a waiting room. "Wait here," he said.

She sat on a wooden chair and dropped her purse on the black-and-white mosaic floor tiles, wondering what she'd gotten herself into. She stared at the tiles, instantly identifying a pattern, much like the one in her brain depicting months of the year she could quickly scroll through backwards and forwards. It was how she visualized sequences, like numbers, or letters of the alphabet, or anything to do with time. For example, decades presented in her mind like dots on a pencil drawing of a face in profile: the present being the top of the forehead, moving back through time as the drawing moved down the nose, the mouth, the chin, below which was the pre-historic period. She had tried once to draw these concepts on paper, but her parents didn't really understand. She continued now to stare at the ground and counted the tesserae that made up each tile: they could easily be the minutes in an hour, or the hours in a day, or the days of the week. She daydreamed herself into the mosaics, searching for centuries, until she noticed one of the corner tiles was chipped, and the void filled in with grout. Her chest tightened. She didn't like symmetrical things to be askew. Her mother's voice entered her head, telling her she had to accept these inconsistencies, that her anxiety was misplaced. She counted to one hundred, as she'd taught herself to do in these circumstances when she couldn't balance the unbalanced, right what was crooked, make order of disorder.

Soon, the young man returned. "Well," he said. "You're cleared so far." He smiled.

"What—" she began.

"We don't ask questions here," the man said. He observed her carefully, then led her down the hall into a spartan room, where from behind a desk rose a slender, elegant woman, who shook Olivia's hand. "Miss Adams will look after you from now on," the man said, depositing her file on the woman's desk before leaving.

"Please," Miss Adams said, motioning Olivia into a chair, then she sat and openly scrutinized Olivia, who remained quiet.

Olivia did her own scrutinizing: the woman's features were familiar, though Olivia couldn't exactly place her. For a moment, she ran through her mind's catalogue of faces to no avail. Some people were able to camouflage themselves in plain view. Olivia, however, could not forget a face if she'd seen it, no matter how fleetingly.

For the next half hour, Olivia answered a variety of simple questions, such as, Could she drive a car? Could she keep secrets? Had she ever been outside Britain? Was she a good walker? Following this, Miss Adams moved on to more personal questions to do with her family background. She knew about her brother's secret socialist club in the coffee shop, her father's deportation to Italy, her other brother's activities with the partisans. She knew where Olivia lived, where she worked, what time she boarded the train home. Did she have contact with Aldo? What was the nature of her relationship to Philip? What had she told her grandparents about the interview? Olivia answered all the questions, disconcerted by how much this woman knew. She imagined herself being followed, photographed, written about. She glanced at the file on Miss Adams's desk, a file the woman had not once opened.

Presently, Miss Adams stood up. "Come with me," she said and led Olivia to another office, where she handed Olivia a stack of reports. "Read these then destroy them."

Olivia did as she was told, then was able to recall the information in them verbatim. Could she follow directives? Memorize instructions? They were testing her, as well as their security. Olivia easily passed all these tests. Was she was willing to go overseas? If so, she would have to join the FANYs — an all-female volunteer group, active in both nursing and intelligence since the early 1900s. This "cover" would allow her to move around freely, though Olivia still had no idea what she would be doing, and where she would be going.

"I've joined the FANYs, but that's all I can tell you," Barbara said, when they met up the following Saturday. "You'll hear soon enough." She smiled, and patted Olivia's hand. "I think you'll enjoy the adventure."

Olivia sighed. Over the past few months, Barbara had blossomed into a glamorous young woman, with wavy blonde hair she pulled off her face in a roll. Olivia envied her fashion sense, admiring her emerald-green suit, whose skirt slightly flared a few inches past her knees, and the fitted jacket with its long row of buttons down the front. She would have loved new clothes, but she was saving every penny she earned for a ticket to Italy.

They walked along a busy sidewalk, stopping for a moment at the bakery section of a large department store, where men and women queued up to buy bread. Olivia breathed in the aroma of fresh baking, thinking of the coffee shop, her mother rolling dough making the prized *cornetti* they sold with coffee. "I'll get some bread for home," she said, and they stopped and stood in line, while on the street, double-decker buses, cars, and military lorries drove past them.

"I'll be leaving soon," Barbara said. "So, you might not be able to contact me. But don't worry. When I can, I'll contact you."

"Where are you going?" Olivia said. She couldn't imagine not having Barbara to confide in, to help her navigate whatever was ahead.

"You know I can't tell you that," Barbara said.

They continued along the sidewalk surrounded by large signs — TO VICTORY R.A.F., GUINNESS IS GOOD FOR YOU, BOVRIL SCHWEPPES TONIC WATER, BUY SAVINGS STAMPS — and soon had to step into the street to avoid a crew of workmen who had dug a trench and were laying cables.

"Overseas?"

Barbara nodded, and Olivia didn't ask anymore, though she supposed Barbara, who spoke perfect French, would be sent to France, into danger.

At the train station, Olivia memorized every nuance of Barbara's voice, her face, her gestures, the fear. "Promise you'll be careful," she said. They held each other tight, then Olivia boarded the train, and watched Barbara recede into the crowd. She tried to still the pounding of her heart, tried to bury the memory of other farewells at train stations, now layered one over the other in a compression of loss.

SECURITY TALK

This is the most important part of your training. You will, therefore, in your own interest, be subject to strict security rules.

GENERAL SECURITY PRECAUTIONS.

You will not be allowed to leave these grounds during the course unless accompanied or specially instructed to do so.

You must never disclose at any time to anyone that you have been at the school or at Beaulieu.

You must never recognize anyone whom you have met here if you happen to see them later on elsewhere, except on official business.

LOCAL SECURITY RULES.

You will hand to me all identity documents now in your possession for inspection.

You will hand to me any firearms, other weapons, cameras or notebooks in your possession for retention during the course.

You will hand to me any money in excess of 5 pounds and any valuables for safekeeping until your departure.

Mail.
Outgoing:
all letters will be handed to me in a stamped, unsealed envelope for censoring. You must not make any reference in your letters to the fact that they are censored.

You will use the postal box address already given to you or the special arrangements for writing overseas.

Your letters will be posted in London.

Incoming.
All letters sent to you will be censored by the Administrative Officer.

Telegrams: Telegrams, which may only be sent in cases of emergency, will be handed to me for censorship and dispatch.

Telephone: you will not use the telephone here or in the locality. (This rule is only relaxed in special cases where H.Q. desires to communicate urgently with a student.)

In the first week of January, Olivia kissed Grandma and Grandpa goodbye and boarded a train for Oxfordshire, for two weeks' training. As the train pulled out, she panicked suddenly, flooded by all the emotions of her other goodbyes, other train stations. What would happen if Kent were bombed, and Grandma and Grandpa killed? She couldn't bear the thought of them gone. She'd be left alone. Stop it! she told herself. She was a woman now. She could take care of herself.

In Oxfordshire, along with two hundred other girls, Olivia began her FANY training in nursing — which she knew well — as well as a series of trials meant to test attitudes, constitutions, and resourcefulness. Their rooms were bugged, Olivia was sure of it, so she said little. Being naturally shy, this was not difficult. Other girls complained about the menial tasks — like dusting or cleaning floors. They'd be told they were going for a half-hour march, then found themselves marching for twenty miles. Everyone was exhausted, and their superiors watched for reactions. Olivia neither grumbled nor objected.

In the final test Olivia had to create a cover story, then sit in a dark room for two or three hours to await interrogation. Olivia imagined herself as a new character, furnishing her imaginary apartment, working at her imaginary job, interacting with her imaginary family. She replayed the scenario in the dark until it became like one of her memories. She passed easily, without breaking her cover story, and soon, she and twelve other girls returned to Baker Street, a nondescript building with many corridors and doors without names on them.

Here Miss Adams continued to test her, focusing on her memory. She gave Olivia reports and books to read — which Olivia could do quickly — then quizzed her on them. In her brain, Olivia could see the pages as if they were frames in a familiar film.

Now, finally, the girls returned to the office of the tall young man Olivia had met weeks before. "You will be working for an organization called Special Operations Executive," he said. "An organization formed two years ago by Winston Churchill." He paused and scanned their faces. "SOE," he said, "is an operation of espionage, sabotage and reconnaissance in occupied Europe. A secret war behind enemy lines, to support resistance armies and to use guerrilla tactics to sabotage German positions. You might have to destroy roads or bridges or railways; you might have to carry messages or weapons or explosives. You will be trained to carry out these operations, but remember, as an SOE agent, you must fit seamlessly into society, and act clandestinely, with bare-bones support staff." He paused again. The girls were so silent Olivia could hear her own heart beating. "None of you," he said, tracing an arc to encompass them all, "would be recognized by us, if you're captured." He let that statement sink in for a moment before proceeding. "If you're caught by the Gestapo, there's a good chance you will be tortured and shot," he said.

The girls shifted a little, and some murmured among themselves. Although none were given concrete information regarding their missions, the danger involved was clearly stated. There would be real consequences of serving as illegal combatants. Instead of fear, Olivia felt only excitement. She'd be going to Italy, where she'd be able to search for her family, and she would make a difference.

"Bravery, courage, and sacrifice is what you must possess," the man said, "and an unflinching desire to aid the war effort at any cost."

Yes, Olivia thought, looking around at the other girls, they were all brave and eager, willing to walk into danger, though their motivations might be all different. They came from the country and the city, teenage girls barely out of school, girls who were bilingual, nursing girls, girls who had a particular talent that had caught the eye of officers on Baker Street, patriotic girls, shy, introverted girls, self-sufficient girls who were used to being alone, brave girls who did not ask questions or share secrets. Soon they'd become couriers, spies, saboteurs, radio operators in the field. They all had to be self-reliant, confident, yet inconspicuous. They would take on secret identities, go on secret missions and be entrusted with their nation's greatest secrets.

Man is born free; and everywhere he is in chains.
One thinks himself the master of others,
and still remains a greater slave than they.

— Jean-Jacques Rousseau

4

Kenya, 1942

The mountain receded as the prisoners filed down to where a convoy awaited to take them on the first leg of their journey to a prisoner camp in Kenya. Nino was packed tight into one of the lorries, along with forty other men, their bodies damp with sweat, dirt and fear. He wanted to object, to tell his captors that he was not even a soldier, that he didn't believe in Mussolini's war, but no one was listening. He stood for hours, jostled against men, his throat dry, dust caked on his face and arms. A couple of the men began humming "Faccetta Nera," Mussolini's marching song, but others shushed them, fearing repercussions. Nino ignored them all, and travelled to a place inside himself where Bianca shimmered like a miraculous apparition. He envisioned her body, her hands, her lips, a desperate longing rising in him. *"The image of her when she starts to smile dissolves within the mind and melts away, a miracle too rich and strange to hold."* La Vita Nuova. She was his Beatrice, his perfect half.

Suddenly, the lorry stopped and men were hurled against each other like dominoes.

"Out!" a voice shouted as the lorry's tailgate was lowered. "*Fuori!*"

Nino jumped out into a vast savanna grassland, where a makeshift camp had been set up. Already other lorries had arrived, and men were settling on the hard ground for the night. Nino found a spot at the edge of the camp and lay down, the cold slipping into his jacket, into the space between sleeve and wrist. Above him, a firmament of stars extended to the horizon. He marvelled at their density, aware he was seeing only a fraction of what was there. Who was he, here, in this desolate place?

In the grey dawn, he was awakened by the British guards, and after a meagre ration of bread and cheese, he joined the others in a long trek headed for Gilgil Camp.

He walked across grasslands, day and night merging, one foot in front of the other, head down, as if he were already dead and didn't know it. He had never felt so absent from himself, so numb, as if his heart had restricted the flow of blood to his nether regions, trying to conserve the brain and itself. Now and then, he looked up to where an endless line of prisoners sliced the landscape. He imagined thousands of feet plodding in front and behind him, a colony of ants. Finally, after two days, they stopped at a rail station and boarded cattle cars that crossed wide plains for hours in the blistering sun.

Midday on the fifth day, the train stopped and Nino stumbled down with the rest. The horizon was dotted with acacia thorn tees, their smooth pale-yellow limbs and spiky white thorns mirrored in the barbed-wire fences connecting guard towers, beyond which the corrugated-iron roofs of barracks shimmered in the sun. A crude sign proclaimed Gilgil Camp. He plodded forward with a column of dejected men, his feet raising dust, his head drooping in the midday sun. Flies buzzed around them all, and from the rail station, the cooing of wood doves mocked their slow reluctant progress.

He thought of his first voyage — was it only three years ago? — when he'd stood on the deck of a ship, clinging to the railings, waving goodbye to Bianca, who stood on shore, a blue scarf billowing behind her. Brimming with excitement, he'd anticipated trips to exotic countries, experiences, freedom. And had not the war intervened, and his ship been requisitioned, he might have lived that dream.

"Long live Italy!" a young man near him shouted, and others responded to the call.

"Look where Italy took you," Nino said.

The young man turned to him, narrowed his eyes. "We'll win this war," he said.

"Sure." Nino turned away, thinking of folly, the lies they'd all been told that Italy was infallible, victorious, while the truth exposed what they really were: disillusioned soldiers, poorly armed, ragged and demoralized.

After a quick round of the camp — here is the commander barrack, the kitchen, the mess hall, the common area for bathroom and washing facilities — Nino followed the others into the barracks, where they all settled in shocked silence, observed from every angle by British and Kenyan guards who patrolled the internal roads leading to the barracks, as well as the external perimeter from the watchtowers. Nino felt as if he were under a microscope, where the slightest movement, the rubbing of an eye, the clenching of a fist, could appear suspicious. He had always valued his privacy, and now found himself exposed, not only to the guards but to the other prisoners.

Bit by bit, he retreated into a small dark area of his mind, only aware of hunger, thirst, sleep. When he could rouse himself, he searched inside his assigned footlocker for family photographs his aunt had sent him, as if to recall a different life. He gazed at his fourteen-year-old self, trying to remember his innocence, his naïve belief in a brilliant future, the promise of travel to Cairo, Bombay, Cape Town, India, Japan, China, names of cities and countries Aunt Isabella had created, like castles, in his mind. He wondered now if he'd been trying to follow his father's heroic adventures, to resurrect him. At times, he felt little more than a child unwittingly thrown into battle, now slipping confusedly out of the war into a limbo of uncertainty, amplified by the fact that he had no access to reliable news. The British had installed a loudspeaker in the camp, and aired broadcasts from Radio Nairobi, but no one knew whether they were hearing propaganda or truth. Other times, he would reread Bianca's letters, as if to ground himself inside her marriage fantasy, to escape this camp, where he felt disoriented, disconnected, starved.

Gradually, the men began to awaken from their torpor. Over the next year, trapped inside this large cage, they had two options: give up and perish, or get up and survive. Several of them took charge and began to identify the various professions in the camp: medics who could help them with their ailments; engineers who could design a church; musicians who could play and sing; teachers who could expand their education; trappers who could catch snakes and mice to supplement their meagre rations, and so on. Nino sighed. His radio telegraph skills were meaningless here. Encouraged, the men began to build a make-believe Italian town inside the camp. The British, happy to see the prisoners occupied, supplied the materials with which to build a church, a library, a stage for theatrical productions, wood for props, fabric for costumes. Some of the men transcribed plays, opera librettos, and scores by heart. They put on productions. They organized soccer teams. They began attending mandatory English classes.

In the early evenings, Nino would often walk to the northern edge of the camp, where he'd befriended an African sentry, to await the passenger train from Mombasa, its cyclops eye piercing the darkness. He'd stare at that beacon, and for a moment, dream himself into a carriage, beside a beautiful woman — Bianca perhaps — slipping away from it all, vanishing in a cloud of steam.

In the daytime, he tried to keep to himself as much as he could, yet of necessity he also spoke to others and laughed with them. Beneath it all he felt a heavy weariness in his bones. He avoided political talk. Antifascists were few, and afraid to voice their views in a camp controlled by fascist sympathizers, who sang patriotic songs that made Nino squirm with humiliation and rage.

One afternoon, lying on his cot in the unbearable heat, he heard a commotion outside. He stood and went out, where to his astonishment, prisoners were singing, banging on the lids of trash cans, leaping on each other's shoulders, kissing, waving tricolour flags improvised from odd clothing, throwing berets, books, plates, shirts, anything unfastened into the air. "Peace! Peace! England has asked for an armistice! The war is over! Long live victorious Italy!" the men shouted, and Nino found himself filled with unimaginable joy. Freedom! He joined the others. "Long live peace!" The celebration lasted several hours, while they awaited the British Command to come and confirm the news.

Finally, an English colonel arrived and all flocked around him, anxious to hear the words from his lips. The colonel paused a moment before speaking, and while most of the men tried to read in his tone and body language the words they wanted, Nino understood the English, and his jubilation was crushed. Finally, the colonel stopped, and his interpreter fell silent also. He stared at them, his face in a sorrowful expression, then said, "Friends, the Colonel said we have to be calm."

"What happened?" one of the men asked.

"What did he say?" several yelled out.

The interpreter shook his head sadly. "The Colonel says there is no armistice. Some troublemaker invented this. The war against the Axis continues, and the British will never bow. So, stay calm."

A hushed disbelief filled them all, as they bent down to gather trashcan lids, to undo the makeshift flags, to search for their books, their plates, their skimpy belongings, now made even more tawdry and pathetic. Nino walked back to his barrack and his cot, thinking in that instant, *freedom* had become even more elusive.

Once again, some men descended into lethargy, but what helped save them for a time were theatrical productions, especially humorous ones that could, for an hour or two, make them forget their captivity.

While working on one of the theatrical productions, Nino met Antonio, who had arrived at the camp several months after him. A gregarious man, Antonio had casually moved among the prisoners, chatting and offering assistance. He spoke both English and Italian flawlessly, had a mysterious past, and divided loyalties, which helped him survive in the camp. Whenever anyone needed something not readily available, Antonio knew exactly how to procure it. Rumours were he either had a wealthy influential family to somehow pay off their British captors, or possibly he was providing some service to them in exchange for these favours.

"I have an idea for a play," Antonio said one day, gathering everyone around him. "A theatre production of the absurd, something Pirandello might have created. Only instead of *Six Characters in Search of an Author*, our play will be about *POWs in Search of Repatriated Life*." He grinned, and everyone clapped.

Nino smiled. It seemed fitting to mount a theatre production of the absurd, given that his existence felt meaningless, controlled by the whims of a war that thrashed and waned like the waves of a tempestuous sea. To survive here, he had to either surrender to invisible forces, or search to make meaning out of his every day.

The premise of Antonio's play was that the POWs, on their return to Italy, would find themselves incapable of integrating seamlessly into Italian society, given their years of "improper behaviour" in the camp, and would need a period of adjustment and re-education. This "improper behaviour" included love affairs, vendettas, thefts, murders, extortion and betrayals, which mirrored and distorted life outside the camp while being crucial to survival within it. Therefore, the returned POWs would set up a tent in the main piazza of their towns, essentially reproducing the all-male POW camp, and from there, would watch the outside world until ready to re-enter it. At any time while in that outside world, should the ex-POW experience any anxiety or distress, he could return to the tent for a period of re-education. Through this stage production, the men would be able to voice their fears for an unknown future, discuss their captivity and its effects on them.

Soon, the men separated themselves into groups: actors, set builders, production assistants, carpenters, and miscellaneous workers. Nino was in charge of communications. He kept everyone up to date, helped diffuse conflicts among the men, and reported on their progress. He became an impromptu interpreter, an interface between the detainees and the British, allowing him a window into the world outside the camp. Six kilometres away, the town of Gilgil and its surroundings were abuzz with Allied soldiers being trained and prepared for campaigns against the Axis forces. Some of the POWS had been selected to work on the town's infrastructure projects: construction workers built barracks, farmers hoed fields, engineers built bridges and roads. For this work, they received a small compensation, as well as extra cigarettes, food, screws and construction materials with which they could build objects — such as tables — for themselves. Nino longed to join them, to feel himself free, even for a few hours a day.

He waited for the right opportunity to speak to one of the British officers who had been helpful in supplying equipment for the camp.

"I wonder, would it be possible for me to work outside the camp?" he asked.

The officer scrutinized him for a moment.

"I've been to London," Nino said, quickly, to set himself apart from the fascists in the camp. "I spent a summer there with my uncle." He stopped, then added, "who lives there."

The officer frowned. "Really? And why does he live there?"

"He doesn't believe in fascism," Nino said. "He's been living in Britain since the early '20s."

The officer watched him carefully, then he turned to the papers on his desk. "You'll have to apply in writing and declare that you won't carry out any acts of sabotage, nor will you fraternize with the British population." He handed Nino the declaration.

The following week, Nino began work at the newly opened African Diatomite Industries processing plant in Kariandusi, ten kilometres from Gilgil. The work was loud and dusty. Yet Nino was glad to be working, which was better than sitting idle in the camp, though the unbearable heat in the plant, and the deafening sounds of diatomite being crushed and dried and milled gave him daily headaches that often turned to migraines. Still, it was better than listening to the cluster of die-hard fascists plan ridiculous escapes, as if they could traverse deserts without water and provisions, as if they could tramp through shrub and sand unseen. They'd all heard of a daring escape at one of the camps, when three mountaineers had climbed Mount Kenya and planted an Italian flag at its summit, after which they'd returned to the camp. Their escape was one from boredom, from the monotony of daily lives. No, Nino figured work was much better. It made him more connected, as if he was contributing something.

"Listen," Antonio said one day, catching up within the shadow of one of the lookout posts. He glanced around, as if afraid someone would hear him. "I have to talk to you." He had hovered around Nino all afternoon, his eyes eager to share some secret Nino assumed had to do with a letter he'd received from his fiancée. Unfortunately, whenever Antonio was on the verge of saying something, one of the other men would approach, so they hadn't yet had the opportunity to speak privately.

Over several months of conversations, Antonio had been hinting of possible ways in which Nino could help the Allies. At first, Nino hadn't understood what Antonio meant, but as time passed, and Antonio trusted him more, Nino had come to believe Antonio was collaborating with the British. "It's dangerous work,"

Antonio had said, "for which one would not be acknowledged if caught." Finally, probably sensing Nino's curiosity and interest, Antonio posed the question: Would Nino be interested in this type of work? Nino shrugged, aware of spies within the camp. Were they trying to entrap him? He smiled at Antonio, neither denying nor agreeing to anything.

Then, one afternoon, in the middle of his shift, a British officer removed Nino to a small airless room, and, amid sounds of rock being smashed, asked him if he would be interested in collaborating. His wireless operator training, his Italian, and English skills would all be valuable to the antifascist cause.

"What exactly am I to do?" Nino asked.

"For now," the officer said, "you will continue working at the factory. When the time is right, you will receive further instructions."

A month later, Antonio approached him after the soccer game. "Take a walk around with me." The rest of the Italian team was celebrating the win, men slapping each other on the back, singing *Vincere, Vincere, Vincere,* a propaganda fascist song about winning the war.

They wandered off in a slow jog, as if to cool down after the game. Once out of earshot, Antonio slowed down until they were both walking. He turned to Nino. "You remember what I told you about —" and here he looked around to make sure no one was listening, "about the... operation," he said.

Nino nodded, though not fully understanding.

"I thought I'd let you know, because I'll be leaving the camp."

"What do you mean?" Nino said. "Where are you going?"

"You mustn't tell anyone," Antonio said, and went on to explain he was headed to Italy to assassinate Mussolini's head henchman Roberto Farinacci, which, he said, would deal a damaging blow to the fascist party. Farinacci was a staunch fascist politician, high up in the regime, pro-German, and detested by the general population. His death would appeal to everyone.

The whole escapade sounded crazy to Nino. It required a series of fortuitous events: Antonio said he would be covertly removed from the camp; dropped into Turkey, unseen, where he would contact the Italian Embassy and claim to have escaped from a POW camp; the Embassy would then repatriate him, and once back in

GENNI GUNN

Italy, he would poison Farinacci, who was known to drink aperitifs in public bars.

"But how can you know that any of this will work, or that you'll be repatriated, and how will you go about getting poison, etc.?" Nino said.

"There'll be contacts along the way. Things will be… arranged." Antonio smiled.

"Are you sure you want to do this?" Nino said. "If you're caught in Italy—"

"I know the risks," Antonio said.

"When?"

"In the next couple of weeks. I'll let you know."

Day in, day out, most of the prisoners wandered around the camp. Hundreds of them, all walking about, stopping to chat here and there, the boredom as oppressive as the air, the mosquitoes, the flies. They all moved through a suspended time, in a kind of mental strain, a giving up on the future, as if afraid whatever else could happen would be worse than what had already occurred.

Nino worked at the factory during the day, but when he returned he, too, joined the others in this endless wandering, trying to make sense of the senseless.

"Are you still going?" he asked Antonio. Ten days had passed since Antonio had told him of his plans.

"Shhhh," Antonio said. He guided Nino farther away from everyone, then leaned in. "Yes, I'm going four days from now."

"So soon?" Nino said. "Are you sure—"

"Don't worry about me," Antonio said, pushing the hair away from his forehead. "I'll tell you a secret. When I get to Turkey, I'm free. I intend to make my own way to Italy and go home. I don't give a damn about Farinacci and Mussolini. Let them," and here he nodded towards one of the British soldiers, "worry about it." He laughed and cuffed Nino on the back of the head. "I'm not stupid," he said.

Nino frowned. In that one statement, he understood Antonio was someone totally different from himself. "What about the others involved?" he asked. "Won't you be putting them in jeopardy?"

64

Antonio shrugged. "I don't owe the British anything," he said. "We're in a war. And as POWs, it's our duty to try to escape." He made a large sweeping motion with his arm. "For the Fatherland."

Nino shuddered inside, but said nothing. He was glad he hadn't shared his inner thoughts with Antonio. They continued their walk around the camp, chatting now about the upcoming football match.

That night, lying on his cot, he thought about Antonio's "escape." Even in the dark, he could see his outstretched arm, the quick fascist salute, and felt a sickening in his stomach as he regressed to his fifteen-year-old self in Britain with his uncle, whose limp was an eternal reminder of the fascists' legacy.

He waited until the day Antonio disappeared from the camp, then sought out the officer who had approached him about collaborating. "I'm not sure if this is appropriate," he began, and the officer's eyebrow raised. "I believe one of the prisoners is working for you," he continued, then revealed Antonio's plan.

The officer listened carefully, then at the end, smiled.

"You think it's funny?" Nino said. "Don't you care about your people?" He turned to go.

"Relax," the officer said. "We know about Antonio."

Nino stopped.

"Just checking loyalties," the officer said.

How to Defend Yourself Against Surveillance

Routine precautions. Whenever you are going anywhere on SECRET work, you must automatically take routine precautions which will make it difficult for you to be secretly watched.

You should always be on the alert to notice strangers hanging about, especially when you're leaving any house.

Do not go straight to your destination.

Make use of a vehicle, either public or private. If you use the former, board it on the run. If you use the latter, do not take one which offers to pick you up, and start by telling the driver the wrong destination. You should never take a vehicle right to your destination, but complete the journey on foot.

Make some innocent visits on the way.

Visit at least one crowded space.

Do not walk or hang about in places where you could easily be watched without detecting it.

5

London, 1942

Nino walked along the busy street, willing himself not to touch the lapels of his overcoat. In the inner breast pocket, the hidden documents appeared to rustle and call out. He was certain he was being watched and resisted the urge to turn around. He continued up the road, away from his destination, until he saw a bus approaching, then he crossed the street at the last moment and boarded the bus on the run. So far so good. Three stops ahead, he hopped off, walked along a crowded street, and ducked into a hat shop. He tried on several caps, turning his head to look out the window to determine whether he was still being followed. A half-block away a man was bent over, slowly tying his shoe laces. Nino sized him up: dark curly hair, about 5'11", grey double-breasted raincoat, grey fedora hat with black band. He knew from his training that he might be asked to provide a description. He tried on two more fedoras, bought a herringbone flat cap, and when he came out, the man was still there, still tying his shoelaces.

Nino would have to postpone his mission until he could shake the man. He concentrated on the options outlined in his training manual. At this point, the best one was to lead the man through a deserted space — to keep the man at a distance — then to either leap into a crowd or onto a bus or taxi. The main thing was to not show any sign of suspicion.

He had already mapped several possibilities before starting out, just in case. He now headed toward a long narrow street, at the end of which was a square he knew would be densely populated. Again, he forced himself not to turn around, and walked purposefully, stopping once to look in a shop window where, from the corner of his eye, he could see the follower. He continued to the end of the street at the same pace, then turned abruptly and zigzagged through the crowded square. As he went, he slid off his greatcoat, slung it over his arm, removed his own fedora and put on the cap. He then continued across the square to another street, where he flagged down a taxi and sped off. He gave the taxi driver an address opposite to where he was going, and finally, when he was certain he was no longer followed, directed the taxi driver to a street corner a few blocks from his destination. From there, he walked to a nondescript building and rang the doorbell.

A tall middle-aged man opened the door.

Nino pulled the document from the overcoat's breast pocket and handed it to him.

"Surveillance?"

"One. Dark curly hair, about 5'11", grey double-breasted raincoat, grey fedora hat with black band."

The man grinned. "Well done, Sergeant Cassar!" He held out his hand.

Nino grinned back and shook the man's hand. Nino was Nardo Cassar now. He stepped inside, pleased with himself. Lt. Paul Adams was the NCO who had been monitoring Nino's progress during his training, and Nino had passed this scheme.

"You'll be heading out soon. Are you ready?"

Nino laughed. "As ready as I'll ever be." He had been in the UK for twelve weeks, first for two weeks of fitness training — which he easily passed — then five days for psychological appraisal, after which he had been sent to Arisaig, a wild, inaccessible area in the Scottish Highlands, for paramilitary training. He was well ahead of the British recruits, already familiar with weapons and radios. What he had had to learn were various "schemes" such as how to make bombs, engage in hand-to-hand combat, and silently kill with his bare hands. He'd passed all those too, though he hadn't had to kill anyone. Following this, he'd had more specialized wireless training, escape and evasion schemes, as well as methods for resistance to interrogation. In short, everything an agent might need to survive in an occupied country.

A knock interrupted them, and when Lt. Adams opened the door, Nino's follower stood there. "Nice trick," he said, holding out his hand to shake Nino's. "I would have done the same to shake me."

"He's one of our prize pupils," Lt. Adams said.

Nino smiled. He needn't have been worried.

"This calls for a celebration," Lt. Adams said. "Drinks and dinner on me at the Criterion."

"I'd love to, but I'm off to tail another unsuspecting agent," the man said. He stepped back out, raised his hand in farewell, and was gone.

"Six-thirty in the lounge for pre-dinner drinks," Lt. Adams said, and Nino nodded.

As he walked back to his room at the nearby hostel, Nino felt fortunate to be in Britain, away from the POW camp. He was certain he'd been selected not only for his English skills, but because he already knew Morse code and radio procedures. The Germans were rapidly advancing, and SOE resources were limited, as was time. Nino's extraction from the POW camp had been relatively easy. He had simply gone to work at the diatomite plant one morning and never returned. Antonio, whose escape adventure had been a ruse, had retrieved his footlocker and delivered it to him in Kariandusi, before his trip to Nairobi to board a flight for London.

Although Nino was ten minutes early, Lt. Adams waved to him from a table by the window. Nino walked over, his eyes drawn to the gilded floral design on the ceiling that he'd heard was created using real gold and was worth millions. He'd never been anywhere so grand. He sat down and Lt. Adams signalled a waiter, who brought them both drinks.

They were about to raise their glasses when Lt. Adams stopped and waved to someone across the room. Nino followed his eye line to where a tall, willowy young woman stood talking to a small circle of people. She smiled at Lt. Adams, lifting her gloved hand in a small wave.

"That's one of the secretaries in the War Office," Lt. Adams said, for explanation. He now raised his glass again. "To the completion of your training!" he said.

Nino raised his glass, clinked and sipped, his eyes drawn to the lovely young woman who was now approaching.

"Viola!" Lt. Adams said, standing up and extending his hand. "Viola, meet Sergeant Nardo Cassar."

Nino stood too, took her hand and held it, momentarily startled by her green liquid eyes.

"Pleased to meet you," she murmured and drew back her hand.

Nino stepped back, embarrassed.

"Do join us for a drink," Lt. Adams said, pulling out a chair.

She hesitated a moment, then smiled and sat down between them. While Lt. Adams signalled a waiter and ordered her drink, Nino tried not to stare at her. Her pale lucent skin and chestnut waves set off the green of her eyes. He had never felt so captivated. He forced himself to look away, to think about Bianca, who until this moment, he had considered the most beautiful woman he'd ever seen. He drew in his breath.

"And what are we celebrating?" Viola asked, looking from one to the other. She undid her coat, but kept it on.

Nino turned to Lt. Adams, who had dropped something and was now reaching for it under the table. "Beauty," he improvised, waving his arm to encompass the opulent white marble, Venetian glass, blue tesserae and gold-foiled ceiling. "And comfort too. We're celebrating the fact that we're here, alive, in the midst of a war." He raised his glass, and Viola and Lt. Adams raised theirs too.

"It's been a terrible year," Lt. Adams said. "Who knew we'd be in a world war during our lifetime?"

They all nodded. At the beginning of the month, Germany had invaded Vichy, France, and now most of Europe was under German occupation. The disaster at Dieppe in August had incurred massive casualties, and in North Africa, the British Army had retreated to Egypt. While Lt. Adams spoke about the British in Africa, Nino superimposed a road on the sheer side of a mountain, Elio, the stench of death.

Viola listened, and said little. It made Nino think that she was intimidated by Lt. Adams.

He turned to her. "And you?" he said. "How have you been faring in this war?"

"I've helped wherever I could," she said. "I'm at the War Office now." She nodded to Lt. Adams. "We're all managing in our own ways."

"Well said!" Lt. Adams raised his glass then downed the rest of its contents. "And now, I think we should be off to dinner. Viola, we'd be pleased if you'd join us, wouldn't we, Cassar?"

"Of course," Nino said.

Viola eyed them both a little hesitantly. "I wouldn't want to intrude—" she began.

"Please," Lt. Adams said, smiling. "It would be our pleasure."

She smiled at them, and shrugged lightly. "If you insist."

They stood to move to the restaurant. Nino walked behind Lt. Adams, following Viola's movements as he went. He felt inexplicably drawn to her. She was beautiful, yes, but he was no stranger to beautiful women. He sensed danger, in the possibility that he could lose himself in her. Perhaps, however, the danger was within himself.

When they were seated at a table, they ordered drinks, and were halfway through them when an officer approached. "A call for you, sir," he said, nodding to Lt. Adams, who stood up.

"I'll be right back," he said. "Have a look at the menus." He followed the officer to the front desk.

Nino sipped his drink, trying to come up with something clever to say now that he was alone with Viola. He wanted to impress her, but felt an unusual awkwardness.

"Do you usually come here for dinner?" he asked, then thought it an impertinent question, and wished he could take it back.

"No. Actually this is my first time." She smiled.

Lt. Adams saved Nino from trying to consider what to say next. "I apologize," he said. "I'm afraid you'll have to excuse me. An urgent matter." He picked up his coat.

Nino stood up, alarmed. "Something urgent? Should I—"

"No, no, nothing like that," Lt. Adams said. "Bureaucracy, I'm afraid." He donned his overcoat, then addressed Viola, who looked uncertain at the sudden change of plans. "Viola, you'll have dinner with Sergeant Cassar in my place, won't you?"

"Yes, sir," she said.

"I'll take care of the bill," Lt. Adams said.

Nino remained standing until Lt. Adams was gone, then took his seat. Viola slowly removed her coat and folded it neatly over the back of the chair beside her. She wore a lovely emerald green dress, over which lay a cream collar embroidered with tiny green flowers. She picked up her menu and studied it.

Nino did the same, stealing glances at her. He could hardly believe the choice of food: two starters, seven main courses, four puddings, coffee or tea. For the past two years, British restaurants had been operating on a non-profit basis, as community feeding centres funded by the government. For nine pence, thousands of people displaced by the bombings could have a meal with one serving of meat, fish, eggs or cheese, and two servings of vegetables. Private restaurants like the Criterion could offer three courses, but the maximum they could charge was five shillings. He looked up, and it occurred to him that she might have a date waiting at another restaurant.

"Have we taken you away from another dinner engagement?" he said. "If so, I'm sorry—"

"No, no," she said, shaking her head. "I came in to relay a message. I was just leaving when Lt. Adams called me over."

Nino relaxed at this. "Then I'm glad he saw you."

She smiled again. "Have you been in the service long, Sergeant Cassar?" she asked, setting her menu aside.

"Almost two years."

"Where were you posted?"

"In Malta through much of it," Nino said, following his cover story. He told her of Malta's importance as a base from which to attack Axis ships. "Churchill's unsinkable aircraft carrier," he said. "Malta might have been unsinkable, but it couldn't avoid fierce fighting and bombings," he said. "We fared worse than the London Blitz."

She frowned, her eyes concerned. "You survived."

"Was there another choice?" He grinned and set his menu down.

A waiter came and took their order.

It seemed miraculous that he could be here in London, in a luxurious restaurant, an enchanting woman across from him. He thought fleetingly about Antonio's play in the POW camp, imagining himself right now inside a large tent, observing the British world he had chosen to inhabit. For a moment, that other world intruded, the cyclops eye of a Kenyan night train, his own longing, the damaged tunnels, the roadblocks, the blown-up bridges, the futile trek to Amba Alagi, the capture, Elio, all a lifetime ago.

Viola leaned forward and her fingers brushed his sleeve just below the elbow. "You have an accent," she said. "Where are you from originally?"

"My parents were Italian so we spoke that at home. I was born in Malta," he lied. "Italian used to be one of Malta's official languages until fairly recently."

Their meals arrived and they ate in silence for a few minutes.

Presently, Viola said, "My father is Italian, though he's been living in London for the past two decades."

Nino wondered if Viola's father had left Italy willingly. He thought of Uncle Claudio and the *squadristi*. Three days before, on his return to London, he had walked past his uncle's house, comforted by seeing it still standing. However, he had been forbidden by his superiors to visit his uncle or cousins or anyone he had been familiar with. They needn't have worried, because Nino hadn't maintained contact with them. He would have liked to tell Viola about his uncle, his self-exile, about his antifascist sentiments years before Italy fell under Mussolini's fist, years before the current war began. Nino had heard that in the mid-1930s, many Italians with antifascist views had been exiled to remote provinces in southern Italy.

"And your parents?" she asked. "Are they still there?

Nino sighed, thinking of his aunt in Pozzecco, probably struggling under German occupation. She had lived through another war, through Austrian occupation. He hoped she was still alive. "No," he told Viola. "They were both killed while visiting my aunt in hospital." The lie weighed heavy in his heart, almost as if he had flung a fatal curse towards his aunt.

"I'm sorry," Viola murmured. She reached across and touched his arm again. A shiver ran through him.

"It's why I left," he said. "I wanted to do more than defend. I wanted to avenge their deaths." This was the truth.

"My brother is in the Navy," Viola said. "I wonder where he is right now. If he's all right."

"Assume the best unless you hear different," Nino said.

"Yes, I suppose you're right." She looked down at her hands and stroked the nails of her left hand with the thumb of her right hand. Their second course arrived.

"What about you," Nino asked presently. "Where are you from?"

"Here," she said. "British through and through." She smiled. "Have you been in Britain long?"

"A few months," he said.

"And what's the verdict?"

"I'm getting used to it," he said.

An invisible thread was drawing them closer. Nino looked away because staring into her eyes disoriented him.

They had finished dinner and were lingering over coffee when three firemen appeared in a doorway and calmly asked everyone to step outside for a few moments. There had been reports of smoke in one of the rooms, and they needed to clear the building to identify the source.

Nino and Viola donned their coats and followed the file of people out into the icy night. It was late November, though it felt more like January or February.

"I do hope it won't be a winter like the last one," Viola said. She pulled up the collar of her coat and fastened the top button.

They stood for a few moments among the other clientele waiting for the signal to return to the restaurant, men and women elegant and privileged. It made Nino think of stars, of their careless brilliance despite the war below. "Look up," he said softly, and Viola followed his lead. "Do you think there are more dimensions than the one we live in?"

"Ummmm, maybe," she said. "It's possible."

He told her that years before, he had visited the Brera Astronomical Observatory in Milan, where for a moment, he'd glimpsed a multi-dimensional world: eight clear acrylic squares stacked six inches apart, each dotted with stars. "Imagine this display as the universe," the guide had said. "From this angle, you see a shelving unit made of acrylic. Come and look down onto it from above. What do you see now?" Nino had stepped forward and looked down. The stacks merged into one plane dense with stars, betraying the eye. He stared into Viola's eyes. "Perhaps we're all like that," he said.

"Disguised," she said, smiling, and for a moment, they were suspended in that thought.

"How long are we to be out here?" a man said, addressing a hotel employee while stamping from one foot to another to keep warm.

The hotel employee shrugged. "Your guess is as good as mine."

Nino's hands were cold. He hadn't brought his gloves. Viola was shivering. "We might as well go," he said reluctantly. "Do you live far?"

"A few blocks," she said. "The walk will warm me." She held out her hand to say goodbye.

"I'll walk you home," he said.

They set out along the street, Nino conscious of Viola's body close to his. The air tingled with frost in the clear black sky. Here and there, puffs of steam floated past them, ethereal, transparent, like time. Nino wondered if he'd ever see her again.

"Do you miss your home?" she asked.

He thought about his aunt in Pozzecco, curved over a bicycle, avoiding German checkpoints on her search for wild greens, or crushing wheat to make bread, or helping orphaned children as she had done in that other war. "I miss them as they were," he said. "I miss our lives before this war." He tried to create a mental picture of his earlier life, his father murdered, his mother dead in the fire, Aunt Isabella his only touchstone. Bianca's face materialized in front of him, as if to remind him of their liaisons, their furtive lovemaking — all so distant now, he could barely recall the sensations. "What about you?" he said. "Do you miss your family?"

"More than I can say." She stumbled over an uneven spot on the sidewalk, and he held her arm to steady her.

For a moment, they were transfixed, close, touching. He leaned towards her until they were inches apart, then she abruptly drew back. He let go of her arm, feeling a strange elation, as if he'd experienced a momentary symmetry.

They walked on, turned down one street, then the next, until she said, "This is my hostel," and stopped in front of a square brick building.

He didn't want to leave. "Can I see you again?" he said.

She opened her purse and rummaged inside. He imagined she was searching for a piece of paper on which to write her number or address. However, as quickly as she'd begun, she snapped shut the purse and looked up. Her eyes were luminous, questioning. He took her hand and held it to his lips, blowing warm air into her palm.

Slowly she drew her hand away. "Are you leaving soon?" she asked. "Is that why you were having dinner with Lt. Adams?"

"Not as far as I know," Nino said lightly. "I've been working in the War Office, just like you." They were so compartmentalized that he didn't have to worry that she'd question the lie. "We could have a drink or see a movie."

"You can leave me a message here," she said.

He wanted to kiss her, to hold her in his arms, to tell her the truth about everything, to tell her that he had no idea when he'd be back, but that if she only waited for him, he would be back. He was elated and perturbed by his own emotions. What about Bianca? Wasn't he in love with Bianca? He moved a little closer towards Viola and she stepped back.

"Good night then," she said wistfully. "Until we meet again."

He watched her walk up the steps, then turn and wave her small gloved hand before unlocking the door and going inside. *Until we meet again*. It sounded both promising and final.

The following morning, Nino arrived at Baker Street, and into Lt. Adams's office, where, behind a desk to one side, sat Viola.

Nino stared at her, shocked, as the realization overcame him that she had been nothing more than a trap, that he'd misread every signal, that he'd believed the attraction was mutual.

Viola avoided his gaze, and stared down at the papers on her desk.

"I guess I've passed this scheme," he said, bitterly.

Lt. Adams got up and greeted him, shook his hand. "I'm sorry I had to do that. Don't blame Viola. She was just doing her job." He clapped Nino on the back. "We need to know you can stick to your cover. It's standard procedure. The Germans will surely test you and if you can't resist a pretty girl here, you certainly won't resist one out in the field, which means you'd put more than yourself at risk."

Nino felt numb, stupid. How could he have believed this woman was interested in him? He narrowed his eyes at her, but she did not look up.

He left, furious with himself and her. Back at his hostel, he packed his suitcase with identity papers, ration cards, and travel permits, all made in SOE's forgery department. He shoved in his clothes created by SOE tailors familiar with European designs and fabrics. It was rumored that German Security Police specialists would examine clothing weaves, because British ones were different from continental ones. He took one of Bianca's letters and slipped it into his coat pocket.

Outside the hostel, Nino joined a group of agents waiting for their ride to Glasgow, then onto a ship bound for North Africa, where they would undertake more training. He thought of the irony of his return to Africa as a different person, with a different loyalty. On deck, the wind assailed him as he listened to emergency procedures. At night, he lay on one of the cots stacked four-high, under a tarpaulin that whipped and flapped around them. He pulled out Bianca's letter and held it against his heart. His hands were frigid, but he didn't need to open the letter. He'd memorized it long ago in the loneliness of the POW camp, and now recited the words in his head. How foolish he'd been, how easily infatuated with Viola's green eyes and pretty face. *A honeytrap.* That's all she was. Well, she hadn't succeeded and for this, he was proud. He wondered how many other agents she'd betrayed, then forced himself to stop thinking of her. He'd escaped.

Points to be Considered in Your Disguise

a) Golden Rule.

Never come out of character. By this we mean not only from the clothes point of view but from the mental side also, e.g., if you are a farm worker, do not wear suit and gloves, have polished nails and behave like an educated woman.

b) Clothes.

Study in every detail the clothes you are going to wear, not forgetting small items such as cut, stockings, handkerchiefs, gloves, etc. Different shapes and kinds of hats will alter type.

c) Personal effects.

Handbag, watches, cigarettes, type of newspaper, contents of paper, etc.

d) Hair.

If it should be long or short, whether it should be tidy or untidy.

e) Your face.

Whether it should be dirty or clean, whether it should be pale or sunburnt.

f). Teeth.

Whether they should be clean or not.

g) Hands.

Nails, dirty or clean, and your hands white or dirty or hard worked.

h) Feet.

Whether you wear shoes or boots, whether these should be clean or dirty.

i) Mannerisms.

Practise until your old mannerisms (such as playing with your hair, etc.) are forgotten and your new mannerisms have become part of you.

j) Walk.

If you had any peculiarity in your carriage or your walk, practise until you have conquered the old ones and obtained new ones.

k) Handwriting

For signature or name if needed, educated or not. Whether you should sign as if you are used to signing it or whether you should handle your pen as though it were strange to you.

6

Algiers / Egypt, 1943

Olivia leafed through *The Secret Agent's Handbook* — a manual of weapons, gadgets, disguises and devices. She had clothes manufactured and aged by SOE to look authentic in Italy — three belted dresses in green, burgundy and tan, with Peter Pan collars, and all flowing loosely to just below the knee, as well as a black pocketbook bag, and black sensible shoes. She was not to dye her hair, put on nail polish, or wear noticeable makeup, as such glamorous touches would be out of place in the rural area where she would probably be going.

The best cover story should echo her own story as much as possible, so she was now Viola, and had two brothers, one in the army, the other in the navy. She didn't know their whereabouts. Her parents were simple people who had lived in the same house all their lives in Musadino, a small village less than two kilometres from Porto Valtravaglia. Her father owned a small plot there, which he farmed on his day off or after his shift as a machine grinder in a factory in Porto Valtravaglia. Her mother had grown silkworms before the war, but now her father had cut down all the mulberry trees to grow maize, so they could eat. Viola was in — and here she was to fill in whatever her location — to find work. Her papers would be falsified to reflect this story.

Soon, Olivia kissed Grandma and Grandpa goodbye, promising to write, promising to be careful. Though she was headed to Algeria for advanced cipher training at Massingham — the main Allied command, supply and training centre for clandestine operations into southwestern Europe — she could only tell them she was going overseas. They'd be shocked if they knew she'd been a successful honeytrap. She was proud of herself. By venturing outside her comfort zone, she had glimpsed a strength she didn't know she possessed. The handsome Nardo intruded in her thoughts... *his face so close to mine...* She squeezed her eyes shut and forced herself to think of Philip, to whom she had bade farewell a few days before, tight in his arms, while he professed love and asked her to write, to come back to him. She had been dating him for the past few months, and though uncertain, she thought this must be love, this feeling of anxious happiness. Despite Philip's many questions, she had told him only that she was working for the government. He begged for her photograph, and she teased him, "Won't you remember me otherwise?" then gave him one before her departure.

On the boat to Liverpool, she fingered the silver heart-shaped locket he'd given her, opened it and stared at his face, wondering if she'd ever see him again. Nothing was certain, the war, her safety, his safety, her parents' wellbeing, Aldo's survival, her brother Mick being on the other side of the world or in the depths of a distant ocean.

"Is he your lover?" one of the girls asked, leaning in to look at Philip's photo.

Olivia blushed. "No," she said. "Not lover. Boyfriend."

"Don't tell me you're still a virgin?" the girl said, laughing.

"I'm afraid so," Olivia said, and smiled.

"I'm Claire," the girl said. "Don't wait too long. You don't want to die a virgin."

Olivia closed the locket and slipped it back inside her shirt, between her breasts. It's not as if she hadn't thought about it. She'd nearly had sex with Philip, but perhaps the place, or the hurried quality of it had put her off. She had the idea — possibly gleaned from novels — that her first time should be romantic, with candles and soft music, not something done in a hasty encounter. "As soon as a suitable candidate comes along," she quipped.

She was happy to have met Claire, who within a short time became her friend. She had not seen Barbara in months. *We don't ask questions here* rang in her head.

When they docked in Algiers, Olivia stumbled off the boat, the ten-day journey a hazy whirlpool of seasickness, explosions and shouts. Her medical and clearance papers were stamped INFILTRATE ON FOOT, because of her motion sickness.

Instead of going to parachute school with the others, she was sent to Massingham — a clandestine advanced command post situated in a former beach club west of Algiers for subversive operations into France, Corsica, Sardinia, Sicily and mainland Italy. Club de Pins was an ideal location for SOE operations. Secluded in a pine forest, it had easy access to the Mediterranean, plenty of space for training, and an airfield nearby at Blida. Here, Olivia joined other women SOE ciphers, who were rapidly tapping out Morse code between London and the battlefield. They were called The Pianists, a name that made her wish she played the piano.

In the first few days, Olivia asked each of her colleagues about Barbara, describing her echoic memory, which would surely set her apart from other agents.

"I think I know who you mean," one of the W/T operators said. "She has a different name...Bernadette. Yes, that's it. She was dropped into France, as far as I recall."

"How long ago was this?" Olivia asked.

The young woman shrugged. "Weeks ago, maybe? We received a few messages from her. . . but... she could be back in London for all we know."

Olivia nodded, but she didn't believe it. Barbara would have contacted her had she been in London when Olivia was there, and would surely have known where to send her a letter. She replayed *London. January 17, 1943...* "*What are your plans when the war is over?" Barbara asks. We're in a café and Barbara is about to be shipped out. "I'm not sure," I say, because it's true. I want to do what my brothers do. "We could become detectives," Barbara says. "We could research way faster than other people, and you could gather information just by being there!" This idea appeals to me. If I were a detective, I'd be able to find Mick and Aldo. "After the war," I say... going away... going away...* Olivia shook the film out of her head.

She counted to one hundred, and placed each foot on the centre of a separate tile under her desk. She would hope for the best.

Olivia worked in one of the larger buildings on the club property, and from there, could hear explosions and weapons firing in the outdoor ranges in the dunes. During paramilitary and demolitions training, she'd often see red flags on the beach as warnings of pending explosions. However, she had no fear, and loved her work and the extra assignments she was given because of her memory. While agents and personnel were generally kept separate for their own safety, Olivia's commanding officer entrusted her with all their identities, as well as the identities of foreign agents. She scanned the agents' photographs and filed them in her memory bank. She could not forget a face, and thus could prove invaluable should a foreign agent try to infiltrate their ranks.

"I want you to meet someone," Claire said one night, on the way to the officers' club. She and Olivia were living in the "Fannery house" with five other young women, on a long expanse of sand dunes adjacent to the Mediterranean. They could swim in the day and dance at the officers' club at night, the war now reduced to telegrams and ciphers. "My current beau." Her eyes twinkled.

"I thought you had someone back home," Olivia said, frowning.

Claire laughed. "Yes, I do, but there's no guarantee any of us will get back alive. We might as well live a little."

Olivia shrugged. Maybe she was too old-fashioned, she thought. War changed everything, created different rules and norms. She wanted to experience as much as possible, but not at the expense of her reputation. That had been drilled into her first by her mother, then by Grandma. She glanced at Claire. Well, maybe those rules didn't apply here across the world.

The club was full, music playing, and various couples dancing. Claire looked around, then waved enthusiastically at a handsome man across the room. "Nardo!" she called.

The man looked up, and, on seeing them, approached. Olivia recognized him immediately, and felt the same magnetic pull she'd felt before, then a deep embarrassment. She wished she could tell him that their exchange back in London hadn't been fake, that she had not stopped thinking about him.

Claire looked from Olivia to Nardo, then took his arm possessively. "This is my friend Viola," she said gaily.

"We've met," he said coolly, "under unpleasant circumstances."
Claire lifted an eyebrow.

Olivia shook his outstretched hand, her heart beating in her
chest so loudly, she was sure he could hear it. His palm was warm,
unlike his demeanour. She recalled London, her hand in his a
moment longer than necessary, how she had felt recalibrated, like
a dissonant instrument finally in tune. She was not a sentimental
person, nor a romantic one. She'd read plenty of novels that spoke
of love at first sight, but she had never actually believed such a thing
existed. *Love at first sight*. Heat rose to her cheeks. He stared intently
at her, as if he could decipher all that was racing through her mind.
She forced herself to look away, and smile at Claire, while she waited
for her heart to calm down. She thought about Philip, conjuring his
face. She'd been in love with him, hadn't she? Was in love with him.
But even as she thought this, Philip faded to a distant memory.

"Let's dance," Claire said, and pulled Nardo away.

Olivia didn't even have a chance to find an empty table, when
one of the officers whisked her onto the dance floor. She forced
herself not to look at Nardo and Claire, and focused instead on her
dance partner, wondering where he'd come from and what he had
experienced. She was accustomed to agents who dropped in and
out of Massingham in various psychological and nervous states —
they could generally remain in the field for about six weeks before
risking being discovered. Some never returned. These men either
settled into the club or kept to themselves. Sometimes, their training
exercises had them parachuting onto the beach, hiding until dark,
then stealthily attacking the dummy ammunitions dump at the club,
which resulted in deafening explosions. Often, when the girls had
to work evening shifts, they hurried back to the villa, frightened
they might meet an agent who would mistake them for the enemy.

She went home alone that night, and shook out and refolded
all her shirts, until they were colour coded and perfectly aligned in
the closet. Claire did not return to their shared room until morning.

Olivia immersed herself in work in the following days, trying
not to think of Nardo and Claire, who now spent most nights
together. Since that first meeting, she had not seen Nardo, and
wondered if Claire was keeping him away from her. *November 30,
1942, cold, clear. We're standing outside my hostel. "Can I see you
again?" he says, and I open my purse to busy my hands so he can't*

*see them trembling. I'm not fit for this job. I want to see him again.
He watches me, expectant, then takes my hand and holds it to his
lips, blows warm air into my palm. I want to stay here forever.* "Are
you leaving soon?" *I ask, wanting to hear him say he doesn't want
to leave. He keeps his cover, asks me to meet him for a drink or a
movie.* "You can leave me a message here," *I say, knowing he'll soon be
gone, and we may never meet again.* You mustn't live in the past, her
mother's voice said, but what if the past contained a memory that
sustained her? She struggled with this, knowing her mother was
right; reliving the past was akin to watching a scene frozen in time
that could not be reanimated. An intermission in her life. Nostalgic,
sentimental. She must no longer think of Nardo.

She focused on her work. She excelled in specialized
instruction, easily memorizing all the codes used by SOE. Her
commanding officer had her attend meetings, knowing she could
type up their content verbatim. She enjoyed these challenges, and
the trust he had in her. For the first time since she'd left her London
home, Olivia felt free, unencumbered. In London, her Italian
heritage had encouraged jeers and insults, and made her afraid she'd
be deported, like her father, to some unknown location. Here, away
from the familiar, she had the sense that anything could happen,
that she could grow into herself.

She still received near daily letters from Philip, though they
sometimes arrived all at once, in batches of threes or fours, letters
that had begun as friendly missives and now were transformed into
passionate love letters, implying more than Olivia felt. At times, she
wished she could embrace that love to mute all thoughts of Nardo.
But Philip was not a crutch, or a distraction. His love for her was
genuine. She wrote him once a week, simply saying she was fine,
and asking news from home.

Two months later, in May, she and Claire were transferred to
the Cairo headquarters due to a staffing crisis. Over the past couple
of years, there had been six commanding officers — one was taken
prisoner, and the others weeded out in London during their annual
inspections. Massive backlogs of telegrams had to be immediately
decoded. She was relieved to be transferred out of Massingham,
with its memories of Nardo.

They arrived in a sweltering ninety-six degrees in the shade,
and along with four other girls, settled into a primitive *pensione*,

alive with a multitude of beetles, cockroaches and other flying creatures impossible to eradicate. Each morning, Olivia shook out her clothes exactly three times before putting them on, then she'd sweep the insects out the door, her mind repeating innocuous words to distract herself.

She and the other Pianists worked long exhausting days on the fourth floor of the Rustum Building — known to all as the "Secret Building." Within two weeks, one of the girls in their *pensione* fell ill and, after a short hospital stay, died. No one knew what disease she had, and though Olivia and the others put on a brave face, knowing they'd been vaccinated against a number of tropical diseases, they felt more vulnerable.

Olivia developed a series of rituals to keep herself safe: she stepped out of bed at exactly 6:54 a.m.; brushed her teeth twenty times on the left, twenty in the middle, and twenty on the right; opened the left-hand armoire door first; incorporated the three shakes of her clothes; carried her shoes outside before putting them on. She knew all this was irrational and superstitious, yet she was rigorous in following her practice.

Back and forth they travelled on a military lorry along hot, dusty streets teeming with people, donkeys, mules, all carrying goods, the scent of animal sweat and excrement mingled with the gas fumes along the road; mangy dogs lay in the shadows; men in long white robes followed by their black-clad wives who kept a respectable distance between them; beggars at the edges of the thoroughfare, often women holding babies around whose faces flies hovered; trams rattled down the main road with people clinging to their sides.

A second girl from another *pensione* took ill and died. And then a third.

A few days later, the Pianists were taken to a basement, where they were vaccinated for smallpox.

Olivia wrote to Philip, intending at first to tell him about the smallpox, but instead wrote of Cairo's poverty and misery while shining limousines glided through the streets, their uniformed drivers staring straight ahead, their businessmen and officials leaned into air-conditioned back seats, bound for workplaces. She didn't tell him about the girls' deaths, protective of a life in which Philip and London had no place.

Following the deaths, Olivia and the girls moved to a paddleboat steamer moored off the island of Gezira. Known as "Jardin des Plantes," the island itself was only a couple of miles long, and boasted grand luxurious villas and gardens with exotic plants from all over the world.

"I've never been anywhere so fantastic," Olivia told Claire, pointing to the tree-lined streets that cast cool shadows along the road. She wiped a bead of perspiration from her lip.

"You haven't seen the best part yet!" Claire exclaimed, leading her to the Gezira Sporting Club. "We are all allowed to join," she said. "We can golf, play tennis, polo and cricket; we can swim in the pool and watch horse races." She grinned.

Olivia had never done any of those sports, nor had she watched horse races, but she was thrilled nonetheless. She could learn. The paddleboat was massive, with three decks and eighty cabins. Soldiers on leave came and went, and for a week or two, their war receded.

"Let's take these," Claire said when they found two cabins that opened to a shared bathroom. They unpacked and settled in, amazed by the cleanliness, the wicker chairs and tables, the dining room, the promenade deck — all so unlike their previous rooms.

Since their arrival in Cairo, without Nardo present, Olivia and Claire had been spending more time together, and although Olivia enjoyed exploring the island in the daytime, she was reluctant to join Claire at night in a series of Cairo hotels and clubs.

"Don't you miss Nardo?" she asked Claire, unable to stop herself, hoping Claire might have some news of Nardo. They were sitting in her cabin, getting ready to go to dinner.

Claire shrugged. "I don't know. Maybe. But who knows where he is, or whether I'll see him again? I'm not waiting around."

Olivia envied Claire's nonchalance. Of course she had to forget Nardo, though he was never hers to begin with. She felt a vague loyalty to Philip, whose letters sounded forlorn and unhappy; he told her he could hardly wait for her return so they could get married.

"I never promised to marry him," Olivia said. "He never even proposed."

Claire laughed. "Well, lucky you! Absence makes the heart grow fonder and all that."

"It's not like that," Olivia said. "I don't know him that well. We haven't. . ." She sighed. "I was only seventeen when I met him…"

"A childhood sweetheart then."

"No, he was a colleague at work. A friend. And then I joined up and before I knew it, I don't know, we went from friends to . . . a bit more. . . we only kissed, for God's sake!"

"It's all the time compression that happens during war," Claire said thoughtfully. "I slept with my boyfriend before I left, mostly because I didn't know if I would live or die, and also because it seemed the right thing to do before I left." She shrugged. "But I don't intend to marry him. At least, I don't think so. I don't want to be tied down right now. Things are too uncertain."

Olivia fingered the locket around her neck. At the moment, it felt like a noose. She opened it and Philip's face made her anxious, as if she were deceiving him. "I'm going to write and set him straight right now." From a drawer, she slid writing paper and pen.

Claire slapped her hand over the paper. "No, no, no," she said. "You can't break his heart like this, long distance. There's a war on. What if he's killed? Do you want him to die totally devastated?"

"He's not going to die!" Olivia said, exasperated. "And besides, I don't want him to make up a life for me."

Claire shrugged. "Suit yourself," but Olivia put the paper away. She didn't want to be responsible for Philip's unhappiness. She rearranged the books on her desk. Besides, she reasoned, she might not ever return home; she might settle in Italy with her parents; her cousins might not relinquish their London house; her brothers might be captured or dead… She took a deep breath. She'd have to wait until she returned home, and see what transpired.

She tried to push Nardo out of her mind, but his memory persisted, infiltrating her thoughts. *He takes my hand and holds it to his lips, blows warm air into my palm… Until we meet again.* Well, they had met again, and he'd been cool towards her. At times, she convinced herself that she'd imagined his interest; other times she wondered if he was thinking of her as he sabotaged bridges, trekked through mountainous terrain, radioed messages, without being caught and tortured. She imagined him parachuting with his transceiver attached to his chest, and knowing how feeble an instrument it was, she listened to all the broadcasts with devotion and concentration.

She hadn't yet learned to read his "fist" — his particular Morse code keying that identified him like a fingerprint — so she treated each message as if it were coming from Nardo. She worked diligently through the contact sheet, listening carefully through the radio noise made by telegraphs, broadcast stations, jammers — continuous white noise that almost obliterated the agents' transmissions. It reminded her of London, of standing in front of a bombed-out building, amid the shouts of emergency workers, cranes and excavators lifting the rubble, listening for the faint sound of a survivor. Often she and the other decoders worked together to decipher a message, fragment by fragment, and tried to do it as quickly as possible so the agent could stop transmitting, aware that danger shrouded every moment while the agent was transmitting.

A few weeks after her arrival in Cairo, she was promoted to instructor in wireless and ciphers. In June, she was startled by Nardo, who had been assigned to her for advanced cipher training. He stood in the doorway, as if hesitant to enter. Her heart beat wildly.

"We meet again," he said. "I seem destined to be in your power."

She frowned. What did he mean by that? Was it their student/teacher dynamic? She was in his power, though she'd never admit it. "There is no power here."

"You had the power to ruin my career," he said.

"And you to save it," she said.

He stared at her for a moment. "Shall we call a truce?"

She nodded, then glanced at his file, trying to keep her hands from trembling. "You've already worked as W/T operator in the war."

"Yes," he said. "I trained for it when I was sixteen."

Olivia concentrated on the work, sequestering the part of herself that couldn't forget their first meeting. Nardo mastered cipher, double transposition. He was smart, charming, easygoing, but showed no further interest in her. Olivia longed for him. And she wasn't the only one. All the women in the Cairo office flirted with Nardo, and he responded to them all equally. Olivia had watched Claire's reaction carefully when she told her Nardo was back, but Claire appeared indifferent. Rumours abounded: Nardo had dated a number of the agents, without commitment; he was married; he was divorced; one of the older young women said he was a womanizer, and they should all be on their guard. This didn't stop anyone from going out with him.

One afternoon, in mid-June, Claire asked her if she'd like go to a party. Olivia hadn't exactly been avoiding parties or social occasions, but when she joined the others at social occasions, she felt awkward. "What kind of party?" she asked.

Claire leaned forward, whispering. "It's one of those best-kept secrets," she said, smiling. "A party at Tara, a villa where famous people go — agents, officers, diplomats — that kind of thing. Very high-spirited kind of party." She raised her eyebrows in mock shock. "Something you've probably never seen before."

Olivia thought for a moment. She'd heard all about Tara, the legendary party villa on the island, named after the ancient seat of the High Kings of Ireland, where four SOE agents and a Countess lived. Everyone knew the stories of wild parties and crazy hijinks, of broken windows, burning sofas in the garden, light bulbs shot out, crates of champagne, but also of kings and writers and war correspondents and diplomats.

"Well, what do you say?"

Olivia hesitated a moment longer. She wondered if Nardo would be there. He seemed exactly like the kind of partygoer who would be there. She forced herself to smile. "Sure."

Later, after dinner, Claire led her up the stairs at Tara, then beneath one of the great arches leading to the loud music and laughter. Although Olivia had seen plenty of splendid villas on the island, she had never been inside one. Claire pulled her into a great ballroom with parquet floors, and she recognized several of the girls from the office, who turned and looked a little surprised to see her. Olivia flushed. Did they think she didn't belong here? It wasn't that she didn't want to join the other girls, or have a good time, but merely that she had been raised in a strict household, and was both shy as well as slightly fearful about how she would be viewed by others. Partying with young men was something her parents would certainly prohibit. It made her wonder why young men could do whatever they wanted, while young women had to be extremely cautious, though right now the other girls from the office were dancing, twirling on the arms of handsome young officers without a care. It's wartime, Olivia thought, rules don't matter anymore.

Then Nardo was at her side, pulling her onto the dance floor.

"I don't know—"

"It's very easy," he said, circling her waist. "Just follow me."

It wasn't exactly true she didn't know how to dance. Back in London, in what felt like a century ago, she and Barbara had practised, in case this opportunity should arise.

"You're a good dancer," Nardo said. "You protest way too much."

She let herself relax, happy to be in his arms. However, this did not last long. Claire came by and playfully pulled Nardo away from her. "You can't monopolize this handsome man," she said, laughing. She put her arms around his neck, and the two of them were away, dancing. Olivia was left staring after them, wishing she'd been able to hang onto Nardo. But she was not the type of girl who would be able to do that, though she envied girls who could freely express themselves.

She was standing there still, staring wistfully at Nardo, when a tall young man came by and touched her elbow.

"Would you like to dance?" he asked

She looked up into his face. He was smiling. He had large straight teeth and hooded dark eyes. His curly black hair was cut short, and he was smoking a cigarette. He didn't wait for her response but whisked her onto the dance floor. He placed his hand flat against her back, and pulled her closer than she was comfortable with. She pushed against his chest, and he relented a little.

"You're one of the new girls, aren't you?" he asked. "I think I've heard about you. You're the one with the weird memory, right?"

"Maybe," she said, startled. She wondered what exactly he'd heard about her. Has she become a party trick for them all?

"What's your name?" he asked, pulling her a tad closer again.

"Viola," she said, pushing against him once again, to create a space between them.

"Viola, huh?" he said and looked into her eyes. "Like the instrument."

She nodded and smiled. "What's your name?" she asked.

"Jaybird," he said, "which suits me perfectly." He let go of her and twirled around a couple of times, then embraced her again. "Get it? Like a bird. Free."

She wondered if he meant it as a personality trait or a warning. She looked away, wishing for the dance to end so she could go and sit down. Nardo was still dancing across the room, with a different girl this time.

"Do you know what they call you? The girls, I mean?" he asked.

She looked at him perplexed. Were they really talking about her? She'd been keeping too much to herself, she thought now, not socializing with the girls like everyone else, turning herself into an outsider, a kind of joke. "No," she said. "What are they calling me?"

"Mnemosyne," he said, and when she frowned, he added, "You know. The goddess of memory, daughter of heaven and earth." He laughed. "A pretty good name, I'd say. You should be flattered."

The music stopped, and Olivia quickly extricated herself, but just as quickly the music began once more, and Jaybird twirled her back onto the dance floor. Over his shoulder, she saw Nardo approach from across the room.

"My name's not really Jaybird," he said confidentially, his breath hot in her ear.

"I didn't think it was," she said, though she had actually believed him.

All at once, as if by some signal, the couples on the dance floor moved to the sides of the ballroom, exposing two young officers in the middle, one who held a great red cape, and the other who had his fingers up by his temples, like two horns.

"*Olé!*" the crowd began to chant, and the two men ran toward each other, in a pantomime bullfight.

I really am in the wrong place, Olivia thought, or at the very least, in an alien place. While everyone was focused on the playacting, a man was slowly circling the room, looking directly at her. He was alone, indifferent to the entertainment. She flipped through her catalogue of faces: *Yesterday. 1:15 p.m. It's lunchtime, I'm on the roof, watching passersby on the street, which is clogged and noisy. The humid air hangs like a transparent scrim. Below, across the street, the man stands alone, watching the building. I think he must be an agent, waiting for a friend.* He had not come upstairs, and she had thought nothing of it. Now, this information took on significance. Who was he and why was he looking in her direction? She frowned. Something about him was not right. The man lingered at the perimeter of the room, then slipped out.

"Did you see that man?" she said.

Jay turned, but the man was gone. "You need to be a little more specific," he said, laughing. "There are a lot of men in this room."

"He wasn't mingling—"

"Probably a newbie," Jay said. "These parties can be a little intimidating."

And then, Nardo tapped Jaybird's shoulder and he turned, surprised. "Cutting in," Nardo said, whisking Olivia away.

"Thank you," she said.

"I could see you needed a little saving," he said, smiling. "And Jay is one of the wilder boys. I'd be careful around him."

"Yes, I figured as much," Olivia said. "I'm afraid I'm not a very good party girl. I'm not used to this kind of thing."

"There's nothing wrong with a little laughing and a little dancing, especially in the middle of the war," he said. "It's the illusion of a healthy normal life."

"I don't even know what a normal life is anymore," she said, with an impassioned seriousness. "Here, I'm surrounded by agents who drop into foreign countries, and may or may not return, while we go to parties." She sighed. "My father was taken away by the police in the middle of the night, my mother is in a little Italian village she's never been to, trying to communicate in a language she's never spoken. My younger brother is lost at sea, we don't even know what that means, and my older brother ran away and joined the partisans or a communist party in Italy. I don't know if any of them are alive or dead. That's my normal life." She took a deep breath. In her head, the words sprang up: *...an agent should not tell people more than they need to know...* "I think I'll go now," she said.

He tightened his grip. "I'm sorry," he said, frowning. "I didn't know." He released her then, and took her hand. "I'll see you back," he said, and led her outside.

The house *sufragi* stood at the top of the steps, his tarboosh held out for a donation. Nardo reached into his jacket pocket, and put some money in the hat. "They're always short of money at Tara," he said, smiling. "Alcohol is hard to come by." He nodded to the young man.

The hot June air was scented with night jasmine that grew around the arches of the villa. Olivia and Nardo descended the steps to the road, Olivia carefully avoiding any cracks in the cement.

"I'm being sent to Italy soon," Nardo said. "But you probably know that already."

She nodded, hoping all would go according to plan. Weeks earlier, British Intelligence had taken the body of a homeless man, dressed him up as a British Marines officer, and planted fictitious documents in a briefcase handcuffed to his wrist, in an effort to disguise the Allied invasion of Sicily. The body had been transported in a submarine and released a mile off the Spanish coast, where it drifted onto the Spanish shore and was discovered the following morning by fishermen. The hope was that the Spanish government, being neutral, would photograph the documents, then pass them to German Intelligence via Nazi sympathizers. The "secret" documents detailed a fake Allied attack on Greece and Sardinia. It appeared that the deception was working, because the Germans had been moving tanks, artillery and boats into those areas.

"I'll be coming too," she said. "Later in the fall with Force 133."

"It's a date," he said, squeezing her hand.

"Will you work with partisans in Italy?" she asked him, thinking of Aldo, wondering where he could be, wondering if Nardo could help her find his whereabouts.

"Probably. But it's all extremely complicated," Nardo said. "In Italy, there aren't two or three easily defined political parties. There are a dozen or more, each with varying degrees of loyalty or disloyalty to Mussolini, with varying degrees of communist or socialist or democratic ideals. Even the partisans have varying affiliations." He paused. "So it's difficult to predict who I'll be working with or where."

"I think my brother might be with the partisans, but I have no idea where or with whom," Olivia said, though she knew *she should not: a) confide in friends just to relieve the strain of nerves; b) answer questions in such a way as to arouse curiosity; c) tell people more than they need to know, no matter how important or how close the association...* She shook the rules out of her head. What's done is done, she thought, They headed along the road towards the river. Soldiers of various nations walked around, in khaki-drill uniforms, corduroy trousers, long baggy shorts and open-necked shirts, army boots or city shoes, their headgear identifying their affiliations.

"Maybe he'll find you," Nardo said. "Are you in touch with your parents?"

"I was," Olivia said, "but that was back in Kent. I've had no news for over a year." Time these days seemed to her slower when she was awaiting news, and quicker when she wanted to slow it down, like right now with Nardo. Although she could recall exactly how they got here, she wished they'd lose their way, so they could wander together longer. She forced her mind back to her parents. Right now, they were a world apart. "I don't even know if they're alive."

"Focus on the positive," he said. "There are many reasons why you haven't heard from them, from delayed mail, to censorship, to lack of paper or stamps..."

"I hope you're right," Olivia said, though she didn't think he was. "Anyway," she said. "I shouldn't have told you all that. Please forget I said anything."

"Be glad I'm not a honeytrap," he said, smiling.

They walked along the river's edge to the paddleboat, and Nardo stopped before they reached the ramp. He turned to her, and she relived the tension between them... *November 30, 1942. I stumble on the sidewalk, and he holds my arm to steady me. For a moment, we are transfixed, close, touching. He leans towards me until we're inches apart, then I abruptly draw back...* but this time, she responded, her arms circling his neck, her body pressed against his in a passionate kiss. She had not felt like this with Philip, this urgency that both surprised and thrilled her. She breathed in Nardo's scent, alive to his lips in her hair, then he slowly released her, and she slipped out of his arms.

"Good night, Viola," he murmured.

"Olivia," she whispered.

"Nino."

Nino, she repeated silently, *Nino*. She walked self-consciously onto the paddleboat, wondering if he was watching her. When she turned just before going inside, however, she could no longer see him.

In her room, she lay in bed, restless, unable to sleep. Water lapped in rhythmic waves, and distant voices of girls and laughter came from the pier. She counted the number of waves against the boat in an hour, then calculated how many there would be in a day, a week, a month, a year, ten years, a hundred, a thousand. *"You protest way too much," he says, his arm around me... My heart is pounding. I hope he can't hear it... The hot June air is scented with night jasmine that grows around the arches of the villa.* She took a deep breath. Most people were still out, perhaps at Tara, dancing. She replayed Nino's arms around her, the dance, the kiss, feeling the same thrill each time, examining the scene for things she may have been too giddy to notice. She saw Jay, and over his shoulder the strange man. He was definitely looking at her. Then, Claire and Nino flitted into her vision, dancing, laughing. She felt a small pang of jealousy, but admonished herself. She had no right to feel this way; Nino was not hers. Presently, she heard sound in the adjoining bathroom. She checked the time: 3:12 a.m. Claire. She got up and rapped on the bathroom door, wondering what other crazy things might have happened at Tara.

"Claire?" she said softly.

The door opened. "You're awake," Claire said. She looked a little dishevelled, and her eyes were glassy.

"Couldn't sleep, though I tried." Olivia sat on the bed.

Claire stood, leaning in the doorway. "What a party!" she said, and combed her hand through her hair.

"Were you there till now?" Olivia said. "What else happened? It seemed rather wild before I left."

Claire laughed a little too loudly. "The mock bullfight was barely the start of it," she said. She weaved forward and fell into a chair.

"Are you all right?" Olivia said. "I think you're drunk."

Claire waved her hand, as if to dismiss the idea. "Maybe a little tipsy," she said. "Where'd you go, anyway?"

"I was a little tired," Olivia said.

"Well, you missed a good party." Claire leaned back in the chair and closed her eyes. "Nardo's a great dancer," she said dreamily. "We'd still be there if someone hadn't called the authorities because we were making too much noise."

A tourniquet twisted around Olivia's heart. So, Nino had returned to the party. Had he walked Claire home? Had he kissed her also? Olivia closed her eyes and fell back. She forced herself not to ask questions.

"I'm off to bed." Claire stumbled up, and blew her a kiss, before going through the bathroom to her own room.

Late Monday afternoon, as she was leaving work, Jay appeared at her elbow. "Hello, Mnemosyne," he said brightly. "I hope you don't mind. You left Tara so early, I didn't get a chance to talk to you." He paused. "I've planned a little surprise."

She frowned. "Whatever do you mean?"

"I thought you'd like to see more of Cairo than the island." He smiled. "We can have dinner first, then walk about and explore."

She began to shake her head, but he persisted. "Come on. A little harmless fun. Don't you want to experience night markets and music? You'll be perfectly safe with me."

Be careful. Nino's words swirled in her head, but he hadn't called or left her any message. His next lesson was on Wednesday. Should he have called her? She didn't know what to make of it all. Maybe it was nothing. A kiss. Big deal. He probably kissed all the girls. She sighed. "All right."

Jay gave her his arm, and they wandered off into the busy streets to a hotel, where they ate dinner. Jay was charming and attentive, and Olivia relaxed. He told her versions of his exploits in France, though she was certain these were compilations of different agents' stories — best of, perhaps. No agent would speak of real missions.

"Close your eyes," he said slowly, reaching across to stroke her hand on the table. "Trust me."

"Really?" she murmured, but she closed her eyes.

"Describe me without looking."

She replayed the last few minutes on the inside of her lids. "You have an oblong face, blue eyes, and hooded lids. Your hair is black, cut short, and curly. You have a small mole under your chin on the right side, and when you're nervous, you touch it. Or maybe," she said, laughing, "you touch it when you lie. Should I go on?"

"You didn't tell me anything I didn't already know," he said sulkily.

She opened her eyes. "Was I supposed to?"

"I'm mesmerized by the idea of your memory," he said, and lit a cigarette. "Imagine how useful you'd be if you could infiltrate some German high command post, and recall every single conversation and every single face." He gave a low whistle.

"That's not likely to happen," she said. "Though I'd like nothing better." She had been told in Cairo that she was needed for coding and cipher, and would not be sent into the field, though she would be going to Italy to set up and continue this work.

After dinner, they strolled down and around narrow streets and pathways, through a labyrinth of alleys, souks and courtyards into an extensive outdoor bazaar, where Olivia felt she was inside a kaleidoscope of glass lanterns in jewel shades, metal ornaments, gold and silver jewellery, baskets, drums, candleholders, elaborate pipes. Merchants called out, children squealed and laughed, men and women bargained, musicians played and sang. She stopped to admire a brass case, and in its sheen, she glimpsed or thought she glimpsed the man she'd seen at Tara.

"There!" she said, her hand on Jay's arm. "Turn around, quick. That man. Do you know who he is?"

Jay turned, but the man was gone. He shook his head. "Are you seeing things?" he said, teasing her. "Don't tell me you have visions too."

She smiled half-heartedly — he was probably right; she was imagining things — yet she couldn't shake away the worry.

They continued along the bazaar, Olivia glancing around as she went, feeling almost breathless in the overwhelming scents of cinnamon, ginger, cardamom, and so many others she couldn't identify. When they came to a display of cotton and silk, she stopped, fingering the fabrics, the textures. She wanted to buy some and turned to Jay, but found herself inexplicably alone.

She frowned, called his name, scanned up and down the kiosks for him — he was taller than most, in uniform, easy to find — but she didn't see him anywhere. Her parents' instructions rose out of her past — *when lost, stay where you are, and we'll find you.* They never understood she couldn't get lost. However, she thought, I'll wait here for Jay to return. This is where he last saw me. For the next half hour, she remained near the cloth stand.

It was full dark now, despite the blinding colours and lights in the bazaar. Where had Jay gone? Surely something had happened to him; he wouldn't have left her there. She was right to have been apprehensive. She had to get back to the paddleboat and get help.

She closed her eyes for a moment, to replay the past several hours in fast-forward motion.

"All right?" A merchant in the cloth stall touched her elbow.

"Yes, thank you," she said, opening her eyes. She quickly retraced her steps past stalls of instruments, mats, toys. The sphinx, camel and pharaoh statues had morphed into sinister creatures. She half-ran through the labyrinth of arches and gates, her heart pounding, and soon was walking towards the river. Up ahead, a crowd was gathered, and a police car and an ambulance were parked on the road. *Jay,* she thought, mind scrolling rapidly to another day, searching. *The man stands alone, watching the building...* She tried to reorient the scene, follow the trajectory of the man's eyes. *Third floor, second window from the left...* She'd check with her CO when she got back...then the party... *why is he looking in her direction? She frowns. Something about him is not right. The man lingers at the perimeter of the room, then slips out...*to the bazaar, *and in its sheen, she glimpses the man she saw at Tara.* What had he done?

She pushed forward, through the crowd. The man was strapped into a stretcher, his shirt wet with blood, his face *mirrored in the sheen of a brass case.* "What happened?" she asked.

"Stabbing," someone said, as the man was wheeled into the waiting ambulance. One of the paramedics pulled the sheet over his face.

"What happened?" she said again.

No one responded, as the ambulance began to pull away from the curb.

Dead. Olivia forced herself to walk casually, normally towards the paddleboat, her mind scanning the SOE manual for the section on Individual Security:

The agent, unlike the soldier, who has many friends, is surrounded by enemies, seen and unseen. He cannot even be certain of the people of his own nationality who are apparently friendly. The agent must, therefore, remember that, like primitive men in the jungle, he has only his alertness, initiative and observation to help him. He has to look after himself...

Was this Jay's doing? She mustn't draw attention to herself, nor look around. She must be alert. She didn't know what to think.

"There you are!" Jay's voice rang out in the darkness.

She turned. "What?" She went to him, and slapped his arm repeatedly. "I thought you were dead!"

He laughed. "That's a bit dramatic, isn't it?" he said. "No. I lost sight of you in the market."

She stared at him, but his face was impassive. "You didn't lose sight of me. You're the one who moved away," she said

"Was I?" He started walking towards the paddleboat.

"Who was that man?" she said, stopping him. "You knew him!"

"What man?"

She was certain he was lying. His demeanour, however, was casual, normal. He was the embodiment of the highly trained agent. He stood facing her, but she couldn't see his eyes in the dark. They continued along the road, Olivia's brain replaying the moment in the market when she found herself alone. She had only looked down for an instant and he was gone. Try as she might, she could not see him leaving. She would speak to her commanding officer. She would replay the scene and let him decide the outcome.

At the paddleboat ramp, she said a curt "Good night," and walked away.

Rail Charge

The charge consists of two ¾-lb. units each comprised of three separately wrapped sticks of Plastic Explosives, the centre one being primed at each end with a one-ounce C.E. primer. These charges are attached to a special cordtex lead, and so spaced along it that there is between them one metre of double cordtex, and at each end, a one-metre single cordtex tail. Each of these units is enclosed in a rubberized fabric sleeve, to which is sewn a webbing strap for fixing to the rail. The whole is packed in a rubberized fabric bag along with a tin containing two fog signals and two No. 8 detonators, these latter being enclosed in a wooden block.

Method Of Use

Detonators are inserted into the two fog signal initiators, and are then taped to each of the single cordtext tails, three or four inches from the end. The charge is then strapped to the railway line with one fog signal at each end.

The locomotive, no matter from which side it approaches, crushes one of the fog signals, which in turn initiates the detonator and the charge. The charge normally removes about one metre of rail.

Italy was an enemy country, not an enemy-occupied one, and anti-Fascist Italians who volunteered to return as secret agents faced a traitor's fate if caught. The courage of those Italians who were prepared to face the firing squads deserves recognition, and stands as an effective counter to enduring images of Italy's fighting abilities.

— Roderick Bailey

7

Paestum / Salerno / Pistoia, 1943

In early September, Nino sailed out of Palermo on the Royal Navy landing ship, headed to Italy's southwest shore. Everything was new to him, as if he'd been reborn into someone he preferred to who he'd been. Until now, he'd never ventured south of Rome. Though Sicily had been under Allied control since mid-August, the mainland was enemy territory. He felt disoriented, viewing his country as enemy territory, but that's what it had become.

He stood on deck, staring at the Sicilian coastline and the promontory Mount Pellegrino, whose pink dolomite Castello Utveggio clung to the top. Built as a luxury hotel, it had been requisitioned by the Fascist government at the beginning of the war to use as an anti-aircraft post. He wondered if it had been bombed by the Allies and was now in ruins, deck chairs upended, windows shattered, turrets crumbling. None of this was visible as he sailed past. He had heard a rumour that the castle had been abandoned by the fascists when the Allies landed in Sicily, and was subsequently looted by the population until only a shell remained, colonized by wild animals.

Along the coast, the citrus orchards and vineyards were in various states of devastation, and among olive groves, remnants of a camouflaged German airstrip were now visible. Nino wondered if the farmers would return once the war was over, and begin anew to cultivate the land as their ancestors had done before them. Would the soil be altered as they had all been? Would it retain the memory of gunpowder and bombs? Would the harvest taste of this terrible era? He felt a nostalgia for his own home, for Bianca, his first love, at a time when love was uncomplicated, when it was enough that two people wanted to be together. He wondered whether Bianca felt the same, or whether she felt abandoned. Had he abandoned her? No, not really. She had given herself to him, and he had believed he loved her. He did love her, or had loved her. However, now, he wasn't sure. He thought of Olivia. What a mess he'd made in Cairo.

After Tara and the kiss, he had forced himself to stay away from her, uncertain how she felt, and even more uncertain how he felt. Then he'd heard she'd gone out with Jay, and wondered if he'd lost his chances with her, all the while pushing Bianca to the back of his mind. The day after Olivia's date with Jay, Nino had approached her desk with a piece of paper he'd placed in front of her. "A stanza from a poem by Ugo Foscolo. Do you know who he is?"

She'd shaken her head, and while she read the poem, he said, "A famous Italian poet from the 18th century. You could read this in Italian, but I translated it to make it more difficult to code break."

> *You make my thoughts wander in steps*
> *that lead to eternal voids; meanwhile*
> *this guilty time escapes, and with it shapes*
> *of cares with which it me destroys;*
> *while I gaze upon your peace, my warlike spirit*
> *sleeps, though yet within me roars.*

"A poem cipher," she said.

These were commonly used by agents, though the Germans had gathered hundreds of well-known poems for deciphering messages. Often, the agents made up their own poems. "This will be our personal cipher," Nino said. "So I can send you messages no one will understand."

She smiled.

"I've given you the whole verse for context," he said, "though we will only use the last two lines: *while I gaze upon your peace, my warlike spirit sleeps, though yet within me roars.*" He wondered if she could read within those words his desire; wondered if she felt the same.

Olivia looked down at the words for a moment, then ripped up the paper in front of him.

"Excellent," he said.

Over the next month, he'd begun to leave her secret messages — at first playful ones — then encouraged by her smiles and looks, he'd composed flirtatious ones, and finally asked her out.

Indicator group: FIJOAH — Peace spirit sleep roars while warlike

LRNI NPI AET LWED EEIS
OITE OUI NAW DEP NTR
YSO OMNE AIO OEU DYU
IAR WOS UBU EDO IEP
HNNE IHEN DGI LEH REL
GLC VAY VTEN MYR ERL
IEK IFU FAY HRA

Hello Viola. I'm
wondering if you'd
have dinner with me.
If you agree, please
be ready at nineteen
hundred hours. I will pick
you up at your residence.

She'd been reluctant at first, unsure perhaps of his intentions, of which he himself was unsure. Wasn't it enough that they were attracted to each other? He'd persisted, and soon they spent all their free time together, their dates ending in passionate kisses Olivia would not go beyond. Now and then, a letter from Bianca plunged Nino into guilt. Yet he wanted only to be near Olivia.

One early July night, when everyone had dispersed to their own quarters, Nino had gone to the paddleboat and coaxed Olivia out. They'd walked along the riverbank, under palms, acacias, sycamores. They both knew he'd be leaving soon.

"Have you seen Jay?" Nino had asked lightly.

"You told me to be careful around him," she said.

He smiled and took her hand. "Careful not to be alone with him."

She'd moved closer to him, their arms touching. "And you? Do I need to be careful around you?"

He laughed. "Depends," he said. In his head, Bianca appeared, framed in the dim glow of a streetlight, leaning against the wall at the front of her house, her head turned to him. He'd taken Olivia's hand, and they'd continued to walk along the river. He hardly knew what they spoke about. He was no longer himself, spiralling into Olivia's vortex, her eyes afire, her hand trembling in his.

"I should have nothing to do with you," she murmured. The air was warm, infused with the scent of night jasmine that climbed stone walls and fell in a cascade of white. Then she laughed. "Though I feel perfectly safe with you."

He held her at arm's length and looked in her eyes. "Maybe you shouldn't."

"And maybe I don't want to be safe with you." Blood rushed to her cheeks.

He pulled her under the canopy of a sycamore and kissed her, drawing her tight against him. Pleasure spread through him, vibrant, urgent, a warmth beyond the physical, so different from what he'd felt with Bianca. Was he fooling himself? Was he giving himself permission to betray Bianca? He had had plenty of sexual encounters that he didn't consider betrayals, because they meant nothing to him. But this... For several minutes, he held Olivia, then slipped his hand between them, and cupped her breast. She closed her eyes, leaned into him.

"Should we...?" he whispered. "Do you want to... there's a hotel down the street..."

She nodded, and he kept his arm around her and led her to a small hotel, where she waited in the lobby, embarrassed, under the eyes of a disapproving clerk, while Nino checked them into a room, pretending they were married.

Upstairs, he slid open the drapes and the streetlight cast a golden beam across the bed. Olivia excused herself for a moment, and went into the bathroom. Nino undressed and lay down, his hand over the raised scar on his chest, just below his left nipple, a memento of the house fire that killed his mother. Throughout his childhood, Aunt Isabella had told him he was blessed with this horn-shaped amulet of good luck.

When Olivia emerged from the bathroom, his arms reached for her. She sat beside him, and he pulled her to him, kissed her, then deftly undid the buttons of her dress, sliding it down her shoulders, his lips brushing her neck.

She sat up abruptly. "I'm a virgin," she said.

He immediately fell back on the bed, as if she'd pushed him. "Oh, Olivia," he said, sighing. "This isn't a good idea."

"What's wrong?" she asked, laying her head on his chest. She traced her fingers along the inside of his arm. "I thought you found me attractive."

"I do, of course I do, but…"

"But what?"

He felt himself withdrawing as he had in Kenya, escaping to an inner place, Olivia's eyes on fire. He reached out and stroked her back, the skin warm, inviting. "It's just that…" and he didn't know how to articulate it, the implied commitment he wasn't ready for.

"I love you," she said.

He sighed again, unsure of himself, afraid to trust his emotions. Hadn't he believed himself in love with Bianca? He and Olivia had only been dating for a little over a month — too soon for declarations. He felt uneasy.

She waited, and when he remained silent said, "But?"

"There's someone back home." He closed his eyes, and conjured Bianca who, in the absence of three years, had become ethereal, an idealized first love. Olivia was flesh and blood, here now, her anxious face questioning, though she surely knew of his lovers in Algiers and Cairo. "Her name is Bianca and…"

Olivia sat up and stared at him coldly. "Why didn't you tell me?" she said.

He paused, embarrassed. "I didn't think it necessary."

"You didn't think it necessary?" She pushed her hand against his chest. "What were you waiting for? Were you waiting until I slept with you? Is this some kind of payback?"

Startled, he said, "I didn't set out to deceive you."

Olivia had stared at him while her eyes filled with tears. He felt a terrible wall descending between them.

She'd drawn the bodice of her dress back up over her shoulders, and given him a brave little smile. "It's all right," she'd said, quickly buttoning up the front. "Nothing happened. Thank you for telling me before something did." She'd gone back into the washroom, while he dressed.

The following week, he'd been sent to Sicily, where he now stood on the deck of the Royal landing ship staring at the small stone walls that stippled the countryside, beyond which rose undulating hills, some green, others scattered with prickly-pear cacti and scrubland that sectioned the landscape into hamlets.

In the distance, Mount Etna rose to a pointed cone. Three years before, it had erupted, and ash had dusted the villages on its flanks.

"Have you never been to Mount Etna?" Jules stood next to Nino, following his line of sight. Same age as Nino, born in Italy, Jules had lived most of his life in the UK, so was fluent in Italian and English. He was quick, friendly. He and Nino had met in Cairo, though they knew little about each other.

Nino shook his head. "It's legendary," he said. "I always meant to go and see it."

He recalled a family story — a myth — in which his father had gone to Sicily before Nino's birth, to see Mt. Etna, and against all advice, had hiked alone towards the summit. Disoriented by steam and noxious fumes, he had wandered for hours, small flames gusting in the imprints of his shoes. At nightfall, he told Nino's mother later, the earth had trembled, become an undulating dragon, with the breath of fire. Vulcan warning him. Smoke swirled in his eyes and nose. Slowly and carefully, he heeded the warning, backtracked away from the flares and incandescent coals beneath his feet.

Below, Nino's mother was frantic.

Near dawn, he emerged triumphant, the soles of his shoes burnt, hair scorched, arms scalded, face smeared with soot. He had survived and thus become a mythological family hero.

"Legendary is right," Jules said, smiling. "In Roman mythology, Vulcan, the god of fire, had his blacksmithing forge under Mount Etna."

"How convenient," Nino said, and laughed.

"Gods are convenient," Jules said. "They can be blamed for everything, even war."

Ares, Athena, Mars, Thor, Chaos. How easy it would be to blame the gods for all human mishaps, for Hitler and Mussolini, who must have been birthed by Satan. Nino, however, didn't believe in gods or devils.

"Maybe we could come back when we get leave," Jules said. "We could climb Mount Etna. Imagine a live volcano underfoot!"

"Count me in," Nino said, "If we can stay alive till then." He had always intended to explore Italy beyond Venetian canals, Tuscan hills and Roman aqueducts, to experience his country as his uncle had done, his feet planted in the burning soil. For a moment, that other fire flared in his thoughts. A searing pain, the cries… He brought a hand up to his ear to stifle the sound, then pressed it over his scar. Fire both attracted and repelled him. He forced himself back to the ship, the countryside, thinking that in another life, perhaps, he might have become a geologist, or a photographer, recording the infinite layers of this earth, and his place in it.

Instead, he was at sea, his feet unsteady on deck, in the roiling waves after each bombing, his hand stroking the airman's watch on his wrist. His talisman. Perhaps it would help bring Olivia back to him.

They were headed to Paestum, south of Naples, as part of AVALANCHE, a codename for the Allied landings in mainland Italy. Nino was one of three agents and two Italian political exiles attached to an Allied Fleet comprising warships filled with infantry, guns, munitions, transport vehicles, torpedo boats and light craft. Behind them, cruisers and battleships. They had advanced silently, without aerial support, to surprise the enemy. Now, as they neared the coastline, however, German fighter planes flew overhead, like giant blackbirds in the clear blue sky, mirrored in the waters of the Tyrrhenian Sea, their whistling bombs exploding around them.

Aboard the ship, the news spread — an armistice had been reached on September 3rd, and had come into force on the 8th — though the bombardments continued. The armistice was no surprise — talks had been ongoing since July when Mussolini was deposed by the Fascist Grand Council. German forces had been arriving in Italy since mid-June, and by late July, they'd successfully occupied the provinces of Bolzano, Belluno and Trento in northern Italy and established The Republic of Salò, a puppet regime intended to be headed by Mussolini, who they planned to free. Despite everyone's hopes that the war would end with the armistice, the Germans had seized control of Rome.

"Bloody Jerrys!" Jules said.

"I hope my aunt is alive," Nino said. "She's in Pozzecco." He hadn't seen her in five years, and her letters were infrequent, probably due to the censors. He was glad Olivia was safe in Cairo, away from active service for now.

"Fingers crossed on that," Jules said.

Pistoia, too, would be occupied. Nino wondered if Bianca was safe. He could not imagine her passively accepting the occupation. Surely, she was active with Lorenzo and the Pistoia Anarchists, as they called themselves, in resistance of some kind.

Shells ricocheted off the deck. They all ran for cover, and fortunately, no one was injured. The Germans' intense fire barraged the landing points. Where were the Italian troops? They had dissolved overnight.

COME ON IN AND GIVE UP, German loudspeakers blasted from the shore. WE HAVE YOU COVERED.

The previous night, Nino had stood on deck staring at the beach lit up by flashes of exploding shells, the sound deafening, like a dystopian New Year's Eve fireworks display. He hadn't set foot on his native land for three years and was aware that if captured by Germans or Fascists, he would be treated as a traitor and would face a firing squad. The thought didn't scare him as it should have. Better to go down fighting for what he believed than to be cowed into submission.

After the landing, the agents' mission was to reach Salerno, then Naples, where the exiles had contacts with an antifascist movement that would help set up a full-scale SOE base in southern Italy, from which they could mount operations against the German occupiers by land, sea and air.

Without warning, clouds drifted in, cotton-ball clumps obstructing the blue, layering into a thick white mattress overhead. They readied to land despite the choppy grey sea. This would be Nino's first landing, though he'd had a lot of practice in Massingham, along with advanced parachute training.

"Let's get going," Rowan, the other agent, said. They had met in Sicily, hours before the mission. He was a tall, muscular man with intense grey eyes.

Nino slung his pack over his shoulder, and joined Jules, Rowan and the exiles in the jeep. They drove up on the pontoon, then onto the beach while shells burst all around them, scattering sand and stones, the air thick with dust and smoke. Shouts mingled in the thunderous gunning and surged through Nino like adrenaline.

Clouds dispersed as quickly as they'd appeared, and the sun blazed on the scorched earth, on the tanks' criss-cross patterns in the sand. The American 45th Division, now landed, advanced towards villages that shimmered in the hills, while the shelling continued. To Nino's left, where the sand met the dunes, a dozen or more soldiers lay dead under blankets. He wondered who had taken the time to line them up and tuck them in so neatly, as if they were sleeping. Violence and tenderness side by side.

On shore, they sped behind hedges, dodging as best they could incoming shelling that ricocheted off the parched ground, flung dirt into the air around them. Nino's excitement and fear turned to astonishment when, in the overgrown forest and brush, rose the columns of an ancient Greek temple. For a moment, he thought he'd inadvertently stumbled into a different century.

"Bloody hell!" Rowan said.

"The Temple of Athena," Jules said. "I always meant to come and see that."

But there was no time to explore it.

Soon, they reached a farmhouse and stopped, hid the jeep in a thicket, then hurried inside, fearful they'd come across a German, or an armed fascist, but they found no one. They settled in to wait for the bombing to end, until they could move again. Nino opened his leather suitcase and set up his B2 set. He alternated among six frequencies, so as not to create a pattern the Germans could detect. With Jules standing watch in the doorway, he began transmitting. He sent two quick messages, one to HQ to say they'd arrived and were in Paestum, and the other to Olivia alone, using their poem cipher. *I'm sorry about Cairo. I miss you.* He didn't wait for a response. Too risky. He'd check again later on a different frequency. He put everything back, closed and locked the suitcase. He replayed his last encounter with Olivia in his head, regretting his response.

"Where are you from?" Rowan asked him. The two of them lay on old couches in the main room and the others in beds upstairs, as if they had accepted the possibility of death and no longer feared it.

"Pozzecco," he said. "Raised by an aunt who had withstood terrible times." He thought about his uncle's chilling story. "When I was fifteen," he said, "a door flung open in my head to let in the truth." When he'd returned to Pozzecco after that summer in London with his uncle Claudio, he had announced that when he turned eighteen, he would not fulfill his military service. He would be a conscientious objector. His aunt had wrung her hands, pleaded with him. Didn't he understand? People were being imprisoned, shot, and exiled for their antifascist views. "To avoid being part of Mussolini's war machine, I joined the Merchant Marines," he said to Rowan. "All that was useless when the war broke out, and I found myself inside that war machine."

"I know that story well," Rowan said. "It was impossible for me to remain in Italy without being imprisoned or worse."

Suffused in shadows, the room resembled another farmhouse, Nino's childhood long dormant, now awakened to Aunt Isabella, who had survived a war in that same house, an odd girl who made uncannily precise predictions, and claimed the dead spoke to her. Throughout WWI, she had accurately predicted deaths and calamities, and the townspeople feared her, avoided her in shops, and crossed themselves when they encountered her on the street. They called her Gondul, referring to the Valkyrie angel of death, who chose who would live and who would die in battle, and of the latter, who would enter Valhalla, the gilded afterlife hall thatched with golden shields, where all who died in combat lived with heroes and kings. Isabella was aware of her nickname, but it didn't bother her. Her visions were real, she'd told Nino, and she, too, dreaded them. The last time he'd seen her, before he went to sea, she had held him tight, and said, "You will die in a foreign land."

"Do you believe it?" Rowan asked.

Did he believe it? Perhaps. Perhaps not. You will die in a foreign land. He had assumed she meant Abyssinia, but he'd survived that. And then Kenya in the POW camp. Yes, he'd survived that too. And Algiers. And Egypt. He'd survived them all. According to her, he was in no danger now, because this was not a foreign land, this was his fatherland. His motherland. Though right now, he hardly recognized it. Still . . .. He shuddered as he heard the dull thud of shells exploding nearby, but shook away the thought. He was here, alive, and had proven her wrong. "And you?" he asked. "Where are you from?"

"It's a long story," Rowan said smiling. "I was born in London, then my parents moved to Siena where I went to school. Then because of my antifascist activities, I was beaten and imprisoned for two years. Eventually, I escaped to Britain." He paused a moment, then added, "I wanted to fight for what I've always believed."

Nino wondered where he'd be in ten years, when he was Rowan's age. The bombing had ceased for the night, and they settled into an uneasy sleep.

Twice a day, Nino set up the B2, but Olivia did not respond though he was certain she must have received his message.

For two days, they hid in the farmhouse, until a low-flying German plane strafed the house and a bullet smashed through a window and barely missed Nino.

In late afternoon on the third day, they set off along the beach, behind hedges, in culverts, edging swampy fields and marshes full of water buffalo, avoiding the road under German control. They stopped only when they reached the river Sele, and crossed on a makeshift, rickety bridge, loose planks flying into the river. On the other side, they drove to the seashore, where they could ride the hard sand. The battle sounds slowly faded, and soon along the beach, appeared helmets, rifles, muskets, machine guns, cartridge belts, jackets and rations, the evidence of the Italian army's sudden flight.

"It's the armistice," Rowan said. "Instead of defending this area, they've gone home as if the war is over."

"For some of them, it is," Jules said.

"They're supposed to continue to fight the Germans," Nino said. "To push them out of the country. Don't they realize they've now become occupied?" He frowned. The Italian soldiers were probably fascists, German sympathizers — or they had been up until a week ago.

They all shook their heads, perplexed, and pressed on, amid the sound of distant gunfire, until at dusk, as they neared Salerno, the battle sounds grew louder. They passed the remnants of an Allied armoured car destroyed by a mine. Nino wondered how safe they were, how many more mines might be ahead of them.

They wove slowly through the rubble and ruins of the town. Crumbling white stone walls exposed the houses' upper levels —

bedrooms and sitting rooms, kitchens and bathrooms — as if the occupants would at any moment return to sleep in their upended beds, sit in the charred parlours, bend over smoking stoves, bathe in the open, like actors in a cautionary theatre production rendering the horrors of war. On the ground lay a large Mussolini photograph, its glass cracked, as if someone had hurled it into the street. In front of a bent Café sign stood an abandoned German gun. The streets were deserted and covered in stones and ash. None of them knew whether Salerno was German or Allied occupied, or perhaps even a buffer zone, a no man's land of collapsed buildings and blackened walls. They continued down flat-stoned streets where doors gaped open, unhinged, until the ground began to echo the footfalls of troops and the motors of vehicles approaching, then quickly abandoned the jeep. Jules pushed open a door and they all rushed inside, crouched in a ground-floor hallway, listening to the muffled sound of tanks and armoured cars advancing.

Their jeep was outside, in plain view.

They held their breaths as the vehicles thundered past, half expecting to hear a command, to watch the door splay open and absorb a barrage of bullets, until they heard the familiar sound of British words.

From the doorway, they watched the procession. Instead of jubilation, however, they could see in the soldiers' faces, in the damaged tanks, that this victory had not come easily. One of the officers stopped and spoke to them. Salerno was in ruins, he said, the port a shambles, no food, and widespread looting. Public utilities were nonexistent, which meant widespread disease would follow. Most inhabitants had either been killed in the air raids, or had fled to the hills. Those few who remained lived in the slums of the old town.

In the midst of this, a message: Mussolini had been rescued from his mountain prison by German paratroopers in a daring assault, and had been installed as de facto ruler of the Republic of Salò. The fascists who had deposed Mussolini were arrested and shot. Those who collaborated with the Germans followed Hitler's orders. Once again, armed gangs roamed the cities and countryside, arresting anyone suspected of being a partisan, terrorizing the population, the madness continuous.

For two weeks, the group remained in Salerno, through daily bombings, and were joined by another SOE unit carrying new instructions, and two more Italian political exiles who needed to reach Naples. They moved into a more protected villa and each day, Nino checked messages, updated their progress, and sent personal ones to Olivia: *I miss you. My warlike spirit roars. Please answer. I'm sorry. I need to see you.* And each day, she did not reply.

New encrypted directives arrived: the men were to split into three groups: Rowan and two of the exiles were to head to Capri where an antifascist movement was growing, the new agents and the other two exiles were to continue to Naples, while Nino and Jules were to retrace their steps and go to the US temporary military airfield at Paestum. More instructions would follow.

One night, two days before full moon in early October, while the Allies continued their advance towards Naples, Nino and Jules were parachuted behind enemy lines on a *coups de main* mission to sabotage railway lines the Germans were using to move supplies and armaments to their troops. Following the successful cutting of the line, they were told to go into the hills and organize resistance groups for the arrival of demolition material by air.

"You're familiar with the area, I believe," the last message had read. "This'll give you an advantage." The target was a tunnel near Pracchia, around twenty kilometres from Pistoia. Surely, Lorenzo would be among the resistance fighters, and possibly Bianca too. At the very least, Nino reasoned, he would be able to inquire whether anyone knew of her.

They landed in a deserted woodland, along with three packages — a B2 transmitter in two water-tight containers, and explosives. They buried all four parachutes, and changed into civilian clothes. Both carried forged documents that identified them as Italian labourers, seeking work in the area.

They hastened into the woods, scanning the dark with their TABBY infrared night scopes, but saw no movement. They opened the packages: each took a section of the B2 in his backpack, then they divided the explosives evenly. They were to set them at two points within a tunnel several miles away. There'd be no train until morning, so they hurried along the railway tracks, mindful of thickets where they could hide, should they hear someone approach. Crickets buzzed a soundtrack, interrupted now and then by the mournful cry of a night heron. In the impenetrable darkness, Nino strained to see a farmhouse, a railway hut, a checkpoint, some evidence of people. Surely sentinels would be guarding the various tunnels that crossed the Apennines, but as he and Jules neared their destination, they saw no one. Were the Germans totally oblivious to their vulnerability, or was it he who was oblivious to his vulnerability?

"We'd better look for a hiding spot," Jules said, as if he'd heard Nino's inner monologue.

The sky was beginning to lighten. They stepped off the tracks and into the woods until they found a dense thicket where they settled in to spend the day.

"I'll take the first shift," Jules said. Explosions sounded in the distance. He frowned. "Pisa, maybe. It sounds far enough."

Nino nodded. "Pistoia will be hit too. Filled with railyards and military targets." He thought about Bianca, hoping she was in the mountains, away from danger.

"Don't you have a sweetheart there?" Jules asked.

"Somewhere," Nino said. He lay down, closed his eyes. "Bianca." However, Olivia's face floated inside his lids. He'd ruined his chances with her. Better to forget. She was not interested in him, or she would have answered his messages. He turned over, and fell, exhausted, into a moving dream of roads filled with rubble, bridges blowing up in front of him, cats mewing forlorn cries, dogs crossing, silent and wary, teeth bared. The maws of shelled buildings haunted him. Ghosts howled. The terrible whistle, boom, followed by screams. Bodies. Torsos, legs, arms, the scaffolding of flesh torn, fragile, blood coagulated around wounds, soaked in the ripped underskirts of sisters, wives, mothers, grandmothers, a torment of spectres who moaned and screamed close to his ears, whose breath was frigid and foreboding.

"Wake up!" Jules shook him awake.

"Whaaat?"

"A nightmare," Jules said, patting his arm. "It's midday. Your turn."

Nino nodded and sat up, the nightmare still howling around his ears. From inside the thicket he could see sun dappled on leaves, branches swaying lazily in the zephyr, the earth's movements continuing despite man's destruction. He sighed. Explosions sounded in the distance, the Allies strafing military targets. He drew out Bianca's letter to reread, though he knew it by heart. Her handwriting was childlike and precise. He spent his shift translating her letter into cipher, as if he were going to send it somewhere, the activity calming his nerves.

All day, they alternated sleep with watch duty until nightfall, when they gathered their things and walked towards the tunnel. All at once, the cricket stridor halted, and in the disconcerting quiet, a violent rustling of leaves and twigs froze them in their tracks. Nino's heart pounded. Jules flicked on his flashlight, and Nino raised his revolver. A wild boar crashed through the bush a few feet past them, grunting and squealing.

"Thank goodness!" Jules said.

Nino exhaled as if he'd been holding his breath.

They resumed their walk to the tunnel, set the explosives and retreated to the woods. Once far enough away, they waited until at 23:30, they heard the massive explosion of the passing munitions train. Satisfied, they set off towards the hills. They'd be hunted now and had to be extremely careful.

For several hours, they walked in darkness, until they began to hear strange whistling calls, and thought themselves caught. What good would their fake identities be now?

"Quick," Nino said. "Pick up branches and twigs. And don't run. We'll say we were collecting firewood." Immediately, he picked up twigs and branches.

"In the middle of the night?" Jules said. However, he, too, bent to pick up loose branches.

Would they be shot? Nino wondered, his body tense, expecting the worst. They were not in uniform, so would not be considered prisoners of war.

Suddenly, six men surrounded them. They were dressed in haphazard military fashion, as if they'd borrowed jackets from one army, pants from another, boots from a third, and so on, but all had rifles and drawn pistols. *Partisans.*

"We've been expecting you," one said, leading them to a brown farm truck hidden under branches, and motioning them into the cargo bed. They drove towards Pistoia, weaving between gravel paths and flattened bush, until a little over an hour later, they reached a ramshackle settlement comprising several huts and tents. A command post, guarded by a sentry, was dug into the side of the mountain. The men ushered Nino and Jules inside, where three men were standing around a table. A fourth man looked up from where he sat, maps spread in front of him.

"Lorenzo!" Nino said, rushing forward to embrace him. His friend looked older but his eyes were bright and focused. He was outfitted in a mismatch of army boots, civilian pants and shirt under an Italian soldier's overcoat.

"Have you come to help us?" Lorenzo said, smiling widely, his tone ironic.

"Nino!" Bianca's voice called out.

He turned. Four years had passed. She was as lovely as he recalled, and no longer a girl. Tall and confident, she stepped towards him and waited. He gathered her in his arms, and for a moment time dissolved, and he was back before the war, longing for her in the evening light. A surge of love overwhelmed him. How could he have forgotten her? Well, here he was now, and that's what mattered.

"How is it possible?" she said. "A miracle."

"Yes," he said, "though I hoped to find you. I thought you might be with Lorenzo and the rest."

"There was no other option," she said. "And you? Who are you working with?" She stared at him quizzically.

"We're working with the Allies," Jules said.

"Good. We need arms and reinforcements," Lorenzo said, interrupting. "We've been raiding the fortress right under the Germans' noses, but it's not enough. And the risk is great." He tapped the map in front of them and Nino and Jules stared at the spot which indicated the Fortress of Santa Barbara's location. "We need to find a secure route in to avoid being ambushed."

"Too bad Viola's not with us," Jules said, and when Lorenzo looked up, he added, "An agent with an eidetic memory — no more than that. She can remember everything that happens to her. She'd be a great scout here." He winked at Nino.

Lorenzo shrugged. "We could all use a better memory." They settled in to talk strategy, future sorties, the nearby encampment of Germans, the strafing of citizens, agreeing and disagreeing on tactics, until Lorenzo frowned, aware of their exhaustion. "I'm sorry," he said. It was almost 5:00 a.m. "We can talk later in the morning and go over terrain."

Bianca, who had been sitting quietly throughout, stood up and motioned to Nino. "Come," she said, "let's walk a while."

They set out along a narrow, well-worn path through the woods. Nino pulled his jacket tight — the late September air crisp— and on the horizon, a dim pinkish hue appeared.

"Where have you been all this time?" Bianca said. "I've had no letters from you for months." She slipped her hand into his.

"We're in wartime," he said, lightly.

"Is that a reason or an excuse?"

"War is not an excuse," he said, then paused. "What about you?"

She shrugged. "I ran away from home. I couldn't face the life my parents envisioned for me."

Nino thought about the lawyer from Torino, wondered if he'd courted her.

"I even returned to Pozzecco and visited your Aunt Isabella," Bianca said. "I thought she might have heard from you."

Nino stopped, startled. She shouldn't have gone the first time, let alone a second time without consulting him. He sighed and continued walking. However, his initial reaction to Bianca began to fade like invisible ink on a page. He was disoriented by his fluctuating desires, as if his emotions were a series of ciphers needing reverse engineering to be read. How far back would he have to go to code-break himself? Bianca must have sensed the change, because she stopped and faced him.

"What's the matter?" she said.

"Nothing."

"Are you sure?" she persisted. "I've been waiting . . . Are we still getting married?"

He started, trying to recall if they'd ever discussed marriage. He didn't think so, though the implication must have been there. "I don't know," he said. "I'm not sure..."

"What aren't you sure about?" she said. "I thought we had an understanding." When he didn't respond, she asked, "Is there someone else?"

He shook his head, avoiding her eyes.

She stopped walking and turned to him. "Who's Viola?"

"A colleague, a friend," he said, startled that she remembered Jules's comment, and told her a little about Olivia, keeping his voice light.

"Are you in love with her?"

"She's a friend," he repeated. "Nothing happened between us." *Déjà vu*, he thought, cringing at his own duplicity, an ouroboros devouring its own tail, in a relentless cycle of destruction and rebirth.

Bianca stared at him, listening, her face impassive. He had the sense that she could see right through him to that part of his heart that contained Olivia.

When he fell silent, she took his hand again and led him back towards one of the shacks. Once inside, she shut the door and pulled him towards her. Her passionate, angry urgency excited him, her hands undid the buttons of his shirt, undressing him deftly. He gave in to sensations he recalled in her arms, made love to her as if to blot out Olivia, as if to remind himself of *this* love.

Later that morning, he awakened to an empty bed, and wandered to the command post where Lorenzo and Jules were consulting the maps. After lunch, the three soon set off in search of appropriate locations for drops, as well as for the landing of the Lysander that would take Nino and Jules back to base.

He avoided Bianca throughout the afternoon, or maybe she avoided him. Lorenzo, too, seemed cool toward him, and he had the uneasy feeling that things were not right between them. He moved away from the camp and sent messages to HQ detailing locations for drops, with Jules as lookout. He hoped they'd be picked up tonight or tomorrow night, the full moon window being three days.

At supper that evening, Bianca arrived late and slipped into the chair beside Lorenzo, who whispered in her ear. She shrugged, stood up, and went to sit next to Nino, who drew in his breath, uncomfortable, as if Bianca's presence had changed the air in the room. No one else seemed aware of this shift. Everyone laughed and chatted. Jules recounted tales of Italians abandoning their weapons and going home. Nino smiled and fidgeted, Bianca's silence disquieting.

"Did you have a good day?" he said, finally.

"*Certo*," she said.

He looked at Lorenzo, who was watching them both.

Lorenzo picked up his spoon and loudly rapped his glass. Everyone stopped talking.

"Congratulations are in order," Lorenzo said, standing. "Our Bianca and Nino here are getting married!"

Everyone erupted into joyous yelling and congratulations. Nino sat dumbly, pasting a smile on his face so as not to humiliate Bianca. He stole a look at her and saw triumph in her eyes. Had she devised this little charade to force him into marriage? Or had Lorenzo, knowing how long she'd waited for Nino? *Perhaps Lorenzo wants Bianca, and this is his way of forcing the issue.* He vacillated among these possibilities, refusing to take any blame himself. He had not mentioned marriage, but he had slept with Bianca right after her mention of it. He felt helpless to speak up and contradict Lorenzo. He would wait, and time would take care of it.

A short while later, two men interrupted the dinner. "Moon's up. We need to go."

Nino and Jules rose, thanked the partisans and gathered their equipment.

Bianca stood in the doorway. "Come back to me," she said.

He smiled, and gave her a hasty embrace before walking past her to the truck that would take them to the landing site. As they drove away, she raised her hand in farewell.

He watched her wane until she became the dark.

Security Standing Orders

No member will be told more about the organization than is necessary for him to do his job.

No member will attempt to find out more about the organization than he is told.

Each member will have a specific job or jobs and will not undertake any other without orders.

Members must only use service names of all other members.

No member will recognize another member in public for other than duty purposes unless they are supposed to know each other in everyday life.

No member will recruit or contact another organization unless ordered to do so.

No member will carry arms unless a cover story is impossible, e.g. during wireless transmission or receptions. Where an agent carries a weapon he must be ready to use it.

Every member will make a daily search of his room, clothes and effects to ensure that he has nothing compromising which can be found.

A member is responsible for ensuring at all times that he is not followed.

Every member will report anything suspicious at once. If he thinks he is suspect himself he must ensure that in doing so he does not bring suspicion on another.

Safety signals will be arranged for all meetings. Danger should always be indicated by something normal, generally the absence of a safety signal.

Not more than two agents will normally meet at the same time.

Passwords and counter signs will be given exactly as arranged and no variations accepted.

For every journey, meeting, or conversation a simple cover story will be prepared in advance.

8

Monopoli / Bari, 1943

Olivia sat in the back of a dusty truck along with three other Pianists. After a long arduous journey from Algiers to Bizerta, then across the Mediterranean, she and the others had finally landed at Taranto, and were now on the way to Monopoli, a small town in southern Italy. The women formed an advance group of coders sent to set up wireless radio communications in the new SOE headquarters in the area, which would shorten transmission distance to agents working with partisans in northern Italy, as well as function as a base for Greek and Albanian operations.

Despite the gruelling journey, Olivia was excited. She was finally in Italy, her father's homeland. It made her feel closer to him and Mamma. She had almost believed they'd be waiting for her at the port. However, although there was no sea between them, or train leaving the station, a more sinister division — the Gustav Line, which stretched north of Naples right across Italy — would keep them apart. . . *The train slides out of the station, and I run alongside, for a final look. . .while I memorize everything: the shouts, the laughter, the warning whistle of an oncoming train, the rain pelting the metal roof, Mamma's soft sobs, Papa's reassuring words, my own heavy heart beating...* Always saying goodbye.

She'd received various messages from Nino, but had not responded. How could she ever trust him? Nevertheless, she'd printed out the last one, and kept it in her purse:

KN YU PY OO RY IE
LO TA UL RO IT WE
LY EI IS MU ST AI

Sorry. I will make
it up to you.
See you in Italy.

She wished she could speak to her mother. They'd been separated too soon. So many questions unanswered. *Be very careful of your reputation... you're too young to go out with boys... you'll understand when you're older... when you're older... when you're older.* Well, here she was, older, and didn't understand at all. Two men in different ventricles of her heart: Philip in London, steady and waiting; Nino somewhere unknown, unattainable, yet all her being longed for him.

In Cairo, soon after the incident in the market, she'd been transferred back to Massingham, "for your own safety," her CO told her. Was she in some danger from Jay? She'd written a report, then scanned through books of photographs of enemy agents, and identified the murdered man. A British MI6 agent, a double agent, perhaps. She wondered why he'd been in Cairo, and what business he'd with Jay, but knew better than to ask questions. Perhaps *Jay* was the double agent, nervous that she had noticed the MI6 agent twice. She wasn't sure what to believe, given that the MI6 agent was dead.

In Massingham, she transmitted to agents working with partisans in northern Italy. She wondered if one of these agents was interacting with Aldo. *We don't ask questions here.* In Massingham, everyone complained about the old equipment, the poor transmission. Why didn't they have better equipment? Olivia worried she'd miss a signal that could lead to an agent's death. As well as interpreting the agent's "fist" to determine whether he'd been compromised, she had to scan for pre-arranged deliberate errors the agent would make to signal he was working under duress. She had to know all the Q-codes — shorthand for common messages

— especially QUG — *I am forced to stop transmitting owing to immediate peril.* Despite the urgency of it all, Olivia worked calmly and efficiently, as if danger quelled her anxieties.

After the armistice, she'd requested the transfer to Italy, saying she could instruct Italian agents from there.

"Is that the only reason you want to be here?" Claire asked as they rode.

"I'm hoping to go and see my parents," Olivia said.

"And?" Claire's eyes twinkled. "Does Nardo figure in all this?"

"You don't know what happened between Nardo and me," Olivia said dramatically, then described the walk along the river, the kiss, the urgency, the hotel, her virgin announcement, her sudden panic, ending with, "You have no idea how devastated I was, my heart broken in a million pieces, my sense of self destroyed . . ."

Claire laughed. "You have no idea how maudlin you sound."

"It wasn't maudlin when it happened," Olivia said, embarrassed.

"No, I'm sure it wasn't," Claire said. "But surely you wanted to have sex with him."

Embarassment rose around Olivia like a red cloud. She wondered for a moment whether Nino had taken Claire to that same hotel in Cairo, whether he took all the women there.

"I don't think you can blush more than that," Claire said playfully, then, "Everyone has someone back home. *You* have someone back home."

"Not really," Olivia began.

"Maybe Nardo feels like you about his someone."

Olivia shook her head. "He told me about her."

Claire sighed. "Why did you tell him you're a virgin? It shouldn't matter. Either you want to sleep with him or not."

"It's not so easy for me," Olivia said. She felt conflicted and foolish after this conversation, and wondered if she could ever feel differently.

After Massingham and Cairo, southern Italy was bleak and anti-climactic. On the drive from Taranto, they stopped three times to change flat tires, and hurried past small town signposts announcing TYPHOID AND SMALLPOX. NO STOPPING. She could now witness firsthand what her Italian instructor in London had said: that the Italian south had been abandoned by Rome. *Italy begins at Florence, he says.* While money flowed to the more industrial north, the south of Italy was neither developed nor were its people helped.

What a strange attitude, Olivia thought. She wondered if her father's tax money had built railway lines and factories in northern Italy, while here people struggled for survival. She gazed at castles and churches, knowing this province of Puglia had a storied past, having been invaded by so many cultures, who left behind castles, cathedrals, churches, yet the Monopoli of 1943 was an impoverished town, dirty, and filled with squalor.

The SOE HQ was a tight-knit group, headed by their CO Stan, and comprising an odd assortment: partisan leaders, who dropped in to discuss missions; a forgery expert, released from a British prison, creating false documents in a house up the hill; paramilitary instructors from the training school at Castello di Santo Stefano, a few miles north; various special agents who were kept in "holding houses" so they could maintain their anonymity; British Liaison Officers from the station at Castellana; pilots from the parachute training airfield nearby; W/T instructors from the wireless training school at La Selva a few miles away; as well as agents from Yugoslav partisan boats, who came into port to pick up arms, ammunition, dynamite — and whose debriefings Olivia attended, then typed up verbatim. They were all connected, rejoicing successes, despairing losses.

Olivia and the Pianists settled into Villa Grazia, a stately villa requisitioned by the Allies, and began working twelve-hour shifts, deciphering, encrypting messages from agents dropped behind enemy lines. Nino's poem ciphers had stopped. Olivia wondered if at any moment he might walk in, and both wished for and feared his return. He was not on her schedule, so she was ignorant of his whereabouts. She didn't want to think of him in the field where he could be captured, his training useless if parachuted into the waiting arms of German soldiers, as had happened to other agents.

The other girls teased her, and asked her if she'd found Nardo yet. She shrugged away their questions, her cheeks burning. Was he alive? *...a shaft of light across the bed, her own rising desire... This is not a good idea, he says. Until we meet again...* Perhaps he was in nearby Bari, where SOE had recently established a base, and where in the evenings, officers often went to bars and restaurants, along with some of the Pianists who found plenty of handsome young men to flirt with, and plenty of clean luxurious rooms in the hotels, where they could bathe. Once, Olivia had joined Claire in one of these excursions, surprised by the number of American and British ships anchored in the harbour, laden with food, clothing, ammunition, fuel, medicines, and everything needed to sustain the 500,000 troops fighting in Italy. It seemed impossible that all around, people were starving, scrounging for food, begging for black-market items, yet in Bari, shop windows overflowed with fruits, cakes, bread, anything you wanted if you had the money. She had spent the entire evening glancing at the hotel entrance, in a state of anxiety and excitement, as if she both anticipated and dreaded seeing Nino, and at the end of the evening, she'd left disappointed.

"Olivia," Stan said one day in late November. "Come with me. I want you to meet someone. "

"What's this about?" she asked as he drove them six, seven kilometres.

"You'll see." He parked the jeep in front of an old building on the outskirts of town. Olivia followed him around the corner, down a narrow gravelled street, crowded with plant urns overflowing with cacti, palms, herbs, wet clothes strung from balconies, faded banners advertising long-forgotten celebrations.

Stan knocked twice on a door, then turned the doorknob.

She recognized the man inside immediately, though she hadn't seen him in months...*tall, oblong face, blue eyes, and hooded lids, straight teeth, black hair, cut short, and curly... a small mole under the chin on the right side he touches when nervous or lying...*

"Hello, Mnemosyne," Jay said, stubbing out his cigarette in the ashtray. He stood to shake Stan's hand, and then hers.

"You remember Jay?" Stan asked.

She raised an eyebrow. "How could I forget?"

"I asked for you specifically," Jay said, and grinned.

"Jay is heading up a rescue mission," Stan said. "You'll go with him."

"Me?" Olivia said, both surprised and pleased.

"We'll be travelling into German territory," Jay told her, adding that he was working as a liaison between SOE and the Americans who were supplying air cover. His job was to survey landing strips for drops, and check up on agents who had disappeared or had not been heard of for a time. She'd be expected to memorize locations, maps, and to possibly identify agents and partisans who were supposed to be in the area, but with whom they'd had no contact. "I thought you might need some excitement in your life," he said. "I hope you're up to it."

She scanned through her brain for faces and files she'd memorized back in Massingham. Identifying agents would be simple, but partisans a more difficult task. The dead MI6 agent rose to the forefront.

"You'll help Jay with identification as necessary, but your main goal will be to carry out a rescue mission for a couple of agents, with whom we've lost contact."

"One of them is your friend Nardo," Jay said.

Olivia took a sharp breath. *Nino*. He was alive. She looked from Jay to Stan, to discern what they knew about her and Nino. "For how long?" she asked. Because she had not been assigned to his schedule, she didn't know when he'd last made contact.

"Several weeks," Jay said. When the agents had gone to their pickup rendezvous, German soldiers awaited them. They'd been kept in an Italian jail for several days, after which they were handed over to the Gestapo, who put them on a train bound for Germany.

"All this sketchy information comes to us from various sources. We can't even be sure it's true," Stan added.

"Here is the miracle if it is true," Jay said. "The agents escaped by jumping from the train and were helped by a couple of farmers onto a different train headed for Pescara, where they were met by partisans and taken to a safe house in the hills."

Olivia frowned, imagining Nino in flight, limbs askew, the slow-motion fall.

"They're both injured," Stan said. "Badly apparently."

She shook her head. It couldn't be. Or as Jay said, perhaps it was miraculous. While right after the armistice, Italian troops and civilians could travel freely without tickets or encountering checkpoints, by late November, the Germans controlled all passenger travel. "Do you trust the source for all this?"

Stan shrugged. "We have to check it out. And this is where you come in, Viola. You and Jay will cross the Winter Line at night. Jay has contacts and will be surveying for drop locations. When you near Pescara, you'll switch to bicycle and go up the hill to the town of Chieti. You'll go in plain clothes, as a school nurse, with papers to match. You will no doubt be stopped and searched at checkpoints, but you'll carry nothing but medical supplies and identity papers." He paused. "Your memory is your secret weapon, Viola. We must make good use of it. You'll be expected to scout the best escape route from the safe house and lead the agents back. Jay will wait to meet you for three days at a pre-arranged location, in case you're captured or something else goes wrong."

The words swirled in Olivia's head: *if something else goes wrong.* What could possibly go wrong? She could be tortured. She could be shot. *Your memory is your secret weapon,* she told herself.

"Of course, I'll go," Olivia said. "I've been waiting for something like this."

Pescara, one of the most important marshalling yards in central Italy, had been under constant bombardment from the Americans, who wanted to halt supplies from reaching the German troops in the south and those in the north. "You'll be our eyes and ears on the ground," Jay said. "On your return, you'll be expected to make sketches and diagrams of everywhere you've been, everything you learned, signalling any permanent checkpoints, any weaknesses that we can exploit." He handed her a rough sketch of a route and farmhouse. "Memorize this so you can find it."

Olivia nodded, thinking of the life schematics in her brain. . . *Olivia, this is not a good idea. . . I love you. . . retribution. . . the train disappears into the cutting. . .*

"We'll need to leave almost immediately," Jay said, "before the lines become impossible to cross." With winter coming, German troops had been hunkering down, searching for escaped prisoners, threatening and bribing Italian civilians and Fascists to become informers. The Germans operated in plain clothes, and once again, Italians were subjected to interrogations, reprisals, destruction of property, executions.

Back at Villa Grazia, Olivia packed a few essentials, reeling with the thought that she might soon see Nino. She pushed him from her mind, telling herself it was useless to speculate, to hope. She wished she'd answered his messages. She wished she'd made love to him, instead of denying what she wanted, and regretting it afterwards.

As soon as her forged papers were ready, she and Jay were in the jeep, both in uniform for the first part of the journey, so if captured they would be treated as POWs. Olivia wondered what would happen if she were captured. Would Nino come to find her? What stupid romantic fantasy was this? she thought, shaking her head. Capture was not something to take lightly. One of the women agents who had been sent to France was captured and had had her fingernails and toenails ripped out. Barbara's shadow flitted across Olivia's mind.

As they drove, Jay carried on a light conversation, explaining that his brother was at the front, and that he was looking forward to seeing him.

"Can I see the agent and partisan list?" Olivia said, and Jay passed it over. She glanced at it, searching for Aldo's name but didn't find it.

"Are you looking for someone?" Jay asked.

She shook her head. "You can destroy that list, you know," she said. "I've already memorized it."

He looked at her with a half frown, then grinned, reminding her of the Jaybird she knew back in Cairo. "I'm counting on you."

Soon they arrived at a railyard just behind the front line. They located the captain in charge, who invited them for lunch while bullets ricocheted around them. The air smelled of gunpowder and sweat. Jay pressed his hand into Olivia's back, and they ducked into a dugout built into the side of the trench.

Jay unfurled a silk map and the three of them pored over it, the captain pointing to possible landing and dropping spots. Olivia noted everything on the map in her head. Then Jay gave the captain the list of people working in that area, and the captain verified those who were authentic partisans or Italian agents. Often, he said, when they occupied a town, half the population would pretend to be partisans, while they were actually fascist sympathizers, so everyone had to be verified. "Olivia can verify the Allied agents," Jay said. "She'll be in contact with them soon."

While they spoke, Olivia marvelled at how calm Jay and the captain were pouring tea, and speaking in normal voices through the wild gunfire, while she flinched at every sound. She thought perhaps that one would get used to it, not hear it any more. Perhaps listening was the same as seeing, in that one saw what one expected to see rather than what was there. If one did not expect to hear gunfire, one wouldn't. She tried to block out the noise, but each sound still made her start.

"Sit tight," the captain said when lunch was over, "I'm going up over the trench to see how things are shaping up."

Jay nodded. He touched Olivia's arm, smiling to reassure her. "I'm going to look for my brother. Wait here and don't venture out."

Jay disappeared along the trench. Olivia stroked the buttons of her uniform from collar to hem and watched the captain climb a ladder to have a look. A bullet whizzed by his head. Olivia caught her breath. How easily one died here, how casually. The captain laughed and ducked into the dugout. "Well," he said, "you can't go back the way you came. Germans have taken over the route."

She shrugged, her mission secret. "Aren't you afraid staying here?"

The captain laughed again. "The Germans can't be bothered to take prisoners," he said. "We'd be nothing but a nuisance. They'll either kill us or leave us here." He shrugged. "You can only die once."

"Hopefully, it won't be today," Olivia said.

When Jay returned, he was sombre. "My brother is a careless fool," he said. "He'll get himself killed unless he's sent home." He folded the silk map into tiny pieces and placed it in his breast pocket. Olivia hoped he wouldn't have to swallow it as others had done when discovered.

They waited till nightfall, then headed in from the coast. Before they crossed the Winter Line, Jay stopped the jeep. "This is the meeting point, Viola," he said. "Fix it in your mind."

Olivia searched for a landmark, something that set this location apart from everything else. Olives and willow sprang up here and there, heather, oaks — the natural vegetation of this area. A little to her left, in the midst of the shrubbery, several pines rose, taller than the rest, their canopy like giant umbrellas. She memorized their details, the number of branches, the sweep of needles, the curves and undulations of the trunks.

"I'll wait for your message," Jay said, "and if I don't get one, I'll be right here in three days. Same time."

Olivia nodded.

"Ready?"

She nodded again. Jay started the jeep and a surge of excitement raced through her. She felt more alive than she ever had. Her heart beat wildly as they careened across the shrubland, turned off onto a narrow mountain road, and climbed. Gravel, stones and rocks began to roll down on them, pinging off the side of the jeep, some landing inside. Olivia ducked and covered her head with her hands, while Jay laughed and rapidly zigzagged around the largest boulders. "Hang on!" he said. Some of the smaller stones hit them on the arms and chest, but not hard enough to injure them.

From a farmhouse up ahead, a man waved madly at them. "The Germans are there!"

Jay turned off the headlights, and sped up. They turned a corner and drove right through a German machine-gun post, the soldiers too startled and sleepy to react. By the time they began firing, Jay and Olivia were out of range. Olivia's legs began to tremble, and Jay laughed uproariously.

"I bet you didn't expect that," he said, as they sped into the dark.

"Will they follow us?" Olivia said.

"Maybe. Probably not."

They raced on until, seeing no pursuit, Jay slowed down, then stopped the jeep.

"I think a kiss is in order," he said. "A reward for keeping you alive."

He reached for her, and in the moment, Olivia kissed him. Then she pulled away, embarrassed, and slapped him playfully. "Behave!" she said, to him, to herself.

Jay laughed. "You might fall in love with me yet," he said. He put the jeep in gear and pressed forward, now keeping away from the main roads. Trees rose around them in witchy silhouettes, brambles and bushes slapping their arms.

Olivia turned to him, wondering how much of his banter was just that, and how much was genuine. She studied his profile: he was a handsome man, on the surface an extrovert, yet she sensed he was secretive and deliberate. "Did you kill that MI6 double agent?" she asked abruptly.

He turned to her, eyebrow raised. "You know I can't talk about that."

"But did you?"

He shrugged.

"I have a theory," she said. "I think you were feeding him false information and he figured it out and came after you."

He shrugged again. "Believe what you want," he said.

When they were close to Pescara, Jay stopped in a secluded area, retrieved the transceiver from under the seat where it was hidden, and set about hiding it inside a thicket. Olivia was to update him as soon as she was able. She took her small case and ducked behind bushes to change into a simple navy dress and a heavy winter jacket.

"You totally look the part," Jay said and grinned. He'd righted the bicycle and held it out to her.

"Let's hope the Germans think so too, should I meet them," she said lightly.

"Be careful," he said.

"You too."

She rode the bicycle along a track parallel to the road, and dismounted and hid whenever she saw the lights of a vehicle. Within the hour, she found a hiding place where she could rest till morning. She lay down. Through the branches, the sky was a harlequin of blacks and greys and stars sparkling in the cool air. She thought of Nino, of their first meeting in London, the two of them staring up, striving to see the layers, the dimensions invisible to the eye. How she wished to return to that moment… *his breath warm on my palm…*

At dawn, worried about the German patrols that could materialize at any moment, she stashed her bag with a small tarp, medical supplies, and change of clothes, and headed out, anxious to avoid checkpoints if possible, Jay's voice in her head: *The Germans will shoot anyone who disobeys their rules: strikers, saboteurs, partisans, curfew breakers, those who assisted anyone in the resistance, anyone caught with a weapon… Eyes and ears are everywhere… Trust no one.*

She headed first for Pescara, to review the damage and see the marshalling yards. The latest bombing had taken place two months before, causing estimates of 600 to 2,000 civilian deaths. She found an abandoned city in ruin, bridge piers half crumbled, buildings askew, others razed. She had to dismount to navigate the rubble through the eerie silence to the city centre, the air redolent with coal dust and wall plaster. A gaping hole was all that remained of the train station. She wondered how many people had died trying to escape the bombing, the smell of burning flesh. The marshalling and rail yards were razed to the ground, but HQ must know that from the American aerial views. Still, she walked around, visually recording. She could see no new construction. Perhaps the Germans had moved their marshalling yard to another city, Ortona maybe.

Once she completed her review of Pescara, she headed straight for the hills toward Chieti, where most of the Pescara population had fled. It seemed impossible that a thick forest of oak and maple could flourish so close to destruction. She pedalled through the woodlands, juniper shrubs scratching her legs, marvelling at the beauty around her, the backdrop of jagged, snow-capped peaks of the Majella and Gran Sasso mountains, their white stone stark against the blue. From her memory, Olivia retrieved the route and sketch of the safe house where Nino and the other agent might be. That locals would keep them safe was a miracle. The American bombs had caused such destruction, Olivia wondered how people could ever accept the Allies as friends. It required a changing of allegiances mid-stream. Though she knew the partisans and resistance groups had been united against the Fascists for decades, she wondered how they now felt about their homes being obliterated, their loved ones killed. As she pedalled up the hill, she also thought of her own parents under German occupation. How were they faring? She had mentioned their whereabouts to her CO, requesting leave to visit them, but, so far, had not had any response.

On the outskirts of Chieti, she stepped off her bicycle and pushed it on the gravel road. Up ahead a German checkpoint. She replayed her cover story; Page 32 of her SOE manual floated to the front of her brain... *Create impression of being an average stupid, honest citizen, trying her best to answer questions intelligently. Interrogators are not impressed by tears or heroics. Always be civil. Avoid replies that lead to further questions.* Her heartbeat quickened, but she squared her shoulders and counted as she approached.

"Papers?" The German soldier held out his hand impatiently.

She reached into her bag and retrieved her identification. She smiled.

The soldier looked at the papers, then scrutinized her, as if to decide whether or not she was what she claimed. "What do you do?" he asked.

"I'm a government school nurse," she said. "I examine the children for diseases, treat headaches, cuts, and any other maladies..." She smiled again.

He held out his hand for her bag.

She handed it over silently. Her heart thrashed in her chest. She made herself return to a summer day in Cornwall when she was eight, on holiday with her parents and brothers. How idyllic her childhood seemed from the distance of time.

"And why are you not at the school now?" the soldier asked.

She smiled again. "I've only just arrived." Stan had assured her that her story could all be verified.

The soldier paused another moment, scrutinizing her once more, then he handed back her papers and bag, and waved her on.

She mounted her bicycle and continued up the hill, thinking she'd have to find an alternate route for the rescue. She mustn't think of Nino, of their reunion, her heartbeat betraying her outward calm. Focus, she told herself. The air was chilly, in the mid-teens, though the sun cast a stippled light through the brush. She dismounted once more, pulled the winter jacket close and zipped it up. She was almost at the town centre, and people were bustling about, opening store fronts, doing errands. She blended into the crowd, as yet another civilian escaping the bombing. Early on in the German occupation, Chieti had been declared an Open City, and because it would not try to defend itself, it was not bombed by either side. The result was an uneasy surrender to the German soldiers who strolled the streets, suspecting everyone. Earlier this year, an infamous camp here, PG21, run by the Fascists, had housed tens of thousands of Allied prisoners and antifascists in inhumane conditions. This summer during the negotiations for the armistice, the British had ordered all POWs to remain in their camps and wait for the Allies. However, with the Germans swiftly advancing, Italian guards had left their posts, some POWs escaped, and when the Germans arrived, the rest were sent to camps in Poland and Germany. Olivia could only imagine their fates, well aware that if caught, she and the agents would face the same destiny.

She walked and rode her bicycle through the town, encountering at one point a haphazard checkpoint — two jeeps staggered ten feet apart across the road, connected by concertina wire and impossible to avoid. A bored German soldier held his hand out for her papers. The fear she'd felt the first time had now settled in her stomach. She answered the questions, and soon was waved on.

Germans stood guard in front of the police station, their grey-green uniforms and guns sinister and imposing. She imagined they had requisitioned houses, evicted residents and now seized what they wanted. She continued until she reached the elementary school where she was to conduct her examinations, and leaned her bike against a wall, intensely aware of her surroundings. She reviewed the diagram in her head. The farmhouse should be along this road on the outskirts of town. A bell pealed, startling her, and children streamed out in black uniforms with white collars, like a flock of magpies chattering as they ran. To her right, a jeep slowly approached, its aerial trying to sniff out contraband radio signals. She wondered how far the Germans patrolled, thinking of her own B2 set hidden down below. Before the jeep reached her, she ducked into the school and waited for it to pass before venturing back out.

She walked her bicycle and looked into store windows as she went, inscribing a map in her head, recording sights, sounds, snatches of conversations. Partway down the hill, away from the centre, where farmhouses and fields of tobacco now dotted the countryside, Olivia identified the farmhouse. Her heart fluttered. Nino was there, injured, helpless. She wished she could go in right now, but instead, she walked past and continued back down the road to where she'd stashed her bag. She hid her bicycle, took a small tarp from her bag, and found a place to rest until dark.

Finally, a quiet settled over the hill, everyone curfewed inside, only the soldiers patrolling. Olivia took the medical supplies and retraced her steps back up to the farmhouse, keeping away from the road, her heart pounding with anticipation. She had not seen Nino in months. A lot could have happened. Did he still feel the same? Or had he moved on given that she hadn't answered his messages? Once again, she admonished herself for reactions she always regretted. Why couldn't she trust herself?

When she was across the street from the farmhouse, she paused, listening, scanned for headlights or flashlights, but heard and saw nothing. She crept up to a door, and rapped.

The door creaked open a few inches. An old man stared at her.

"Viola," she said.

He opened the door enough for her to come in and shut it quickly behind her. "Dario," he said, holding out his hand.

He led her through the house and out the back to one of the stables.

"Are they—" she began, but he motioned for her to be quiet, then handed her a flashlight.

"I'll keep watch," he said. "Be quick."

It took a moment for her eyes to adjust to the darkness inside the stable. The two men were lying on makeshift beds behind bales of hay. She rushed forward. "Nardo!" she said, tears springing to her eyes.

"Viola, it's Jules," a voice said. "Nardo's not here."

"What do you mean? Where is he?" She turned on the flashlight for a moment. Another man lay beside Jules.

"Nardo was well enough to try his luck getting back, so he could radio our co-ordinates," Jules said. "This is Paolo, one of the partisans captured with us."

Olivia sank down next to them. "Are you sure Nardo was all right?"

"He was able to get up and move. Unlike us…"

She opened her medical bag of supplies, letting her FANY training overtake her massive disappointment. "Let me have a look at your injury."

"My leg. It's broken. And Paolo's ribs…"

She examined both of them, using the flashlight sparingly. Jules' leg had been set with a rough splint, and Paolo had a broken ankle as well as cracked ribs. They'd not be able to walk down the hill. She sat back, weighing her options. She could scout for a landing spot and radio Jay to send a Lysander to pick them up, but she'd still have to get them down the hill. She turned off the flashlight and went to the door. "I'll be back," she said. "I have to make arrangements."

Dario stood outside, a few feet away, keeping watch. She told him she had transportation arranged to take the men back, but that they'd have to make their way down the hill first. "Can we make stretchers and take them down through the brush?" she asked. "Do you have men available to help?"

At first, Dario was reluctant to put his men in danger. They'd only be able to travel at night, during curfew. Olivia was firm. If he could construct a stretcher, she'd drag each of them down herself. Finally, he agreed to make inquiries and let her know.

She headed through the brush down the hill, as silently as possible, making a wide circle around the checkpoint. She'd pick up the bicycle tomorrow. An hour later, she reached the hidden transceiver, and sent Jay a message. The two men were too injured to walk far. He had to drive back across the Winter Line and meet her where they'd stashed the radio. Tomorrow night. She sat back, breathless, imagining the German jeep circling around sniffing her signal. She would wait five minutes.

"Agreed," Jay's response came almost immediately.

She sighed and turned off the transceiver, re-stashed it, then snuck back up to where she'd left her bicycle. She ate the biscuits in her pack, gathered her bag, then returned to the barn.

Paolo was asleep. Olivia set the small tarp beside Jules, and sat down. "What state was Nardo in?" she asked.

"He was a little roughed up, as you can imagine," Jules said, "but nothing broken. We had no radio though, and were fortunate enough to be helped by the locals." He lay back and closed his eyes.

"Did he make it across the line?" she asked. "Have you heard anything?"

"Nothing," Jules said. "How could we in this condition?" He sighed. "And now we've become a burden and danger to anyone who hides us."

"We thought Nardo must've found a way to radio in our coordinates," Paolo said in the darkness. "How else did you find us?"

Olivia shrugged though they couldn't see her. Stan had said there'd been no contact with Nino. "Someone radioed in. Another agent. Partisans, perhaps, or a resistance fighter. We weren't even sure whether to trust the information." She lay back against the hay, letting her mind conjure Nino, his smile, his hands at her shoulders, his lips on hers…Perhaps he was still with the partisans. Perhaps he didn't intend to return. She wished she could join the resistance movement herself, maybe find Aldo. She sighed. *Let it go. Let it go.* "We should try to get some sleep," she said.

A little past six, the farmer came in with a meagre breakfast. "A change of plans," he said. He had made arrangements for the men to be hidden inside the false bottom of a cart owned by a peddler who daily travelled between Pescara and Chieti. "You'll have to move during daylight," Dario said. "And go through the checkpoints."

Olivia considered this, though she had no other option. If they made it down the hill safely, she'd have to hide the men until night, when Jay could come and pick them up. "Can we trust the peddler?" she said.

Dario nodded. "He's a good man. He could be shot for doing this." He paused. "Stay quiet, prepare, and pray for the best. He'll be here mid-morning."

Olivia got up. "I'll be back," she said, and headed down the hill through the woods in the cool morning air. The stiff peaks of the snowcapped mountains sparkled in the morning sun, while black shadows created sinister horizontal ridges. A mere ten kilometres away, the Adriatic lapped the shoreline. Her thoughts turned to Nino, Cairo. *June 8, 1943... 'We should run away,' Nino says, his voice light. 'And where would we go?' I ask, ready to follow him anywhere. He laughs. 'Where no one could find us.'* She replayed the words, his face, his eyes. Right now, the only escape was forthcoming. She hoped Jay would cross without incident; she hoped they would all return safely.

Later that morning, Olivia watched the peddler's cart pass through the checkpoint. She waited a half hour, then rode her bike through the checkpoint as well, smiling at the same soldier, who waved her through. She rode on slowly, casually, until she reached the fork in the road leading to Pescara, where the cart was stopped on the shoulder, the peddler pretending to inspect the donkey's shoes. They both scanned right and left, then quickly drove the cart further into the bush, out of sight of the road. Together, they half-dragged, half-carried the two men into thickets.

"I can't thank you enough," Olivia said, squeezing the peddler's hand.

"May God be with you." He nodded, and resumed his trip to Pescara.

Olivia made sure the men were as hidden and comfortable as possible. "Do not talk," she said. "Sound carries, and you don't know who might be on the road. Try to sleep." She was exhausted, but knew she shouldn't stay near them, in case of capture. She went to the meeting point and waited for Jay.

A couple of hours after dark, she heard the engine before she saw the jeep, and leapt up, relieved, amazed that everything had gone as planned. Jay sprang out and embraced her. "Good girl," he said. He had brought a stretcher, and together, he and Olivia retrieved the two men, one at a time, motioning them to be silent. Jay had brought penicillin, gotten from the Americans, just in case of infection. He also had pain killers to help the two men get through the ordeal.

They rode without headlights, taking a different route than the one Olivia recalled, deftly skirting two different checkpoints. Jay drove silently, confidently, cautioning them with his hand, now and then, as if he possessed a special sense that perceived danger. He was accustomed to this, Olivia thought, adrenaline surging through her. She remained in this state of suspended fear and excitement, until Jay let out a large sigh. "We're across," he said. "This is Allied territory."

Debriefing took several days, during which Olivia, Jules and Paolo were kept in a separate house, *a holding house* — separated from everyone. Olivia drew maps, sketched checkpoints, searched through photographs to identify anyone she might have encountered, and typed up everything she'd experienced, omitting the frantic beating of her heart every time she replayed her approach to the barn.

When she was done, Jay stood up. "Time for me to head out," he said. He brought Olivia's hand to his lips, and kissed it.

She smiled, wondering where he was going next, whether she'd see him again. "Feel free to call on me anytime," she said, smiling.

"I may take you up on that," he said.

Back at her residence in Monopoli, she found an envelope addressed to her. She turned it over. No return address. Inside, the indicator group IOAH then:

MEX EMX OSE AHX EYL
LML ION IRE IEX TSX
LIW NLX AVX LYA VUC
IOX HLX IIX OSD EYX
ALX HLA RSX

She spoke the Foscolo poem's stanza in her head, while decrypting. An ode to night, to peaceful night, while battles rage: *while I gaze upon your peace, my warlike spirit / sleeps, though yet within me roars.* His warlike spirit, she thought.

> Hello Olivia.
> I am here in
> Italy. Miss your
> lovely smile.
> Shall we dance?

He must have made it back. Relief and happiness surged through her. Where was Nino now? Did he know she'd gone to find him? That she was back? How could she find him?

She slept four or five hours a night, trying to not think about him. Sometimes, she took out the message and reread it, looking for clues. *Shall we dance?* She was convinced they had unfinished business, a spark, an unspoken promise.

November 12, 1943

My dear Nino,
How difficult it is to have little or no news from you. I worry every moment of every day, and pray for your safe return.
I have great faith in the belief that everything happens for a purpose. You're safe now that you're here in your own country.
I had the most wonderful surprise. Your lovely fiancée came to visit me. I am thrilled to hear you're getting married, and I only hope you'll wait until this war is over, so I can be there to witness your happiness. Bianca is an admirable woman — brave and beautiful, always willing to help. She told me all about her activities in Pistoia. You must be so proud of her. She has been a great comfort to me, and I am half in love with her myself.
Take good care, my dear boy, and don't forget your old aunt, who thinks of you constantly. I send you blessings and love.
Aunt Isabella

9

Monopoli / Bari, December 1943

A week later, Olivia was alone at her desk when Nino walked in. He was as handsome as she recalled, his eyes shining. She rushed to him, and he folded her in his arms, murmuring her name in her hair. "I've missed you so much," he whispered.

Olivia's eyes filled with tears, her cheeks burned. She was almost hysterical with relief and happiness. "I've been so worried about you," she said. "If anything happened to you—"

"Nothing's going to happen to me," he said, holding her at arm's length. He bent toward her, and kissed each tear on her face, before pressing his mouth on hers.

The door opened and they sprang apart. Stan looked at them and grinned. "As you were," he said, and walked back out. They burst out laughing, their hands touching, unwilling to let go.

"I have to get back to work," Olivia said after a moment.

Nino encircled her waist and pulled her to him. "Only if you promise to come out with me afterwards."

At 4:00 p.m. sharp, Olivia left work and walked to her room, where she washed her face, fixed her hair, and changed into the green dress and wool double-breasted coat. Her stomach ached, as if it were both too full and too empty, stretched with both happiness and doubt.

Nino had borrowed a jeep to take her to Bari for the evening. "We'll walk along the Lungomare, and eat at a wonderful restaurant overlooking the ocean," he said.

They arrived in Bari around 5:00 p.m. and Olivia was once again struck by the large modern buildings, fountains and shops, by the wide wide streets lined with palms.

Of course," Nino said, "there is also the old Bari, but it's dirty and frequented by shady characters — certainly not the kind of place I would take you to."

They crossed the piazza. American and British soldiers rode their jeeps lazily along the waterfront. Vibrant laughter and music emanated from night clubs and restaurants. Elegant men in woollen coats and women in feathered hats strolled about as if the war didn't exist.

She and Nino walked along the waterfront, a manicured sidewalk of paving stones with palm trees and lamps at regular intervals. In twilight, the harbour shimmered with lights, and the ships were silhouettes of masts and guns and ropes. Sailors unloaded cargos; couples, singles, officers, soldiers, civilians all walked along, chatting, skirting the port, impervious to the hint of sulphur mingled with sea salt, gas, and diesel fumes. Beside them rose old historic buildings, which had all been requisitioned and taken over by the Allies as their offices and headquarters. Groups of sailors passed them, their white uniforms stiff and pressed, their laughter echoing in Olivia's ears.

They stopped at one of the outdoor cafés and Nino ordered them both beer, which they drank while people-watching. Nino slid his arm around her, and they sat for a while, gazing at the ships, mired in their own thoughts. Olivia was tense, confused by Nino's attentions given what he'd said to her about another woman, and even more by her own nervous longing.

"How did you get back?" she asked. "After the mission."

He squeezed her shoulder. "I can't talk about it, you know that. But you," he said, "are now considered a heroine. Jules said you managed a daring escape."

She smiled. "It took a village." She paused. "I know I'm not supposed to tell you things outside of my cover," she said, to break her own spell. The beer had turned her cheeks a pale pink. "But I need your help."

Nino smiled and nodded. "You can trust me," he said.

"It's still about my brother Aldo," she said. "I wish I could have news of him. I wish I knew if he was even alive." She paused. "You've been with the partisans. Do you think you could ask some of the agents who drop into the north? Maybe someone would know him."

Nino leaned back in his chair, frowning. "It's a big country," he said. "The likelihood of someone I know knowing him is probably less than finding the proverbial needle in a haystack." He shook his head. "He might be using a different name as well." He reached into his pocket for a cigarette pack, then tapped one out and offered it to Olivia.

She didn't smoke, but she thought she'd try anyway. Singers and film stars held cigarettes between manicured fingers, while smoke rose like haloes around them. Olivia thought them sophisticated. Nino tapped out another for himself, and lit both their cigarettes. Olivia did not inhale the smoke that burned in her mouth, but neither did she cough.

A German reconnaissance aircraft circled high above them, a blackbird in a deep blue sky. Nino looked up and followed the path of the aircraft; none of the port crews paid any attention. "But could you try?" Olivia asked. "What harm would it do?"

Nino turned to her. "Do you have any idea where he might be? A region? An area?"

"All I know is where my parents are supposed to be, a little village called Musadino. I think it's in Lombardy." She sighed. "Oh, what's the use? They should be sending *me* news. They know my address in the UK. They're probably all dead!"

"Oh, don't say that." Nino took her hand and squeezed it. "It's not easy getting word out in the middle of the war, especially up north, where the Germans would be watching every move. But I'll ask around, and we'll see if anything develops."

They finished their beer, and Nino told her he was taking her to dinner at a restaurant facing the harbour. "As soon as dusk comes," he said, "those cranes," and he pointed to them all along the harbour, "will switch on their spotlights, so the merchantmen can continue to unload the ships. It's rather beautiful."

Olivia smiled happily and they walked to the restaurant. She fantasized he'd changed his mind and would soon declare his love. He led her up six stairs and into a luxurious room with marble floors, polished columns, mirrored walls, cutlery gleaming on white tablecloths, a bar in one corner of the room, and an ornate stage housing a jazz trio and singer, set up in the opposite corner, behind a dance floor of varnished oak. Olivia's mind scrolled to *the gilded floral design of the Criterion ceiling... I wait until Lt. Adams and the new agent are seated, before I enter the room...* This room, this time, was even more splendid. A waiter escorted them to their table next to the floor-to-ceiling glass wall, through which they could see the American and British warships moored in the harbour, and beyond them, the white ripples of the Mediterranean. What a paradox that this luxury could exist during a war when most of the country was starving and dispossessed. She was both lucky and ashamed to be there. She wondered how Nino could afford this restaurant. She felt special that he'd brought her here, and pushed back her hair, thinking she wasn't dressed well enough. Not like some of the other women.

"Have you been in Italy all this time?" she asked him, once they'd ordered.

He grinned, then reached across the table and took her hand. "I'm almost sorry I wasn't badly injured. Then you could have rescued me."

"Jay needs some credit," she said, lightly.

"And you?" he said. "I'm sorry I didn't know you were in Italy until yesterday."

She thought he must be able to read her heart. Was she so totally transparent? "Oh, don't be sorry," she said lightly. "I didn't expect you to keep track of me." As soon as the words were out, she wanted to take them back. They implied exactly the opposite.

He laughed. "How was Cairo?"

Safer ground. "I returned to Massingham for a while, before coming here."

"Is your friend Claire here too?" he asked.

Olivia made herself keep an indifferent expression on her face, while a small twist of jealousy turned into a tornado in her chest. Could he sense it? She swallowed. Smiled. "Oh, Claire. Yes, she is," she said, when she could keep her voice from giving her away.

"I'm glad she's here," he said. "It makes all this much easier when you have a friend, don't you think?"

She smiled again and nodded. Was he thinking of her or of himself?

They had barely begun their soup when a flare dropped from the sky. Then gunfire.

"Anti-aircraft," Nino said. "Probably a mistake." But he sat up, all aware.

Suddenly, a blinding flash was followed by a terrific blast.

The port's only anti-aircraft battery opened fire. Then a long whining whistling sound, followed by a tremendous boom. Ships exploded, and flames swirled and rose high into a blazing panorama. Shells rained down, and massive black smoke engulfed the port. Nino shouted, "Get down!", grabbed Olivia by the hand and pulled her under the table. A waitress screamed. A bomb exploded in the water in front of them, causing all the windows to blow in. A crescendo of screams pierced the air, and Olivia realized her own throat was open and gasping. A second explosion splashed water into the room. Female customers screamed in unison. One of the chandeliers crashed to the ground, its crystal teardrops sliding across the floor in all directions. The mirrored walls cracked and crumpled into the room. The jazz musicians were huddled in a corner, their instruments tight against their chests and the vocalist was sobbing, "I can't hear the music. I can't hear the music."

"Oh my God, we're going to die," Olivia said.

"No, we're not," Nino said, his voice calm. "Don't get hysterical, Olivia." He placed his hand on her arm and pressed his fingers into the flesh until Olivia shut her eyes in pain. But this achieved the right effect. Olivia bit her lip and made herself breathe deeply.

Finally, there was a lull in the bombing, and Nino said, "Quick. Let's get out of here. We have to get away from the harbour. The Germans will be back." When they stood up, the harbour was a massive tower of flames amid multiple deafening explosions. "An ammunitions ship," Nino said.

Together, they ran past the splintered tables and chairs, the glass, until they reached the street, and even then, they continued on, running away from the harbour, into the centre of the old city, which had also been bombed, whether accidentally or not.

Before they could decide which way to go, a siren sounded, and they scrambled toward the nearest bomb shelter packed with nearly a hundred men, women and children. A water main must have been damaged, and the small stream they'd seen flowing down the street seeped into the shelter. Olivia closed her eyes, and held on to Nino's arm, praying to God, while all around them people wept and sobbed and screamed until Olivia thought she'd go mad. She was claustrophobic. She began to pant. Nino pushed her head down between her knees and said, "Breathe, breathe!"

For over two hours they stood in that shelter, water rising up to their ankles, the oxygen depleting with their every breath. Then a new explosion shook them all, its sound deafening, and dust particles filled the air. Everyone surged forward toward the entry to the shelter which they all assumed had caved in. Nino held Olivia tight against the crush of people, the terror. In moments, however, the dust cleared, and they realized the shelter was not caving in. One of the men took charge and made everyone move back. They stood trembling in huddled silence for hours, until the all-clear sounded around 11:00 p.m.

Outside, the air smelled of garlic and gas fumes and crude oil and thick suffocating smoke. "Come," Nino said, "We'll go to the Grande Albergo delle Nazioni. Someone there will have information." They wove through the blare of sirens, the hysterical screams and moans of the injured, children's cries and mothers' shouts. *Aiuto! Aiuto!* Olivia became aware her own sobs were mingling with others. "Shh, shhh," Nino said. "It's going to be all right." But how could it be all right, when everyone was suffering? She was vaguely aware of pockets of fire that emitted thick black smoke and dust. She couldn't breathe.

Nino spoke softly, and though she couldn't hear what he was saying, she understood from the tone of his voice that he was trying to calm her. Along the street, he held her hand tight, as they dodged fractured doors which had been wrenched from hinges, shards of glass, bricks fallen and still falling from facades and chimneys. The blasts had knocked out power, and troops were now searching for survivors, their flashlight beams circling in the dark. Nearby, a massive fire was growing, and residents were desperately trying to save whatever possessions were dear to them.

They reached the lobby of the hotel, in which hurricane lamps had been lit. Nino and Olivia approached a group of Allied officers, who were debriefing. And so, they discovered little by little what had happened: seventeen ammunition and gasoline ships had been hit in the harbour. The massive explosions had whipped up a wind that tore through the city like a tornado. Houses in the old section of Bari crumpled like cardboard boxes, sending glass, doors, frames, the interiors of houses into the air, so the sky itself became a danger zone. And worst of all, when one of the American ships — the USS *John Harvey* — had exploded, it released a poisonous cloud of sulphur into the air and an oily substance into the sea that burned the American sailors who had jumped into the water to save themselves. Any contact with their skin caused massive excruciating blisters. The hospital was without power, and overflowing with burn victims and death. Across the city, too, people were dying, buried under rubble. The bombing had taken only twenty minutes, yet the havoc it caused would linger through generations.

Well past midnight, the officers stood up to go. During the discussion, Olivia had regained her composure, but was now shivering in shock. She wondered how these men could speak so calmly, so evenly, while surrounded by a maelstrom of destruction.

As soon as they were alone, Nino turned to her. "It will be impossible to travel in this pandemonium," he said, "not to mention that I can't even imagine if the jeep is still in one piece." He ran a hand through his hair. "We'll go back to my residence and see if it's standing. It's a twenty-minute walk. Can you make it?"

Olivia nodded, though the last thing she wanted to do was to walk through more devastation and human suffering.

"We can rest there."

Olivia was trembling uncontrollably now, and Nino circled her in his arms and guided her forward. Slowly, the farther they walked, the less the ruins until they reached Nino's residence — a house requisitioned by the British — which stood more or less intact.

"You'll feel better once you've washed your face and drunk some water," he said, urging her towards the washroom.

Olivia stopped at the door. "I'm frightened," she said.

"I'll be right here."

In the washroom, she stood at the window and ran the tap water over her hands. Even this far away, she could see the horizon burning, and in its flames, the shadows of smoke funnels. She thought about Aldo and Mick and her parents. Where were they? How many bombings had they been subjected to? She wanted to go home. But where was home now? She filled her hands with water and splashed her face, then she cupped water into her hands and drank deeply.

Nino was waiting for her outside the door, as he promised. He took her to his room, and closed the door. The power was out even here. Nino slid back the curtains, and the room was bathed in a dim echo of the inferno burning at the port.

"I have something for you," he said, and slid the watch out of his pocket.

Olivia turned it over in her hands. "It's beautiful," she said.

"It's for safekeeping," Nino said. "It's kept me safe and now it'll do the same for you."

Olivia sighed. She pressed the watch to her chest and sat on Nino's bed, thinking she could die tomorrow; she could die tonight. She took his hand and pulled him down beside her. He put his arm around her, and then his lips were on hers, and she clung to him, recalling their kiss back in Cairo, the urgency of this kiss now. She ran her hands down his chest, unbuttoned his shirt and pushed it off his shoulders, while his hands unzipped her dress. They fell into each other on the bed, and Olivia's heart thudded against his. She clung to him, breathless in the twilight of the room, her body flushed with desire.

"Are you still…?" he whispered.

"Shhh," she said.

10

Monopoli / Bari, 1944

All that night of the Bari bombing, merchant seamen were rescued from burning ships, plucked from the sea. Over a thousand American and British servicemen died, as well as hundreds of civilians. The garlic smell, blisters, and burns that killed many were due to mustard gas stored in one of the American ships. *Classified*, given that mustard gas was prohibited by the Geneva Protocol of 1925. Nino felt the burden of this dark secret. "We're at war," one of the commanders said, as justification. But Nino was stunned, horrified that the Americans were willing to use chemical warfare against the Germans, knowing the Italian civilian population would also be affected.

He and Olivia had not had much time together in the weeks following the bombing and the chaos that ensued. Romantic liaisons between agents were forbidden, given that both would be vulnerable if one were captured. However, neither Nino nor Olivia were so naïve as to believe no one knew their secret. Just before New Year's, they both asked for a few days' leave, and three days after Christmas, Nino rented a hotel room overlooking the ocean at Torre a Mare, between Monopoli and Bari, a perfect place for a secret rendezvous. The two spent long idyllic days together, leaving their room only to eat and walk along the shoreline.

Nino yearned to know everything about Olivia, and asked her about herself while they lay, drenched in sweat after lovemaking. She was playful in her retelling, minimizing her experiences. "Before the war," she said, "my life was uneventful, in the way ordinary people believe their lives to be uneventful, despite the intrigues, longings, resentments and startling joys secreted in their inner lives."

He smiled, though she couldn't see this in the darkness, and said he wasn't convinced, because he imagined everyone believed their life to be exceptional and original in some way. Why else would people write memoirs, if not to document their particular experiences?

Olivia didn't agree. "If you ask people about their lives," she said, "they will tell you they have no story to tell, though they may imagine some slight, some particular pea beneath a mattress they carry into adulthood. For example," she said, "when I was small, in winter, Mamma would carve my initials into the skin of a large potato, which I would bring to school to be baked in the coal-oven at lunch. I didn't realize how poor we were, and to this day, I can't bear the taste of potatoes." She paused. "But this was not out of the ordinary. The Great Depression had left everyone wanting."

Nino thought of his own school days in Pozzecco. His aunt had been frugal, but she had not invested in the stock market. He had never been hungry, nor poor, not in the way Olivia described.

"But your parents did well in the end," he said. "They had a café and a house . . ."

"Yes, it's true. Later on. They worked hard for everything they had." She paused for a moment, and Nino was certain she was reliving it all inside her mind, exactly as it had happened. "I had a sister," Olivia said presently. "She is my family's great sorrow." She turned to him, her eyes filled with tears. "She died of diphtheria when she was six."

He gathered her in his arms. "I'm so sorry."

She shook her head. "Though I was only eight, I felt immense guilt, because I had always been envious of her smooth white-marble skin, her small cherub lips. Had I inadvertently wished her death? My mother's friends would stroke Rosa's hair and murmur, *She is like an angel, in looks and temperament.*" Olivia frowned, as if hearing those words right then. "Angels were forever smiling and doing nothing," she said, "while I was restless and unsettled. I wanted to do the things my brothers were doing, I wanted to ride a train to see where it could take me."

Nino thought about that as a mirror-yearning to his own feelings — something unspecified but anticipated, a physical need for movement, for displacement and discovery. Olivia was his twin soul in the midst of a confusing, complicated world.

"And what about you?" she asked. "How was your childhood?"

He was reluctant to speak about himself. What could he say other than he'd had a happy enough childhood with his aunt Isabella, though his memories were clouded by the *squadristi* violence, his dead mother and father, women moaning, sobbing, and fire, fire, fire — memories ignited at the most unexpected times. Violence, he thought, lives on inside all those who have experienced it. It damages in ways one can't comprehend. "I longed to have parents and siblings," he said. "I grew up with adults, and was often lonely."

These small intimate disclosures bound him to Olivia, exhilarated him in unexpected ways. This must be how Bianca felt about him, he thought, uncomfortable in that knowledge. *L'amore domina senza regole.* Love rules without rules. Bianca, he thought, guiltily, tortured by the fact that he hadn't told Olivia about the engagement, which he didn't consider anything more than an entrapment. Guilty that he had been unfaithful. How could he tell her that? And guilty that he hadn't told Bianca the truth. Perhaps Olivia sensed something, because she was wary, unsure of his love.

This wariness did not abate, especially when in the new year, he became increasingly busy, and often travelled back and forth to Bari, sometimes Brindisi, acting as interpreter during the interrogation of rogue agents or the debriefing of returning agents, clandestine meetings he could not discuss. Olivia wrongly interpreted some of these evenings as parties Nino was frequenting without her.

"What aren't you telling me?" she said one evening, as they walked along the waterfront.

Nino shook his head. She knew he couldn't divulge secrets, and he was hurt by her suspicion.

"Yesterday, I saw two women in the garden of your residence," she said.

He frowned. A couple of weeks earlier, he and several agents had been transferred to Bari to train wireless operators and ciphers. As a result, the British had requisitioned a villa in a small nearby town. Nino had acquired a motorcycle and daily made the twenty-kilometre ride between Bari and Villa Guarnieri. Olivia could not have seen his residence unless she specifically had gone there by bicycle. "There are many officers there for women to visit," he said. He often stopped and talked to these women, possibly even flirted. Women were attracted to him, and he enjoyed the attention. But they meant nothing to him. "Why can't you trust me?" he said.

She raised her eyebrows at him. "Because you're a man," she said.

"That's not fair," he protested.

"Before the war," Olivia said, "I was innocent, in the way young girls were innocent in the 1930s, sheltered, protected, watched over by adults, kept away from boys and men, from provocative clothing and compromising scenarios. One of my brothers — usually Mick, my younger one — would tail me to the store, to visit a girlfriend; would wait for me when school ended." She was unperturbed by this close custody, she told Nino. It was simply what everyone did. Her mother told her that her brothers were guarding her reputation, as if this were something that could escape and cause havoc. She smiled, then shook her head. "I was headstrong and innocent," she said, "a terrible combination in a time when young women were easily taken advantage of, when there was no recourse for men's bad behaviour. One of my friends was raped, yet the blame settled on her. The young man was sent away, with a slap on the wrist. My friend would have been headed for a life of disrespect had she lived in Italy." Olivia stopped and looked at Nino, her face serious, her brow wrinkled. "Thank goodness she lived in London."

"Not all men are like that," Nino said.

"Still… better to be safe than sorry," she said.

He laughed and kissed away her doubts, though they persisted.

He was almost relieved when, at the end of January, he was sent to be part of a second Allied landing, at Anzio this time, through German bombardment, and weeks of fighting that felt more like suicide.

On Nino's return at the end of March, he, Olivia, Claire, Rowan and two other agents went to Bari to celebrate Jules's birthday. They were in high spirits, having survived the last mission. Every moment was precious. Olivia sat near Nino, anxious to speak to him privately.

"I had a letter from my mother," she whispered, "and it's possible that Aldo is in or around Rome. If only there were some way to contact him."

Nino nodded, though he didn't see how they could find Aldo, when there were thousands of resistance fighters all over Italy. He had not even tried to locate her brother, believing it to be virtually impossible. He tried to explain to Olivia that the Italian partisans were not one homogenous group. They comprised many factions of various political or religious affiliations. Often, they fought with each other over ideological issues. In Udine — twenty kilometres from Pozzecco — for example, the Osoppo Brigade, formed the previous December, included partisans of secular, Catholic, socialist and liberal ideologies. They were all eager to fight the German occupiers, but because that particular area of Italy — the Friuli-Venezia Giulia — was mired in ethnic and territorial conflicts, the Osoppo Brigades were also at odds with the Garibaldi Brigades, and the Slovenian-Yugoslav partisans. "This difficult, complex political-military history dates back not only decades but centuries," he told Olivia. "How could I possibly find one man, without knowing which faction he belongs to?"

Olivia stared mournfully at him. "But what about Rome?" she insisted. "You have contacts."

Nino shook his head. Since the beginning of the German occupation of Rome in September of the previous year, SOE had been trying to establish communications with antifascists, but had been largely unsuccessful. Still the Allies continued to advance towards the city — a German stronghold they thought they'd never conquer. Recently, partisans had returned with terrible stories of hunger and oppression in Rome, of torture, imprisonment and death, often helped by Fascist collaborators. More than a thousand Italian Jews had been deported to Auschwitz. It bewildered Nino that these Fascists could betray their own neighbours, as if his father's death had been futile. "I wish I had better news," he said.

"Enough with all your whispering!" Claire said, and both Nino and Olivia looked up. "Let's drink to the birthday boy!" Claire raised her glass.

They all raised theirs, exclaiming, "Hear, hear."

Jules, who had had a lot to drink, began a long-winded speech about comradery, friendship in the face of danger… Nino tuned out and listened to Olivia, who continued to fret about her brother.

"I'm sure we'll take Rome soon," Nino told her, optimistically. "And then we'll see."

"Perhaps my brother was there and helped set that bomb that killed those Germans."

Nino shook his head. "That bomb also caused the death of 335 Italian civilians." He thought about those innocent people, marched to the Saint Calixtus catacombs, shot, and pushed into a mass grave, some buried alive. "There's no silver lining there." He did wonder whether Aldo had been involved, and if so, whether he'd gotten away. If they could make contact, he might prove very useful.

"And," Jules continued, his voice rising, "I'm not the only one we should be celebrating tonight." He looked at and pointed to Nino. "I believe congratulations are in order."

Olivia turned, startled, and the others also faced Nino, awaiting confirmation of whatever he was to be congratulated on.

"This is your celebration, Jules," Nino said waving his hand, as if to bat away Jules's words.

"Nino is engaged…" Jules began.

Olivia face reddened. She put her hand on Nino's arm.

"…to a beautiful young woman named Bianca. I met her on our mission last year."

Olivia stiffened beside Nino. He reached for her hand, but she pulled it back. Her face was now blanched and masked. Why hadn't he told her? While everyone burst into a congratulatory song that made no sense, he leaned into her and whispered, "I can explain." Before she could respond, Rowan slapped him playfully on the back. Claire frowned at Olivia. Nino felt completely helpless, yet he knew this was all his fault.

He got through the evening, and Olivia, too, did her best to act normally, but he was sure they could all see how upset she was. She feigned a headache, and returned to Monopoli with Claire and one of the agents.

The following day, he was waiting for her at the end of her shift. She walked past him, ignoring him.

"Olivia, I can explain," he said, and she stopped.

"I was expecting this," she said. "Oh, not exactly this, but something to ruin what's between us." She began walking again, and he followed. "My mother warned me about this," she said, her voice breaking, then went on to tell him how on her twelfth birthday — as a kind of rite of adulthood — her mother had taken her to an astrologer who had compiled her nativity horoscope, and in the area of LOVE, he had pronounced that she would make *sacrificial demands*. "Is this what I'm doing? Asking you to be truthful? Is this a *sacrificial demand*?"

Nino didn't believe in astrologers or horoscopes, and he was pretty sure neither did Olivia, but this phrase now soared up between them. He envisioned an altar and offerings to some idol. "Of course not," he said. "I can explain. It's not what you think."

"Really," she said.

"Come. We need to talk."

She crossed her arms. "What good will that do?"

"Please," he said, touching her elbow. "Give me a chance to explain."

She stared at him for a moment, then followed him, in slow, deliberate steps, as if she were counting each one, and weighing them against her own reluctance.

It was now late afternoon, the air cooling. Nino drove them into the countryside, to a place called Lama San Giorgio. He had heard of it from one of the agents, who was interested in archeology. They did not speak during the drive, and Nino practised in his head how to explain that he had not intended to get engaged, and that he should have made that clear to Bianca immediately. Now too much time had passed, and he felt he couldn't tell her in a letter. He needed to do it face to face.

He parked the jeep, then led Olivia along a Roman bridge formed by a series of stone arches, on one side of which was an outcrop of limestone rocks among thick scrubby vegetation. They walked in silence until they heard the roar of a motorbike approaching and looked up the road. A young man — a boy really — was riding towards them. To their astonishment, the boy maneuvered his front wheel up an incline onto one of the stone walls bordering the bridge — not more than a foot wide —in a daredevil move. They sprang back just in time as he rode past them, exhaust in their faces, and Nino yelled at the boy that he could be killed.

"There's a war on, in case you haven't noticed," the boy said, dropping onto the bridge and stopping, one foot on the ground. "Come on. Get on, Mr. English. I'll give you a ride you'll never forget."

Four other boys came running along the road, excited by the jeep, by the two of them, possibly hoping for money or cigarettes. Children often surrounded the soldiers in the hopes of getting something that could be traded for food.

"Well?" said the boy on the bike. "Are you afraid?" He was a tough one; his friends were watching him in both awe and fear.

"Come back when you're old enough to be in uniform," Nino said, and waved him off.

The boy paused for a moment, and Nino thought of himself at that age, all bravado, no idea what that uniform signified. He wanted to take back the words, but before he could think what to say, the boy lost interest in him and turned to the other boys, who now ran back up the road. Nino watched them go, innocent still, yet also wild and wary.

"Let's go down and have a look at the Roman arches," he said, glad for the interruption, trying to stall the inevitable.

"I'm waiting," she said.

"It's a total misunderstanding," he said, heading toward the embankment at the end of the bridge.

Olivia scrambled after him. He thought of all the months awaiting her reply to his ciphers. Would things have been different between him and Bianca if Olivia had responded, had given him hope? A part of him knew he was grasping for excuses. He rambled through oak trees, prickly-pear, almonds and oleander bushes someone may have planted years before, but now grew wild. "Be careful," he said and turned. "My friend said there could be snakes."

Olivia narrowed her eyes at him. "All snakes should carry warnings."

Nino's senses tuned to the rising tension, worse than any serpent. At the bottom, he turned to face the Roman stone arcade that formed the road above. "Let's sit. Let me explain."

"I don't see how that'll change anything," she said, and bent down to pick a wild daisy next to a laurel bush.

"I did not intentionally get engaged," he said.

"Oh?" She gave a sarcastic laugh. "How does one get *unintentionally engaged*?"

He explained what had occurred, the entrapment he felt. "I love you," he said, startled by his own words, reaching for her hand.

"But you let the deception go on," she said, slapping his hand away. "Not only with her, but with me too."

He sighed. "I didn't mean to—"

"Don't take me for a fool," she said. "If you really felt trapped, you should have told her immediately, and you should have told me too."

He frowned. She was right. He had hoped the situation would dissipate in time, not wanting to face Bianca, to go against his aunt's ethics, to admit that he had slept with Bianca during the mission.

"Are you going to marry her?" Olivia's eyes were cold.

"I love *you*," Nino said.

Olivia turned and scrambled back up the embankment in silence. Nino followed.

"I'm sorry. You have to believe me," he said. "I don't love Bianca. I didn't ask her to marry me. I love you, and I think you love me too."

She did not respond, and back up on the road, got in the car and sat, staring straight ahead while Nino drove the few miles to Monopoli, where he dropped her off, with a strained "Good-bye."

He returned to Villa Guarnieri, disheartened by Olivia's refusal to believe him. Until he spoke to Bianca and cleared up the misunderstanding, he had nothing to offer Olivia. For the next two months, he avoided Monopoli and spent more time in Bari. However, he sent Olivia impassioned love letters that she ignored. *Olivia my love, I'm trying to stay away from you, but I'm terrified to lose you... My love for you is inexhaustible and I believe you love me too. I swear I would never betray you... You are mine. You are everything. You alone can have me, not only with the senses, but with all my soul...* However, no amount of words on paper seemed to move her heart. Could she not hear his anguish? Finally, he rode his motorcycle to Monopoli, only to find that Olivia had taken her leave and gone to find her parents. He wondered if he'd ever see her again.

11

Musadino, 1944

A train to Milan then Porto Valtravaglia on Lago Maggiore, to the tiny village of Musadino, in Lombardy, where her father was born. Olivia arrived in late afternoon and asked directions to the house where her father was born. A small boy pointed up a dirt path to an old stone building she recognized by Mamma's description in her letter.

Pasted on the old wooden double door was a public-order poster in Italian and German, listing twenty points, each one ending with "… will be punished by death." The crimes ranged from helping partisans, to being caught out after curfew, or tearing down posters. *"If crimes of outstanding violence are committed, especially against German soldiers, an appropriate number of hostages will be hanged. In such cases the whole population of the place will be assembled to witness the executions. After the bodies have been left hanging for twelve hours, the public will be ordered to bury them without ceremony and without the assistance of any priest."*

Olivia knocked tentatively, and as soon as her mother saw her, she wrapped Olivia in her arms and began sobbing. "My child, my child," she said.

Olivia held her tight, crying with her, so relieved that her mother had survived, yet alarmed by the protruding bones, the thin, malnourished frame.

Her mother held her at arm's length. "You are alive and well provided for."

"Yes, Mamma." Olivia wasn't prepared to see her mother in patched clothes, without proper shoes, only her bare feet in crude, carved wooden soles held on by a leather strap. Her chestnut waves were pulled into a tight bun, veined with grey; her face creased with worry, her hands rough. She had aged a dozen years.

"Papa? Where is Papa?" Olivia asked. "Is he all right?"

"Working," Mamma said, and crossed herself. "Thank the Lord he has a job." She pulled Olivia inside a small vestibule and closed the door.

"I thought he was sent to Dalmatia," Olivia said.

"When Italy changed sides, he was abruptly discharged." She crossed herself again. "We are still alive, as you can see."

The main room was spacious — Papa's large family had all lived here at one time — but sparsely furnished with an old wooden table and four mismatched chairs, a wood stove against one wall, and beside it, a crude credenza for food storage. In the corner, a large steel bucket was full of water. Four different-sized pots hung on the wall, and various plates and cups were turned upside down on the stone ledge that circled the room.

Mamma sighed and sat down heavily. "I have nothing to offer you," she said. "And we are a few of the lucky ones." Papa knew each mushroom and wild edible plant. "We catch and eat every kind of animal, every sort of bird — frogs, snails, freshwater shrimp, hedgehogs, even a squirrel once. Only salt we can't get. We are the lucky ones," she repeated.

"Oh, Mamma, I am so sorry you're going through all this. This war will be over soon, you'll see." Olive sighed. "What about Aldo? Has he contacted you?"

Mamma shook her head. "He came to see Papa maybe a year ago now," she whispered, as if someone could hear them. "He is somewhere with the Resistance. We are all in danger if we even mention it. I pray the Lord he is all right."

Olivia thought of her brother — how she wished to see him — and about the fact that Mamma had thanked the Lord twice, as if she had found solace in religion here in this small village where evil lurked around every corner.

"The Germans," Mamma said, "have deported all the Italian soldiers stationed here, and sent them as slave labour to Germany. Here, they continue to have *rastrellamenti* — they search and round up young men between fourteen and fifty and send them to Germany. They call it 'recruiting' but there is no option to refuse. Thank goodness Papa is fifty-three." She crossed herself once more and told Olivia about her father's work at a factory in Porto Valtravaglia, where he was a machine grinder. He worked ten-hour days, then would go up the mountain to cut wood for fuel, and when the season was right, to cultivate a little piece of land, where he planted maize. "There is a ration system," she said, "but few goods are available in the village. What about you? You look well. Tell me everything."

Olivia opened her bag and withdrew what few provisions she had been able to carry — cans of condensed milk and packets of crackers, tea — and set them on the table. She had carefully rehearsed a cover story for herself. Better for her parents to know as little as possible, lest she put them in danger. She told Mamma a vague story of government work, from which she had saved enough money to come and find them. However, she couldn't stay long.

The truth was that the previous week, Stan had called her into his office and shut the door. "You have family living in Musadino, if I'm not mistaken."

She'd nodded.

"We need you to do some covert work up there."

"Yes, of course," Olivia said. "Will I be able to visit my parents?"

"Yes. In fact, that's what makes you perfect for this mission, because it will all look natural."

Olivia's heart had begun to race. Finally, she would be able to see her parents again, possibly discover Aldo's whereabouts. She had made herself breathe in and out slowly while Stan explained that the agents working with the partisans in the mountains had had their communications compromised. Two drop-offs had been ambushed, implying Germans were intercepting calls. Fortunately, the partisans had been tipped off by farmers before they could be arrested or shot. However, they had lost the provisions. Olivia would need to contact the agent with information about new drop-offs and strategy. And she had to do it in daylight, because of the curfew. "When you're outside, a village cowherder will lead you to the meeting point. Here is his photograph."

Olivia nodded again.

"You'll memorize the message, and won't have to worry if you're caught," Stan continued. "Though you will have to bring a map, but this we can easily hide."

Other than this, she was not to ask or answer questions.

"The cowherder is in the Resistance," Stan had told her. "But he will have no information other than to lead you to a particular spot." This was the way agents and partisans were kept safe. The less they knew, the safer everyone was.

Olivia looked at her mother now, wishing she could share information, take her into her confidence.

"What news of Mick? And Grandfather?" Mamma asked. From the wall, she retrieved a pot, filled it with water from the bucket, and set it on the wood stove. "And I trust everyone else is all right?" She looked at Olivia, anxiously.

"I haven't had word about Mick," Olivia said, trying to keep the disappointment from her voice. She had hoped, however improbably, that her parents might have received news of Mick, possibly from her aunt. "He was on the other side of the world last I heard." This wasn't exactly true, but she decided her mother did not need another worry. "As long as we don't hear otherwise, we can only assume all is well," she said, echoing Nino's words to her.

Mamma looked at her dubiously. "They wouldn't know how to contact us." She measured out maize and set three bowls aside.

Olivia opened the canned milk she had brought and set it beside the maize. "But they do know how to contact Grandma and Grandpa in Kent. As for the rest, I believe they are all fine," Olivia said slowly. "I joined the war effort, Mamma, and I've been working in Egypt."

"Egypt?" her mother exclaimed. "Whatever could you be doing there?"

"I'm not allowed to disclose anything about my work. But I assure you, I'm perfectly safe."

"You're living on your own, then?"

"With other young women. But don't worry. I can take care of myself. This war has made us all grow up."

Mamma sighed. "It has reduced us all to paupers."

"Surely you can go home now that Britain and Italy are on the same side?"

"Can we? We've had no word. And how would we get there without money? Papa's wages barely cover expenses. We don't even know if we still have a house in London."

"Of course, you do," Olivia said firmly, fighting *the muffled sound, the men's agitated voices... One of my cousins, Alba, stands behind the counter, and when I approach, she leans forward and whispers, "Go away. We don't want any trouble. " ...Alba pushes a hand into my back. "It's not safe," she whispers. "You'll be the ruin of us all." Then she shuts the door firmly behind her.*

The door opened and Papa stamped his feet on the sill before entering. His clothes were patched like Mamma's, his eyes sunken into creased skin. Olivia ran to him and tearfully embraced him.

"Why have you come?" Papa said. "This is not a safe place for a young woman." He eyed her up and down, as if disbelieving she could be his daughter. Four years of war had changed them both.

"Papa, what are you saying?" Olivia exclaimed through her tears. "I've thought of nothing but the two of you, and Aldo, and Mick—"

"It's not safe here," he said. "Haven't you seen the Germans everywhere? One wrong move and you're shot." He frowned. "You don't know what these animals can do." He sat down heavily, blood rising to his face. "The Fascists are no better," he said. "Why do you think I left Italy?" he said.

"Papa, don't upset yourself," Mamma said. She went to stand behind him and rubbed his shoulders.

"This is no place for a young woman," he said, listing various occurrences in the village, times when people had been punished for showing courage and fortitude in the face of the German atrocities. "It's like going back in time," he said. "Like your memory, Olivia." He sighed. "I see it all clearly even now, the Fascist atrocities in the early years, the ferocious beatings with the *manganello*, the doses of castor oil the Fascists forced their opponents to drink, and the murders." He spoke quietly, as if under a spell, a witness, an oral historian reciting a terrible archive, so it was not forgotten. "I am a member now of the Partito Socialista di Unità Proletaria, the Socialist Party."

Olivia supposed he was trying to explain why it was unsafe for her to be there, unsafe for all of them. She sat between them, holding each of their hands. How she loved them. She wished she could tell them about her involvement in SOE. They'd be so proud of her.

When she returned to HQ, she would ask Stan if he could help her get her parents back to London. But what good would that do? London was under constant bombardment, the dangers everywhere.

After a meagre dinner, Papa pushed away from the table, exclaiming, "It's almost dark. Draw the curtains, Mamma." He patted Olivia's hand. "Pippo will be here soon. We cannot have any light, or he'll bomb us."

"Who is Pippo?" Olivia asked. She recalled a silly song her father used to sing:

"...ma Pippo, Pippo non lo sa, che quando passa ride tutta la città;
si crede bello come un Apollo, e saltella come un pollo."

"...but Pippo, Pippo doesn't know, that when he passes all the city laughs;
He believes himself beautiful like Apollo, and struts around like a chicken."

Papa shook his head. "Pippo is an airplane that flies in the night. Nobody knows who Pippo is. Could be German, American, could be Italian. But we all agree we can hear him. Only after dark. And if Pippo sees a light, he drops a bomb. You'll hear it yourself."

Olivia frowned. This sounded like a story people invented to make children compliant, or maybe to warn themselves. A bogeyman. "It must be German, "she said. "The Americans are our allies now."

Her father shrugged. "Won't stop them as long as there are Germans here." Mamma pulled all the curtains tight and lit a candle. Then she turned off the light. They sat in semi-darkness for a few moments, listening. However, the night was silent, though Olivia thought that if she were outside, she would surely be hearing nocturnal animals in the woods around them.

"We go to bed early here," Papa said, standing up. "Not like back home." He ran a hand through his hair, and pushed in his chair. "We're under curfew. Without light, we might as well go to bed. Besides, I'm up at dawn." In the summers, he told her, he and Mamma moved to the cellar at night, where they could light candles without worry of being discovered by Pippo. Now, however, the cellar was damp and cold, and they couldn't risk becoming sick. One of their neighbours had succumbed to tuberculosis.

As he spoke, Olivia was overcome with sorrow. Her father had aged so much. How she wished her parents were back in London in their comfortable life, with their family around them.

Mamma led her outside, up the stone staircase to a second-floor bedroom, made up the bed, then she and Papa went up to their room.

Olivia lay in the total darkness, wishing the war was over, wishing her parents were not hungry and afraid. This, however, was the norm here where the Germans were entrenched. She had been lucky to have bypassed this brutal experience, having arrived in Italy after the Allies had secured the area. Had she been kept out of danger because she was a woman? Her mind circled around the events of the past few months, her work, Nino. Soon, the silence was pierced by the insistent cries of an owl, a mournful sound like grief. She thought of Nino, his voice in her ear, his mouth on hers, his breath against her heart. He could be somewhere nearby for all she knew, or he could be dead. She could not stop loving him, despite his betrayals. Tears spilled on her cheeks, for her parents, her brothers, herself, for her heart aching, until finally she fell into a troubled sleep.

When she arose in the morning, her father had already left for work. Her mother was sweeping the floor, her back bent over like someone bearing a heavy weight. Olivia startled at the sight. Her mother was only forty-six, yet right now she looked like an old woman. She opened her bag and drew out the three sweaters, two scarves, a skirt and heavy socks she had packed for them. One of the sweaters was large, as were the socks, and she hoped they would fit Papa. She wished she could have brought more, but she couldn't risk being searched. Her eyes welled with tears, and her mother seeing this, leaned her broom against the wall, and gathered Olivia in her arms, patting her back, saying, "There, there," which made Olivia cry harder. She should be the one comforting her mother. She had been playing at being an agent, with nothing at stake really, not for her. She hadn't had to suffer hunger, live in a German-occupied town, fear for her life at every moment. She had been living in a cocoon of safety, and guilt now threatened to submerge her. Had she been more concerned about Nino — whom even now she couldn't banish from her thoughts — than about her day-to-day workings? Had she been turned away from the terrible conditions her parents were in? She clung tighter to her mother for a moment, then wiped her eyes.

"It's not so bad," her mother said, "we are alive, and we have a little food. Others are in a worse state. Come and have some tea."

She spent the morning helping her mother with various chores, walked with her to the town well to collect water, and listened to the life of the occupied village. Fear permeated the air; her mother flinched at the slightest sound.

In the afternoon, when her mother went to lie down, Olivia said she was going for a walk, and headed up the path towards the hillside, as per her instructions. Two sets of large boot prints extended in front of her, and she wondered if the cowherder or partisans were up ahead. Her steps crunched in the snow and sounded in her ears like beacons to the Germans; her heart pounded, and she forced herself to walk at an even pace. At the end of the path, exactly as her commander had explained, two trails appeared, and she took the left one, walking at the same pace, her feet stepping carefully inside the tracks in the snow, making hers less obvious. The underbrush thickened, and the path narrowed.

"*Sombre but sunlit is my path,*" a voice said behind her.

She turned. A young man of seventeen or eighteen approached the path. He had a long face, pale blue eyes, bushy black hair, and a thin moustache over his upper lip. He wore a wool greatcoat, probably taken from one of the military barracks when the Italians abandoned them. All the insignia had been ripped off, leaving dark ghost shapes.

"*And all within it, till the shadow is in light,*" she said, recognizing him.

He nodded, then overtook her and continued up the hill. She followed a few steps behind, alert and aware of her surroundings. He soon turned left onto a trail barely discernible from the brush. All around, the forest was thick, its canopy dark and foreboding. As they climbed, here and there they came across geometric snow-covered plateaus cut into the mountainside for planting and grazing animals. At one point, she turned, and the village below resembled a romantic hamlet of ancient stone houses.

Up ahead, a man swiftly emerged from the woods and spoke to the cowherder, who turned and nodded to her. She stopped and waited. The cowherder continued up the trail.

When he was out of sight, the agent approached her. She recognized him, too, from the photograph she'd been shown back in Monopoli, and spoke the message she'd memorized, then, unbuttoning her coat, she quickly ripped open a tiny seam in the lining to extract the silk map she had folded flat and hidden inside.

"Halt!" a voice rang out in the distance, and they looked up, alarmed.

The agent grabbed the map, signalled for her to go back down, and touching his hat, bounded into the woods.

Olivia stood fixed for a moment. Then she stepped off the path, and crept towards the sound, keeping hidden.

Up ahead, two German soldiers stood in front of the cowherder. One was reading the identity papers of the boy, and the other was gesticulating with his gun. Olivia couldn't hear what was said, but she could see the young man pointing to one of the plateaus, probably to explain where he was going.

Without warning, in one quick movement, the German soldier raised his gun and shot the cowherder in the head.

Olivia caught her breath. As if in slow motion, the boy's body hovered for a moment before crumpling to the ground, an explosion of blood staining the snow. *This was her fault. Her fault.* She remained rooted, terrified to move, terrified to stay. The soldiers began arguing, then one threw the identity papers on the boy's body, and taking the other soldier's arm, urged him down the path. Olivia crouched, then flattened herself beneath the underbrush, replaying the training she'd received back in England. *She had a backstory; she was walking for fresh air. She had every right to be here. She had seen nothing,* knowing full well she wouldn't be able to explain why she was hiding, and if caught in civilian clothes, she would fare no better than the boy. *She was guilty.* After a harrowing wait, the two soldiers, still arguing, walked past her down the path toward town.

She remained in the underbrush, hoping they wouldn't notice the smaller footprints within theirs in the snow, and listened for any sudden change in the tone of their voices.

When she could no longer hear them, she slowly stood up, and brushing the snow from her coat, walked cautiously down the hill, keeping off the trail, until she reached the path at the end of her parents' house. She saw no one.

Once inside the house, she collapsed against the closed door, her knees weak, her heart pounding. Her mother was still upstairs napping. The whole ordeal had taken a little over two hours.

With trembling hands, she removed her coat, extracted a needle and thread from her purse, and meticulously sewed the seam closed. She made herself think of a time before all this happened, a time when she was innocent and happy simply to be asked to dance with a boy. *Jerry. July 16. A hot, muggy day. The end-of-term school dance. I'm helping at the coat check, when Jerry walks towards me. My cheeks are burning, my breathing pounds in my ears. He stops in front of me, and asks me to dance.* She panicked suddenly, as if this boy were in front of her right now, his hand extended, his headless body—

"Olivia, is that you?" her mother's anxious voice called out.

She was startled back into this small village, the panic now shifting to *as if in slow motion, the boy's body hovered for a moment before crumpling to the ground, a massive amount of blood staining the snow on the path.* "Yes, Mamma, it's me."

All day, as she helped her mother patch clothes, recut those beyond mending and sew them into blankets, she was anxious at every sound, wondering if someone had discovered the boy, wondering if someone might have seen her coming out of the woods.

When her father came home late, around 7:00 p.m., he was quiet and distracted.

"What's the matter?" her mother asked, taking his coat, leading him to the table where a bowl of soup awaited.

"There's been a murder," Papa said, "A young innocent boy who had gone to the mountain to prepare it for the village cows."

Mamma crossed herself. "I do hope there won't be repercussions—"

"He came across a German checkpoint — one of those arbitrary ones they erect here and there, as if to catch unsuspecting criminals." Papa let out a long sigh. "They shot him in the head, and said he was *resisting arrest*. What were they arresting him for?" He paced up and down, agitated.

Olivia forced herself to count, to ward away *the boy's body hovered for a moment before crumpling to the ground… sombre but sunlit…* She tapped the table edge in front of her repeatedly. Her mother covered her hands with hers.

"Papa, please come and sit," Mamma said. "This is not our concern."

Papa slammed his fist on the table, and Mamma began to cry. "It *is* our concern," he said, firmly. "That boy could have been me. He could have been Olivia!" He sat down heavily, and dropped his head in his hands. Mamma stood behind him, stroking his back.

They ate in a strained silence, then a loud knock startled them. Papa held his finger up to his lips, and went to the door.

"It's almost curfew," Mamma whispered, wringing her hands at the sound of men's murmurings. "Who could that be?"

This is all my fault. My fault… till the shadow…blood in the snow… Olivia made herself breathe and count, count, while her mother sat still, her chest heaving.

Soon Papa returned. "The Germans said we have to leave him there all night, on the snow. We can get him tomorrow before curfew. But this is not what we're going to do!"

Mamma looked up, alarmed. "What do you mean, Papa? You're going to get yourself killed!"

"We've had enough!" he said. "We are all going to do something decent." The village men, he told them, were going to unite and go up the mountain after curfew and bring the boy's body down.

While Olivia and Mamma stayed back, frightened and anxious, the men of Musadino waited until past midnight, lit torches and climbed the mountain through the snow, in defiance of the strict curfew. Neither Olivia nor her mother could even think of sleeping, so they stayed at the table, in a vigil, one small candle casting an eerie glow across their worried faces.

A little before dawn, the men returned to the village. Papa came in cold and panting with fatigue, but he was victorious. They had brought the boy's body down on an improvised stretcher, taking turns to carry it four at a time. They had defied the Germans and won, at least for now. He washed his face and changed his clothes. He would go to work now, he said, and later there would be a funeral. The coffin would be carried across the village to the cemetery. "We will all go," he said.

After he left, Olivia and her mother waited to see what the Germans would do; an uneasy tense silence fell over the village.

A crude coffin was built, and although the Germans said only family members could attend the funeral, as the coffin advanced through the village, men, women and children silently streamed out of their homes — some carrying wildflowers, most dressed in black — and joined the procession, as did Mamma, Papa and Olivia, until they were all assembled at the cemetery in a spontaneous gesture of defiance.

After the burial, they all walked home quietly, heads down, half expecting some terrible fate. Olivia wondered if they'd all be corralled and shot into a common grave. However, there were no *rastrellementi*. Nothing occurred out of the ordinary.

Once home, Papa was joyous. "This is how we regain our humanity," he said, while Mamma shook her head sadly. "And it's not only the Germans we have to worry about. Those bands of fascists roam around and, if they find partisans, they torture and kill them. One of Aldo's friends had his eyes clawed out." He shuddered. "We're in the Republic of Salò, with that monster Mussolini." Papa spat on the ground. "Olivia, you must go as soon as possible. It's not safe here for you."

The following morning, she kissed her father goodbye, promising to be careful. Then, after Papa left for work, and before she had to take the train, Olivia went out for a walk, to hew this village and surroundings into her memory. Who knew if she'd ever see her parents again? If any of them would survive? If only she could do something to help the partisans. She headed off on the mountain trail she'd taken the previous day, a trail now trampled with muddy footprints, wishing she'd been brave enough to confront the murderous soldiers. She felt helpless and frustrated. If only Aldo were near, she'd happily abandon SOE and join the resistance. Oh, what was the use of pondering any of this? She continued to walk, adrift, as if by causing this brutal unnecessary death, she had lost her own purpose, had become untethered from herself.

Mamma walked her to the train, despite Olivia's warnings that she shouldn't draw attention to them in any way. They held each other tight in the midst of a crowded station, both of them crying.

Olivia slipped Nino's watch from her wrist and slid it onto her mother's. "This will keep you safe," she said. Then the train whistle blew, and Olivia stepped up and into the jam-packed train, with people clinging to its sides.

A hand grasped her arm — the grip firm — and propelled her into the buffer between two carriages and detained her there, while the countryside flowed past. She held her breath, watched a long train slowly rumble past— an entire German division heading south, flat car after flat car loaded with tanks, and at the front and back of each, German steel-helmeted soldiers, their rifles aimed.

Night and Fog Decree

Persons who committed offences against the Reich or the German forces in occupied territories, except where the death sentence was certain, were to be taken secretly to Germany and handed over to the Sipo and SD for trial or punishment in Germany. After these civilians arrived in Germany, no word of them was permitted to reach the country from which they came, or their relatives; even in cases when they died awaiting trial, the families were not informed, the purpose being to create anxiety in the minds of the family of the arrested person.

Whoever knows where a band is hiding and does not inform the German authorities forthwith
WILL BE SHOT IMMEDIATELY!

Whoever harbours or feeds a band or individual bandits
WILL BE SHOT IMMEDIATELY!

Every house or building in which a bandit is found or in which a bandit has been harboured
WILL BE BLOWN UP!

The same applies to any house from which shots are fired at members of the German forces. To all such cases stocks of hay, straw, and provisions will be burned, the cattle requisitioned, and the
INHABITANTS SHOT IMMEDIATELY!

Every village which has given assistance to the bands
WILL BE DESTROYED BY FIRE AND THE
INHABITANTS SHOT!

12

Northern Italy, 1945

Three months had passed since Olivia's disappearance.

In late February, when the sky was an inky black and the air frigid, Nino, Jules, Rowan and three other agents drove from Bari to Gioia del Colle Air Base, then boarded a plane that would take them north. Winter had been harsh, and would be more so in the mountains where they were headed, about a hundred kilometres south of Turin, where Rowan would lead this mission aimed at training partisans at sabotage, identifying air drop locations, as well as carrying out operations against the Germans.

Since late November, Nino had been in a state of near panic, imagining Olivia in a German concentration camp, or tortured in an Italian jail, or worse still, dead. She simply had not returned from her Musadino mission. He asked everyone at HQ for information, but no one could—or would—tell him where Olivia was or what might have happened to her. He called Claire. Surely she would know Olivia's whereabouts.

"I know her frequencies," Claire said. "She hasn't used them."

"Maybe she's compromised, or lost her set," Nino said, hopefully.

"Maybe," Claire said, her voice unconvinced.

Next he thought he should go to Musadino and find her parents. Perhaps Olivia was there. However, everyone dissuaded him from this. What if her parents had heard nothing? What right did he have to worry them? He asked Stan if he could contact a partisan in the area, someone who could go to the Musadino house and see whether Olivia was there. But this, too, proved fruitless. He spoke to Rowan, Jay, anyone who would listen, to no avail. He sent a message to Miss Adams in London, but received a curt reply. Olivia was MIA.

Nino now sat in the DC-3, silent, his heart a chasm. Was he the cause of Olivia's disappearance? If only he could hold her in his arms, love her, reassure her — things he should have done when he had the chance. He took a deep breath and forced himself to contemplate his immediate future, which, according to other drops, could be as successful as it could be disastrous. What did it matter what happened to him now?

The plane's motor droned, though no one spoke. The six of them knew each other well; there was no need for chitchat. A dim bulb inside the plane tinted their faces an eerie green. Beside them, the door was open, and beyond it, an immense darkness, as if the world had fallen away. Nino wondered if this was what one experienced in death, an endless black nothingness, an emotional eclipse.

Rowan sat across from Nino, his face serious, his forehead creased. He urged them all to think of the many antifascist friends and colleagues scattered across prisons in Italy, who were counting on them to carry on their work. "I see them all now in my mind's eye," he said, "all the people I've known who gave up their lives, people whose sacrifices must not be in vain."

They all watched him silently. He looked calm and thoughtful, though Nino wondered what he was really feeling as they flew in the black above mountain peaks.

"People who died not only in Italy," Rowan continued, "but also Spain, France, Africa; people who fought for freedom, though their own had been taken from them."

Nino thought of Antonio Gramsci, imprisoned in 1926 in Turi, near Bari, of Elio on that African mountain, of agents who were shot while sitting in a jeep beside him, of the countless soldiers whose faces he didn't know, but who had bled into the earth.

He thought of Rowan and Jules heading into danger with him, of Lorenzo and the partisans, of Olivia, who now existed in the liminal space between hope and despair, of Bianca, from whom he'd received a letter this past week, a letter telling him she had returned to Pozzecco and had been welcomed by his aunt. She was either ignoring or misunderstanding his silence. *When we're married,* she wrote, *your aunt should come and live with us.* He thought of Aunt Isabella, her views on honour, duty, loyalty, a woman who had remained a spinster after her betrothed died in the great War. Bianca had not misunderstood anything, he thought; she'd outsmarted him, probably with Lorenzo's help. He lay his hand against the scar on his chest. Instead of lucky, he felt betrayed, by love, by country, by politics, perhaps even by himself. He closed his eyes and lived a daydream in which he and Olivia were happily living in London, or travelling the world of adventure and discovery. Instead, here he was in this metal box filled with the stench of gasoline, with Sten guns, revolvers and daggers, as if he were a mafioso, fleeing the police.

A couple of hours in, the pilot yelled, "Ready!"

They stood up as if in a trance, arranged themselves in single file, and passed around a flask of brandy. From the open door, a frigid wind whistled past them. They lowered their goggles, preparing to jump. Beside the door two RAF non-commissioned officers smiled at them, ready to push them if they showed any reluctance.

The pilot made a wide circle, then called out, "No lights. We'll have to go back."

A reprieve. They all sat down, relieved. Perhaps they'd try again tomorrow, Nino thought. Below, partisans were waiting, probably hiding, prey for the German troops that patrolled the area, and who would surely have heard the drone of the plane.

The pilot, however, decided to circle once more, then sharply yelled, "Ready!" and they all stood up again, somewhat disconcerted, and filed towards the green light by the door. One by one, they took a step forward, then Nino was at the front, without a moment to reflect on the cold air on his face, on the nothingness he hurled himself into.

When his parachute opened, all his anxiety dissipated in the silent calm, as if the earth had stopped revolving, as if everyone no longer existed, as if only night would prevail from now on. His eyes quickly became accustomed to the moonlight as he floated towards mountain ridges, snow-covered pastures and dark tracts of bush. Below, rivers and lakes mirrored the moon; above, he imagined the sky brilliant with stars, and himself dwarfed into the most insignificant being.

As he approached the ground, the landscape appeared like a child's drawing of miniature farmhouses, haylofts, fields and forests that grew until his field of vision focused only on the bonfires circling a clearing where he hit ground, and sank deep into snow. For a moment, he gave himself up to this strange sensation.

"Hurry! Germans!"

As if awakened, he stood up, stripped off his parachute and plodded towards the voice, his feet sinking deep into the soft snow, until he reached a group of partisans who pulled him forward urgently, while others rapidly gathered the parachutes, and the arms and ammunitions dropped.

"Help!" Jules called.

Nino turned. Jules had dropped heavily and was now half-buried in snow. Nino moved towards him, but one of the partisans took his arm. "Keep moving. Too late," he said. "Germans will be here in a moment."

"But—"

"Move or you'll get us all killed," Rowan's voice said.

Nino shook his head. "I'm not leaving him," he said, and started once more toward Jules, who, realizing what had happened, waved him away. "Go!" he said. "You've got the radio. You can't be taken."

Rowan grabbed Nino's arm and pulled him forward, away from Jules, whose panicked eyes burned into Nino's brain. He turned and hurried along behind the partisans, away from the clearing until they reached a hill, dense with trees and shrubs that formed a canopy above them. Two of the partisans took the arms and ammunitions and left, to store them in a church in a nearby village.

From here, they had a clear view of the road where now, a jeep and a truck of German soldiers were headed for the clearing. Then a shot rang out.

Jules! Nino forced himself to breathe, hysteria rising in his chest. Two partisans stood next to him, the others gone.

"Quick," one said, and motioned Nino to follow him to a barn up a small hill, where he settled into the hayloft, shivering with cold and misapprehension. How could it end like this, so abruptly, so unforeseen? He closed his eyes and saw Jules beside him in Sicily, Salerno, Pistoia, Monopoli, Bari, his face, the panic, recalled their pact of a trip to Etna when the war was over, their feet sinking into the burning earth. He cried silently, suppressed tears for Jules, for their friendship, for Olivia, for himself, for not risking more, for being alive while others perished.

Something scurried in the barn. Rats. He was certain the Germans would no doubt be searching for them all. A *rastrellamento*. Rakes scraped across his restless dreams, stamping out fires. At dawn, two partisans awakened him from a fitful sleep, and led him to the others in the hills. The partisans were constantly on the move. Familiar with hills and terrain, they mostly managed to avoid capture.

At their meeting place, Rowan patted his back, head shaking. "We'll get him home," Rowan said.

Nino set up at Casa Rosa, a large farmhouse. On the hill above it, hidden by trees and rocks, was a half-ruined shack that, for the past year, had been a wireless station. He settled in to send and receive messages. The ciphers told of civilians shot or arrested in nearby Turin, of German trains moving through tunnels, of armament drops and trip movements, of supplies intercepted by the Germans, of agents killed or taken prisoner, of atrocities being perpetrated in Trieste by Tito's Partisans against Italians — ciphers Nino relayed to HQ. Each day, he also sent Olivia the same cipher — *my warlike spirit sleeps / though yet within me roars.*

He received no reply. No cipher mentioned Jules. No cipher told of Olivia's whereabouts.

Through February, March and early April, they were constantly on the move, evading ambushes, while sabotaging roads and bridges. Each day or two, Nino crept back to the wireless station above Casa Rosa to relay their progress and pick up messages from HQ. Of the four agents left after Jules's death, one had been captured, one had been shot during a *rastrellamento* and now, only Nino and Rowan remained.

The days blended one into the other, and Nino was constantly on edge, listening for the sound of Germans approaching, ready to flee into open fields, to hide in cowsheds, or haystacks, or woods, or caverns. High on adrenaline and fear, he responded instinctually to the dangers around him, following the partisans' lead, often into caves with concealed entrances. Nino and the partisans huddled there, sometimes for days, without food, while listening to the Germans' footsteps as they patrolled, throwing hand grenades into the mouths of these caves. Nino held his breath in those moments, imagining his throat aflame, thinking about death, how vulnerable they all were, not only in wartime, but in their everyday lives, when they least expected it: a car accident, a heart attack, a fall from a ladder, a forest fire, a flood, an avalanche of peril lurking in every living moment. How did he end up here, cold and alone, in his own unrecognizable country, fighting a foreign occupier? Were they destined to never live in peace?

In mid-April, Nino, Rowan and the partisans slowly moved towards Milan, where chaos was evident: fascists were fleeing, trying to reach the Switzerland border to save their skins; demoralized German troops wandered about listlessly. Then on the 28th of April came word that Mussolini and his mistress Claretta Petacci had been arrested while also trying to flee to Switzerland, and were executed by a partisan, without trial. The foreign press considered this an act of barbarism, but for Nino and the Italians who had lived for twenty-five years under Mussolini's brutal regime and had suffered countless casualties, Mussolini's was a deserved end. Mussolini's and Petacci's corpses were then driven to Piazzale Loreto in Milan, and dumped in the square where months earlier, Germans had dumped the bodies of partisans. A mob kicked, beat, spit, and shot at the corpses before hanging them upside down from the metal girder above a service station in the square.

Soon, Nino received a cipher urging that under no circumstances were the partisans to occupy the cities until the Allies arrived. However, the partisans, having done all the fighting here and shed their blood for this victory, were not going to let the Allies take the credit. As the Germans began to pull out, the partisans immediately entered towns like warriors, strutting down main streets lined with crowds who cheered and clapped. Nino and Rowan followed, resigned, and, as they neared Turin, they heard gunfire, and soon came upon a grisly scene: in the gardens of a large mansion, partisans had shot fascists and half-buried them, so their arms and legs stuck out of the ground. Inside Turin, the firing intensified. Fascists occupied the top floors of buildings and were firing down on them. For twenty-four hours they fought, until the partisans rushed buildings and killed every fascist in their sights. The following day, the first Allied troops marched into the city.

At the end of April, Nino and Rowan returned to SOE HQ, which had moved to Siena while they were on their mission. Once again, Nino sought news of Olivia in vain. It was as if she had vanished. Could she have deserted and joined the partisans? But this, surely, his superiors would know. Perhaps when she went home, she had found her brother and joined him.

He took a week's leave and boarded a train for Monopoli, where he wandered aimlessly, as if he'd find Olivia in the abandoned Villa Grazia, or the Bari Lungomare, or the seaside hotel where they'd spent Christmas, or Lama San Giorgio where he'd last seen her. He tortured himself with scenarios he could not substantiate, and when he returned to Siena, despite the camaraderie of colleagues and agents, all rejoicing that they'd survived the war, Nino held himself apart, still reeling from Jules's death, and the fears that populated his dreams. The war's final days proved brutal. Revenge killings, enraged killings — no one knew who killed whom. The partisans, after years of fighting and being hunted, did not spare fascists or collaborators.

Nino had been in Siena only a couple of weeks, when to his surprise, Antonio arrived. Nino had not seen him since Kenya, though he'd assumed Antonio had been sent to another country perhaps.

"You're surprised to see me," Antonio exclaimed, pulling Nino into a bear hug.

"Where have you been?" Nino asked, pleased to see a familiar face. "Did you ever poison that Farinacci?"

Antonio shook his head and laughed. "I wish."

"Too bad," Nino said.

"It's good to see you, my friend," Antonio said. "Let's go for a ride."

Nino pulled his light jacket from the back of a chair and followed Antonio to his motorcycle. They rode down the hill to the centre of the city and found a small bar.

"And where have you been since I saw you last?" Antonio said.

Nino sighed. "In more barns and woods than I care to remember."

"Italy, I presume?"

"Yes," Nino said. "And you?"

"Yugoslavia, mostly."

"That's where most of the drops went," Nino said, recalling the repeated requests for arms and ammunition that didn't come. "I should have known you were involved. Thank God the war is over."

"It might be over here, but it's not over everywhere," Antonio said. "I've just returned from Trieste."

Nino nodded and leaned forward. "What's it like?" he asked.

"Occupied. By Tito's Communist Partisans." He ran a hand through his hair. "The Yugoslavs have been arresting Italians, seizing bank accounts and property, requisitioning large amounts of grain and other supplies." He shook his head. "And worst of all," he said, "several thousand people have vanished — both Italians and Yugoslavs who opposed Tito's takeover —sent to Yugoslav concentration camps, or murdered and dumped into mine shafts and sinkholes in the Karst." He took a deep breath.

"How is it possible?" Nino said, though he knew these ethnic cleansings had persisted in the area for decades. During the Italian occupation of the province of Lubiana a couple of years previously, Italian soldiers had shot thousands of people, burned hundreds of villages, imprisoned, tortured and deported citizens — an ethnic cleansing of fifty thousand Slovenians the generals were proud of. "We are killing too few!" General Robotti had said. Soldiers had brought back horrific photographs of men, women and children on their knees, their praying hands raised, imploring the soldiers not to kill their loved ones. Nino shuddered. "An eternal history of reprisals," he said.

They sat in silence, sipping their beer, until Antonio said, "The Allies will soon arrive and push them out. After that, I'll be stationed in Trieste with the Allied Military Government. Special Branch, Security Section. They'll be administering military rule until things settle."

"I wouldn't mind working in Trieste," Nino said. His SOE colleagues were all returning to their countries and lives, their friendships and loyalties easily abandoned now that the war was over, as if they had never been real.

They chatted a while longer, then mounted Antonio's motorcycle to return up the hill to HQ. In a curve, the front wheel skidded, slid five metres along the ground and toppled in front of a small crumbling church.

"Damn!" Antonio said. He'd been knocked clear of the bike and was struggling to get up. "Are you okay?"

"I think so," Nino said. He'd been flung against the church door, and when he tried to stand up, he felt a sharp pain in his left leg. He gingerly massaged it, to no avail. Then he raised his pant leg, and struck a match. A deep gash slashed across his knee.

"Ouch," Antonio said. "That'll need stitches."

Nino shuddered at the blood, and to test the extent of the injury, moved his leg a little. "At least the bone's not broken," he said.

Antonio hobbled to the motorcycle and righted it. "Can you get back on?"

"I think so," Nino said again. After a painful struggle, he was able to remount the motorcycle and the two of them rode to the hospital emergency, where a doctor sewed eighteen stitches into his knee.

Antonio had fared better. He had several scratches and bruises, but was able to return to work. "Hope to see you in Trieste," he said to Nino, and rode off.

Over the next three weeks, trapped in bed, because any movement would open his wound, Nino began writing letters to Olivia, and although he thought she might never see them, the act comforted him. *Not an instant goes by that my thoughts aren't turned towards you, who are my everything, my only reason to go on living,* he wrote. *If only tonight I could dream of you, I'd lose all my pain.* But the more time passed, the more despondent he felt, as if he were once again imprisoned. His yearning for Olivia created its own suffering, his life a void without her, a suspended state.

One afternoon, a knock awakened him from a listless dream.

"I heard about the accident," a woman's voice said. "How terrible."

"Claire!" Seeing her stirred him. "I thought you were in Bari," he said.

"I was. I am. But I'm clearing up some paperwork, then getting married." She smiled. "I'm going to stay in Italy."

"Congratulations," he said, then after a moment, "Viola? Any news?"

She shook her head. "I know what you know," she said, which was simply that she had not returned from Musadino last November. She sat on a chair beside the bed, and took his hand. "You have to move on, Nardo."

He closed his eyes. "I can't," he said. "I need to know what happened."

Claire frowned. "Unless she was captured — which we probably would have heard about — what likely happened is that having heard about your engagement, she decided to remove herself from a harmful situation." When she saw his surprise, she added, "Of course she told me about your fiancée. What do you think?"

"It wasn't like that," he said. "You don't know the story."

"I don't need to know your particular story. It's the most common of all — the fiancée back home, the wartime affair." She shook her head. "Viola wasn't cut out for that…"

"I never intended to marry this fiancée," he said slowly. "It was all a misunderstanding…"

"Nardo, listen to me," she said gently. "You need to let go. Whether Viola is alive or dead, she is now beyond you."

"You've heard from her!" he said, half rising in the bed, then falling back from the pain.

"No. I'm just saying, if she's alive, she knows where to find us."

Claire stayed on for an hour or so, talking about people they knew in Monopoli, in Bari, and about her coming marriage to a young Italian agent there. Nino listened, downhearted.

After she left, he lay there thinking about her words: *You have to move on.* Well, he didn't want to move on, though he knew he had to. For one, there was Bianca, who he still had not dealt with. She would now be expecting him to go to her. The thought chilled him. Every few days now, he received letters from her, sometimes four or five at once, written weeks before. *Nino my love,* she wrote, *I haven't heard from you. What's happened? Don't you know when you are so far away and I'm waiting, every moment seems like a century? Why do you want to worry me? Can you not at least send me a postcard? I love you so much Nino. Don't break my life. My Nino, reassure me. All my love, your Bianca.*

If only Olivia were here. Sometimes he wanted to fall asleep and not wake up… other times he was seized by fits of fury against himself, against everyone, against this wretched war. He needed her presence, her comfort; he needed pure air, wide seas, much sun. Instead, he struggled, his heart bleak as the sky.

Finally in early June, when he'd healed, Nino's service with SOE ended, and he was given two weeks leave, before being sent for training in Gorizia for the Allied Military Government Civil Police. As Antonio had predicted, the Yugolavs were pushed out of Trieste by the Allies on May 1, with military rule established by the AMG. Nino was pleased to continue his service with the British. He gathered his few possessions and boarded a train for Pozzecco, anxious to see Aunt Isabella, anxious to start working again.

The train chugged through a devastated landscape of towns, factories, bridges, villages, all destroyed by the bombings — his country a wasteland. In early evening, he neared an Udine he hardly recognized, made of burned-out buildings and rubble.

When he reached his family home in Pozzecco, his breath caught in his throat: the two-storey rectangular building was pockmarked by gunfire, windows boarded up, and the large wooden doors chained and padlocked. *Abandoned.* How could it be? He had heard from his aunt a couple of months ago. Something must have happened. He stood perplexed for a few moments, looking around at other houses, some of which were also boarded up. Finally, he knocked on a neighbour's door and asked.

"You must be Nino," the woman said. "Praise be the Lord you're alive."

Nino nodded. "My aunt? Donna Isabella. Do you know where I can find her?" He pointed to the house.

The woman grasped his arm. "The Germans…" She paused, and her eyes filled with tears. "Donna Isabella was helping partisans… I'm sorry," she said.

A roaring began in Nino's ears — explosions and fire. No. Not Aunt Isabella. "Are you sure?" he said, hopefully.

"I'm sorry," the woman said again, and moved aside. "Do you want to come in?"

Nino shook his head. "How long ago?"

"A couple of days before the end of the war," the woman said. "Many were killed in those final days… my daughter…"

"Where can I find her?"

The woman pointed to the church several blocks away. "Padre Pio took care of the burials. He probably has your house key, or maybe try city hall. They had to board everything up. Looters, you know." She made a sign of the cross. "Is there no decency left?"

He thanked the woman and walked slowly towards the church, his feet heavy, his heart exploding with grief. Padre Pio led him behind the church to the cemetery and after a blessing, left Nino alone.

Nino stared at his aunt's grave, unable to reconcile the freshly dug black earth with her vibrant being. Had she predicted her own demise? Awaited it? Aunt Isabella was his anchor, the one person who loved him unconditionally. That tie now severed, he found himself unmoored. He sank to his knees. He had lost everyone he loved. What was the point of carrying on? His tears fell into the earth, until his heart felt empty and compressed into a hard little ball. He had crossed a boundary and would never be able to return to himself.

A week into his leave, Nino lay fully clothed in his old bedroom in the family home. For a few minutes, he fell into a pleasurable dream of visiting the past, imagining his child self atop a hay wagon, in awe of the swallow's nest perched on a ceiling beam in the portico that extended to an inner courtyard of stalls and pens, now long deserted. He smelled damp hay, old house, abandonment. The chickens pecked at his feet, dairy cows lowed, donkeys brayed, while Aunt Isabella pitched hay into the stalls. He soared up through air, though he couldn't see or feel his body, flying at the speed of thought, hundreds of miles, surrounded by a black universe, crammed with constellations of stars. Exhilarated at first, he tried to capture the immense beauty, his mind a film he would later develop. Yet the infinite, the desolate silence oppressed him. He wanted to return home. He listened for the familiar sounds of his aunt calling his name, her footsteps quick on the cobblestoned portico, but the moment he did this, he was swooping down full tilt, then jolted awake by repeated knocking downstairs.

He forced himself up, dizzy at first, disoriented. Opened the blinds to let in the mid-afternoon sun. The knocking persisted. He went down to open the door.

Bianca stood there. She threw her arms around his neck, kissed him. "I was so worried," she said. "Not hearing from you. I only now heard about your aunt. I'm so sorry. I know how much you loved her and she you."

Nino blinked, and slowly disengaged himself.

She picked up a suitcase and her bag and walked past him into the main room. He followed, as if he were the guest. He had no idea what to say to her.

Bianca started chatting about the last time she was here, visiting Aunt Isabella, all the while removing her sky-blue jacket. She wore a mid-calf matching skirt and a white blouse with tiny mother-of-pearl buttons down the front. She moved her head as she spoke, and her shoulder-length hair swung from side to side. Nino watched her, thinking she was still as beautiful as he recalled, but his heart was closed to her. He would have to set her straight. The idea exhausted him.

She stopped talking, as if sensing his reticence, his sorrow, and efficiently went about straightening up in the kitchen, washing up dishes he'd abandoned, while he sat in one of the faded antique chairs, and breathed the fabric, searching for his aunt's scent. She was here — alive — five, six weeks ago. He wondered how she'd survived throughout the war. Did her neighbours help? Perhaps the partisans looked out for her. Guilt rose in his throat, and he swallowed. It seemed everyone he loved was always just out of reach.

"It's clear that you can't stay here alone. You're not looking after yourself," she said. "I'm going out to get us some food."

He sighed, and made a motion to stand up, but she shook her head. "Just stay here," she said. "I'll be back in a few minutes." She picked up her jacket and went out.

He hadn't said anything, and this felt right. He sank back into the chair, unwilling to return to life.

She returned with provolone, mortadella and fresh bread, which she cut and placed on a plate for them. "I realize this must have all come as a shock, but we'll figure this out together," she said.

"Bianca, I'm sorry—" he began, but she shook her head.

"No need for apologies," she said. "This war has taken from everyone."

He hadn't even asked about her family. "Are your parents all right?"

"Yes, they're all shaken but fine. Nothing is as it was…" She sat at the table, made an open-faced sandwich of cheese and mortadella and handed it to him. "But Lorenzo…" She burst into tears.

"No, not him too," Nino said, resigned. He reached across and took her hand. "This damned war," he said. "I'm sorry."

She continued to cry while he patted her hand.

Finally, she wiped her eyes and looked up. "I'll stay here with you," she said. "I don't think anyone cares any more about impropriety."

He thought about how easy it would be to simply fall into this comfort, to let Bianca take care of him. He felt emptied out.

"Talk to me," she said.

"I'll only be here another week," he said. "Then I'm off to Gradisca for training."

"I don't mind," she said. "I'll stay here and wait for you."

Olivia is dead, he thought. What difference would this make?

Bianca installed herself as the mistress of the house. She opened shutters to flood the rooms in light, turned out mattresses in the sun, swept and dusted, shopped and cooked — her presence a pallid echo of Aunt Isabella. Nino left the house for hours each day, and walked in the countryside, relieved to be alone with his grief, which continued to expand. Bianca moved into his bed and made love to him. He responded to the sensations, though none opened his heart.

Soon he left for his six-week training, grateful, relieved to flee Bianca's tearful farewell. In Gradisca, he blocked her out, as well as Olivia, Aunt Isabella, Jules, and Lorenzo, the deaths of other agents, the fears. This was what he'd hoped for — to continue to work with the British. However, instead of exhilaration, he felt only a languid acceptance, as if he had been flung into a stormy sea and had abandoned himself to the waves.

He concentrated on his studies and exams which he passed with high grades. He was to go to further training after another leave. He tried to fill his leisure hours with work, to push away all regrets and grief.

On his return, Bianca met him with unexpected news: she was pregnant. "We'll get married as soon as the banns are published," she said matter-of-factly. "I've already contacted the priest."

INTERMISSION

Pozzecco, Italy 2010

At the hospital, I sit silently, thinking of love and secrets, while I stare at my father. Despite the yellowing bruises, the scabs on his cheeks, he looks peaceful, asleep, the lines on his face softened to reveal the outline of my childhood father.

I recount for him black sand beaches, a holiday in Hawaii one year when I was twelve. We were a happy family then. My father had just returned from five months at sea. We'd gone to the Big Island first, up to the rim of Kilauea, where puffs of steam rose from the black earth concealing red-hot magma churning below. He told me the story of his father, his heroic trek on Mount Etna, and how easily danger is disguised. "You wanted to climb down, to feel the heat against your hands, as if you could ignore the depth of that caldera, the fierceness of its soil," I tell him. "You promised we'd go to Mount Etna one day, but we never did." And later, on the beach below, the gently lapping waves on that black sand turned into rip currents dragging us thigh-high into the sea. Another illusion, another unseen depth. Black lava, obsidian, the glass sharp like memory. I wonder if he can hear me, if he's remembering too.

I hold his hand and tell him that I fall in love with men like him, and they turn out to be as silent and absent as he was during my youth. I tell him I have no children. I'm afraid of disclosures. I tell him I want him to awaken.

"I'm planning to take him home to Canada," I tell his nurse when she comes to check on him. "When will he be able to travel?"

She raises her eyebrows. "Only time will tell," she says, and goes on to explain that an induced coma is similar to hypothermia. "It's all about slowing the blood flow," she says, "to give the brain time to heal." I wonder about Antarctic explorers who died in the cold. Could they hear the wind in the ice caves, or the ocean waves smashing to shore, or the ice rupturing beneath them? Could they feel the blizzards sealing their eyes shut? Did they welcome the whiteout?

I return to Pozzecco, discouraged, but I am patient. I will stay until he wakes, and I will take him home with me.

Upstairs in the family home, I tiptoe down the hall, recalling my father's childhood fears of ghosts who emerged from the paintings and roamed the courtyard. Some nights, I glimpse a trembling haze, and huddle under the covers.

From the drawer of my father's bedside table, I withdraw a bundle of photos of African landscapes; of men playing soccer; uniformed officers in a canteen; my father landing in a field, his parachute open, laughing at whoever is taking the photo; the Temple of Athena. Olivia — in front of a transceiver. I stare at the photo, trying to divine who she was and what happened to her. She must have died.

In a shoebox in the wardrobe, a bundle of letters from Olivia, dated between 1943 and 1944. They are the voice of the beloved: *Nino, my love, moments ago, my eyes fixed on the place where we spent many happy evenings, quivering, savouring the beautiful night…My thoughts keep straying relentlessly to you. There's so much I want to tell you, if only it were possible!… Nino my love, when can we sit in moonlight without fear of being seen? Why do I have to keep my joy to myself?… I want to see you, to be surrounded by your arms. Wait for me, I will do everything possible to reach you… Nino, my heart is numb. Are you free to want me? I fear a dream has ended…*

The words trail through my fingers. I rebundle the letters, and replace them in the shoebox. No wonder my mother was always suspicious.

An envelope labelled "Bianca" is thick with photographs of my mother. I spread them out, settle on one particular portrait. My mother is in soft focus, her hair backlit, her dark lips lightly open. She is as glamorous as a silent-movie star. This both is and is not the mother I recall from my childhood, the kaleidoscopic arrivals and departures, the laughter and tears, my mother's unpredictable moods, tuned and untuned by my father's entrances and exits.

"Why do you always have to be so hostile?" my mother says, her lips tight. Her face is pallid, and her eyes puffy from crying. I'm sixteen, and we're in the cardiac ward of an Ottawa hospital.

"I'm not hostile!" I say, though my tone implies otherwise. I stare at my mother, wondering why, despite my father's betrayals, she continues to be so devoted to him. Of course, she loves him. We both do.

"When he comes home," my mother says in a furious whisper, "and he will get better and come home, you will not upset him with your questions and accusations." She pauses. "Let this be the end."

I stare back, partly defiant, but also frightened that I may have caused my father's heart attack. I run my thumb along the seat's edge where metal meets black leatherette. It sends me spinning into black asphalt highways across mountains, into the blackshirt militia of Italy's Fascism, into the black caverns of the Karst, into that accusation.

"Bella?" my mother says, her voice anxious. In the dingy light of the hospital waiting room, my mother looks grey and tired in her black suit, the skirt wrinkled, her eyeliner faded, or perhaps wiped away by tears.

"Please," my mother implores. "We mustn't upset him. Promise me."

My stomach clenches, my chest tightens. Does my mother blame me simply because I asked a question? My eyes begin to fill, and I turn my head.

My mother waits and we sit in silence for a minute or two, her eyes burrowing into me.

"Bella?" my mother says, softly.

I sigh and nod.

The postcard of Bari's rotunda Lungomare depicts a spacious promenade along the Adriatic, ripples of whitecaps rolling into shore, the sun just above the horizon, a sky of brilliant blue. The rotunda is a half-circle jutting into the sea. Not a single person is visible, as if whoever took the photo cleared out the area, or possibly shot it at dawn. There are no warships, no towering funnels of smoke.

I turn the postcard over. No writing, only the small print Rotonda Lungomare 1971. Was my father in Italy then? I think back. That was the year my mother came to visit me in Vancouver.

"I could have married a resistance fighter," she said.

"I could have stayed in Italy," she said.

"We choose our own futures," she said.

My mother was tentative, her speech halting, searching for words, as if she were trying to tell me something. Or possibly trying not to tell me something. She had arrived in Vancouver unexpectedly, had phoned me from the airport. I was eighteen, living in residence at the university.

"I've left your father," she'd said, while we waited for her luggage to come down the baggage carousel. Her eyes were bright and glassy, as if she'd been both crying and laughing. She was a beautiful woman, in her forties, her skin smooth, her hair soft and wavy around her face. She wore an elegant linen dress with thin black-and-white vertical stripes, and a soft white cardigan over her shoulders.

"He was barely there," I say. My father Ulysses. At sea. Always at sea.

My mother nodded.

I said nothing, waiting for more, but none came. I wondered what had occurred between them this time.

We collected my mother's bags, then in the car on the way to my apartment, my mother said, "It's been a long time coming."

"Why now? What's different?" I asked.

"You don't know anything," my mother said.

"Both you and Dad have seen to that," I said, to which my mother remained silent. Presently, I asked, "What are your plans?"

"I'm meeting a friend in a few days, then I'm not sure."

My mother left as unexpectedly as she'd appeared. Three days later, I returned from class to find a note, saying her friend had arrived, and she'd be in touch as soon as she was settled.

I received postcards from Rome, Barcelona, Paris, as if my mother were on a whirlwind European tour, or a honeymoon. The postcards said nothing about her situation.

I wonder now if my mother knew about the lung cancer and was trying on another life. I didn't see her again until two years later, when she was in hospice in Toronto, so diminished as to be unrecognizable. She was alone.

"Olivia," my mother said, her lips trembling with the effort, "was a spectre who haunted all our married life."

"Who is Olivia?" I said, but she shook her head. "Ask your father."

I turn the Bari Lungomare postcard over in my hands once more, wondering if my father went to Bari on a sentimental whim, to remind himself of happier days. My mother must have known that she could never compete with the dead.

How I wish she had confided in me, helped me understand both her and my father. Instead, she taught me to hold my feelings close.

"Everyone," she said, "will betray you."

Part 2

AFTER

13

Trieste, 1948

During the first three years of Nino and Bianca's marriage, their relationship turned to dissonance, brought about by a sense of distrust which had begun with that supper in the mountains of Pistoia and continued when Nino returned to Pozzecco from his second round of training in 1945, and Bianca tearfully told him that she had miscarried. He wanted to be happy, to fulfill Aunt Isabella's dreams for him, to rekindle the love he'd had for Bianca so many years before. He wanted to believe her, but in the back of his mind was the entrapment of the engagement and now of the marriage itself.

They had been living in Trieste since 1947, when the UN had established the city as a free port, and divided it into two zones: Zone A, administered by the Allies, and Zone B, by the Yugoslavs. Trieste was in turmoil, being fought over by those who believed Trieste belonged to Italy; those who supported Trieste's annexation to Yugoslavia; and those who wanted Trieste to be an independent state. As Inspector in the AMG Civic Police, Nino had to protect the citizens of Zone A, both from internal violence and from that perpetrated by those from Zone B, maneuvering within three ideologies, trying to maintain peace, keep everyone happy, or at least prevent them from killing each other.

He responded to events that ranged from the absurd — a man brandishing a pistol in a bar because some of the patrons were singing partisan songs — to acts of intimidation aimed at the police; to having to break up fights between neo-fascists and communists; to managing right-wing anti-Slavic parades. It was a difficult time for the Slovene citizens of Trieste, and as the Allies tried to protect them, they were perceived by the nationalists as anti-Italian.

He couldn't share the details of his work with Bianca, who viewed these missions as Nino's "secrecy." He tried to reason with her, by reminding her of her resistance days. "It's a matter of security," he'd say, "not secrecy."

"You can trust me," she'd say.

Nino, however, didn't trust her any more or less than the representatives of the myriad factions within the city, who were not necessarily what they seemed, their motives often hidden behind agendas. His SOE training reinforced that he could trust no one.

One night, Slovenian partisans demonstrated near the boundary between Zone B and A. In response, the Italian Premier mobilized a platoon of Italian soldiers to march on their side of the border, to show Italy's readiness in case of an invasion. Tito then brought his Yugoslavian troops up to face the platoon in a stand-off, and Nino had to go and defuse the escalating tensions.

"Why are you showering and changing your shirt?" Bianca said, as she often did when Nino was on call and had to go out in the evenings.

"It's work, Bianca. You know I can't discuss details," he said. Antonio from the Security Office liaised with him, and often called him out to strategize against perceived threats to the citizens and Allied Military Government in Trieste.

"You don't need a second shower to do that. Why are you always lying to me?" Bianca said. "Who are you meeting? Is it that social worker? Do you think I'm stupid?"

Nino shook his head and left. They had settled into this ritual of accusation and silence, both of them resentful and angry. Yet, Nino thought, they'd had good times too, sweet moments between them. He knew Bianca loved him, and he was trying his best not to disappoint her. In a moment of weakness, he had told Bianca about Olivia — framing her as someone he had loved once. Bianca's reaction had stunned him. She accused him of being unfaithful, of lying to her, and Nino reminded her that he had never made promises, and that he had not even proposed. This set them on an edge neither could abandon.

Demonstrations continued on both sides of the border until the AMG banned them all, but when the Yugoslavs broke the ban and entered the Zone, the British didn't react until violent clashes began.

"Communist lovers!" people yelled at Nino and his unit, the words summoning the *squadristi* violence of Nino's childhood, history in a perpetual repetition.

The tension continued, with daily bombings and nighttime disturbances. East against West. British trying to protect the Mediterranean from Soviet encroachment, and Americans hoping for co-operation with the Soviets. Nino had to navigate the treacherous pits of underground organizations, dark networks, weapons depots. He was a target for neofascists and Blackshirts, many of whom daily paraded through the streets with fanfare, carrying Italian flags, often congregating in Piazza della Borsa, the same piazza from which only days before they had been expelled, chanting fascist slogans and singing nationalistic songs of the last regime. They confronted peaceful demonstrations and tore down commemorative flags for the four Basovizza Heroes — Slovenian partisans executed by the fascists in 1930.

In the midst of this chaos, one spring morning, Nino received a letter from Rowan, with whom he'd kept in sporadic touch since the war's end. Rowan was planning a trip to Italy and would be in Trieste the following week.

Bianca was excited to meet Rowan, a friend from his former life. She sewed herself a new dress, using lining bought at a discount store, and cut a coat from a green wool blanket. Nino was glad that she was making such an effort to please him and Rowan.

He booked them an outdoor table at Cafè degli Specchi in Piazza Unità, from which they could see the Adriatic and ships anchored in the port. To the right, Trieste rose up to the Karst and Opicina. Beyond it, Yugoslavia.

Rowan looked much as he had five years before, only now he'd put on a few pounds, and had a beard. He'd been living in London, and was planning a move to America.

"I saw Claire in Bari," Rowan said, when they were settled and awaiting their lunch.

"Who is Claire?" Bianca asked, sitting up a little straighter.

"She was working with us," Nino said, deliberately vague. They were still sworn to secrecy, and couldn't even divulge the existence of SOE.

"What did she do?" Bianca said.

Rowan smiled. "What people do in wartime," he said.

Bianca frowned. "That's all I hear from Nino. Everything is secret. I don't understand how everything can be secret." She pretend-pouted.

Rowan laughed. "It's security more than secret," he said. "Speaking of which, have you any news of Jay?"

"Jay!" Nino said, recalling that Olivia had gone out with him. "Not a word. Maybe he's back in London too. A colourful fellow, that's for sure." This set them off on the topic of people they'd known in Monopoli and Bari, while Bianca fidgeted with her utensils.

"…and Olivia is working for MI5," Rowan said, and both Nino and Bianca looked up, startled.

"You said she was dead," Bianca said, looking at Nino.

"You didn't know she was alive?" Rowan frowned. "I'm sorry. I thought you knew. One of those miracles," he said, and went on to tell them that Olivia had been captured and tortured by the Gestapo. She'd had a hot poker branded into her back, and still she refused to give up any information. "Heroic, really," Rowan said. "Better than some male agents. " Following this interrogation, she had been sent to Ravensbrück concentration camp, where she managed to survive until the end of the war. "Others did not fare as well," Rowan said, shaking his head.

Nino was too shocked to speak. Olivia, alive! His heart pounded in his ears, and he felt the blood in his face. Bianca scrutinized him while he tried to recover. "I'm happy to hear that," he said, in as normal a voice as he could muster. "No one knew what had happened to her…"

"Or they didn't want to say," Rowan said. "Possibly she was recruited into MI5, and they wanted to keep it quiet."

"Secrets! Always secrets," Bianca said. "We're not at war any more."

Nino thought about work, the daily skirmishes along the border, which felt very much like a continuation of war.

"You don't understand," Rowan said, and smiled. "We've been trained to forget."

After a pleasant visit, Rowan departed to see his family in Siena and Nino and Bianca walked home in an uneasy silence, Nino's heart filled with turbulent emotions, his head with Olivia's face, her smile, her lips.

"You really didn't know?" Bianca said, when they were back in their apartment.

"Of course not. Why would I have lied about it?"

"I suppose you wouldn't have married me if you'd known. I always knew you were unfaithful! It's been my curse to love you." She sat down heavily, and began to cry.

Nino stood apart, thinking she was right, reluctant to console her with what now would be a lie. He pulled out his daily *Police News Digest*, which had a summary of police news appearing in the local press, and sat down to scan it.

"What are you going to do?" Bianca said after a few minutes.

He looked up. He wasn't sure yet. "I don't know."

"I suppose you're going to go to her. That's what you'll do!" She burst into new tears.

He sighed and looked back down at the *Digest*: murders, suicides, stolen arms, drownings, thefts, traffic accidents, political kidnappings — all too predictable and exhausting. Bianca was right. What he really wanted to do was go to London and see Olivia, clear up whatever was or wasn't still between them.

The following Saturday, he left Bianca sobbing, threatening to leave him, though nothing would change his mind. He flew into London and called Rowan to ask him to arrange a meeting with Olivia. He was afraid if he called her, she wouldn't come.

He waited with Rowan at the Criterion, and watched her enter as he had all those years before, his heart thumping in his chest. She spotted Rowan and waved, then stopped when she saw Nino, and pressed her hand to her chest. He stood up as she approached, unsure whether to embrace her or shake her hand.

Rowan took her hands, and kissed her on both cheeks. "You remember Nino," he said, pulling out a chair for her.

"Of course," she murmured, her cheeks red. "Hello."

He smiled. "Olivia. You look well. Life is treating you well." He felt idiotic mouthing a cliché, while the rush of emotions he had felt when he first met her in that dining room in London were now overwhelming him. He wondered if she were feeling the same.

Rowan smoothed the meeting with talk of people they all knew, of his recent trip to Bari and Monopoli. Olivia and Nino both listened and nodded in the right places. Throughout the light lunch, the tension between Nino and Olivia grew. So much unspoken.

Finally, they were done and stood up to leave. Outside the restaurant, Nino turned to Olivia and quickly said, "Walk with me a bit."

Rowan looked from one to the other, then his watch. "I have to go. So great to see you both." He shook Nino's hand and lightly pecked Olivia on the cheek.

Nino watched Rowan go, his chest tight. "So," he said, when they were alone. They began walking the same route they'd taken all those years before. A déjà vu of suppressed emotions.

She stopped and stared at him, her green eyes intense. "Yes."

He sighed. "I tried to find you," he said falteringly, "after the war. No one knew where you were. Or maybe they didn't want to say."

She shrugged. "It was difficult," she said, and continued walking.

"Rowan told me," Nino said, not wanting to upset her, to bring back terrible memories.

"I'm all right now." Her voice trembled.

"Olivia, I've thought about you constantly—"

"It's too late," she said. "I searched for you too. But you had already married." She brought a hand up to her chest. "It's too late. I'm married now."

He reached for her hand and held it, felt the ring on her finger, his stomach knotted. Then he pulled her into an embrace. "I love you," he said in her hair, "I've always loved you."

She slowly disengaged herself, shaking her head. "It seems we're always out of synch." She reached up and kissed him on the lips. He held her tight once more. Then she stepped back. "Goodbye."

He stood rooted, and watched her walk away, thinking once more how quickly one's life can detour, with accidental words, unforeseen events, hesitation, reluctance, fear.

When he returned, Bianca was gone. He made no attempt to bring her back. She had returned to her family in Pistoia. Eventually, she enrolled at the university and rented a small apartment. Nino sent her monthly cheques and moved into the barracks, which felt more secure.

Vulnerable, unfairly targeted in his work, and desolate, as time went on, he dreamed himself into a different life in which Olivia would be at his side. Women still gravitated to him, so he embarked on a series of fleeting affairs, but they left him lonelier than before. He immersed himself in sports, in friendships, but these lost their lustre. All he could think of was that Olivia was alive yet beyond him.

All through the next year, he was consumed with work, which had become increasingly hostile and dangerous. The police had to maintain continuous twenty-four-hour service, because of the ongoing crisis regarding Trieste. Was it to be Italian, Yugoslavian or a Free Territory? Daily skirmishes broke out along the border, bombs exploded, shots ricocheted off walls, the police precinct was attacked. In short, a guerilla warfare was in process, a struggle that had crystallized, pitting Italians vs non-Italians, nationalists vs Communists.

Nino began to think of Bianca, the pre-war Bianca, his first love, the Bianca his aunt loved too. Her hands reached for him across the years from the alley behind her house; from the meetings they attended, thighs pressed against each other, her fervour in the cause ignited; from the idealistic dreams of his youth. He blamed himself for ruining their relationship.

He took a week's leave and drove down to Pistoia, as if to return to that Utopia. He called her on his arrival, and Bianca falteringly told him that she was involved with someone else now, a baron. "Don't be so surprised," she said. "What did you expect?"

Indeed, what had he expected? He was surprised, yes, but was mostly disappointed at the dwindling of his youthful expectations. On board the train for Trieste the following day, he thought about their strained relationship, the intrinsic tie between her and Aunt Isabella. Bianca had been the chosen one and he was glad his aunt had not had to witness his defection.

14

London / Trieste, 1951

Olivia had finally resettled into her life when the letter dropped in the mail. For the past three years, Nino, the war and Italy had receded into a Pandora's box in her mind. She recognized the handwriting as Nino's, and her heart lurched. She took a deep breath, wondering how she could still feel so strongly about a man she met eight years before, a man who had betrayed her not once, but twice. Their last meeting had shaken her, and his final words, *I love you. I've always loved you*, replayed in her head at the oddest times, set her trembling and weepy. She climbed the stairs to the apartment, where she hung up her coat, and slipped the letter into her skirt pocket. Philip was in the living room reading a newspaper. He looked up when she came in. "Any mail?"

She handed him the bundle, and he smiled fondly. She felt instant guilt, though she tried to push it down. She hadn't done anything. She hadn't even read the letter. She came up behind Philip and massaged his shoulders, reassured by his warmth under her hands. He'd been home for the past week, due to a sudden onslaught of severe headaches. It reminded her of Nino's migraines, of which he'd spoken, though she hadn't ever witnessed them. Now, she wished she'd listened more carefully to cures Nino may have mentioned. She scrolled through her memory bank to an evening walk in Bari in 1943, before the bombing of the harbour, following her younger self along the Lungomare, past battleships, beyond which sky and sea merged. *Marconi therapy*, Nino was saying, adding it was some kind of electric wave. She wished now she'd asked questions instead of just listening. She would ask Philip's doctor if he'd heard of it.

Philip reached up and stroked her hand on his shoulder. "Thanks."

"Are you feeling a little better?" she asked.

He nodded. "Much better today. I'm anxious to get back to work."

"I'm sure they miss you," she said, "but I'd rather you wait till you feel totally well."

He nodded again, and turned back to the newspaper. She read the headlines over his shoulder: BRITISH SUBMARINE AFFRAY SINKS IN ENGLISH CHANNEL, KILLING 75; US PERFORMS ATMOSPHERIC NUCLEAR TEST AT ENWETAK. Apparently, there was no learning from history. She shuddered at the thought of another more deadly war, one to possibly obliterate the entire planet.

She, too, had learned nothing from history, she thought, her love affair with Nino ending as swiftly as it had resumed, plunging her into a deep depression from which she had struggled to surface. In her room in Monopoli those years ago, she had sat in near darkness, replaying their time together, as if to determine where she might have gone wrong. Although Nino had told her about his childhood sweetheart, she was shocked that he had become secretly engaged, while he professed love to her. An insurmountable betrayal. Claire had helped pull her out of that slump, telling her Nino was not worth moping over. Life is too short, she told Olivia, especially during war. If you fell in love once, you can do it again. And I believe —and here Claire had smiled knowingly— you've been in love already twice. Isn't there a young man back home waiting for a wedding? Olivia had blushed and tried to wave Claire away. In her heart, she was convinced she would never love again, not like she loved Nino. However, here she was, married to Philip.

When she'd returned after the war, Philip had listened to her plight, consoled her, filled the gap with his affection. In Ravensbrück, she'd told him, she was forced to stitch German uniforms — which she sabotaged by loosely stitching them so they would fall apart, by stiching the pant legs together, by not adding pockets — and to refurbish artillery shells, which she filled with only half the explosive charge, or dampened it with water. There were few inspections before despatch, so it was difficult to pinpoint a culprit. Her mind reeled to those barracks… *how lucky I am to escape the gas chambers… I search for Barbara, but there are 10,000 of us… the medical experiments… the scar branded into my back… forced prostitution… Nino, Nino, Nino.* Then into another time, her return to Britain, her debriefing, she had searched for him, and discovered his *unintentional engagement* had resulted in a very real marriage. She had felt as if the oxygen had been sucked out of her heart… *I must forget him. I must forget him…* Once done in London, she had gone back to her parents in Musadino and waited for Aldo.

Her mother had tearfully returned the watch. "It should have kept *you* safe," she said.

Finally, when they had not heard from Aldo for six months, they'd resigned themselves to the fact that he was most likely dead. In fact, he might be one of the casualties in the Karst caverns and ravines around Trieste. She didn't want to think of her brother bound with wire and dropped alive into one of the bottomless fissures. *Le foibe*, the Italians said. To this day, they had no idea what had happened to Aldo. Nor to Mick, who was MIA and presumed dead. Nor to Barbara, for that matter. The missing, the loved ones, were scars on her heart.

She and her parents had returned to London, where her parents had repossessed their house, and Olivia was offered a job at the Home Office. She had gone to Orchard Court, where Miss Adams had confirmed that Barbara had been sent to France, but had not returned. Miss Adams assured Olivia that she would continue to search for information until she could account for all the girls she had sent overseas.

She sighed, and touched the letter in her pocket. Nino was working in Trieste. Maybe he had news. Her fingers massaged Philip's shoulders absent-mindedly. As soon as she could, she casually went to the washroom, where she eagerly opened the letter and read:

Trieste, September 1951

Dear Olivia,

I'm not even sure you'll read this letter. I think of you often. Bianca and I separated three years ago, and I am still here, in Trieste.

How are you? Are you still working for the British government? I've been promoted to Chief Inspector of the Allied Military Government civilian police. Trieste is a rather lively place, cosmopolitan, filled with entertainment venues to keep the Allied forces happy. I believe talks are ongoing between the British, Americans and Tito, and there will be a solution at some point. Meantime, alongside the cheerful façade, is the threat from the Titini, so we are constantly having to defend the border with Yugoslavia.

You're wondering why I'm writing, I'm sure. I know you said a final goodbye when we met in London, but I can't stop thinking about you, and about our time together. I feel I didn't get a chance to fully explain myself.

I searched for you in every way I could without success. I would never have married Bianca if I'd known you were alive.

I'm not trying to be sentimental, nor to bother you. I hope this finds you well and healthy and happy. I don't know your current circumstances, but I have a 10-day leave coming up, and I'm wondering if you would consider joining me. We could travel up north closer to the Alps. Have a holiday and catch up on each other's lives. Is this too presumptuous? Please be frank with me in your reply. For old times' sake:

IOAH
LLX MAX UHO GDX OIN
YAC CEE LNO SWX AEX
OME SLX YAX ERC AIM
MTE AYX ELX REN SSX
LIR DEA THX

I look forward to your letter.
Your Nino always

Olivia reread the letter twice more, her heart pounding, decrypting the cipher in her head —

*Do you
recall my last
message? I am
here in Italy.
Shall we dance
once more?*

— before folding it into its envelope and replacing it in her pocket. She flushed the toilet and went into the living room, glad Philip was engrossed in the paper and wouldn't see her flaming cheeks. She crossed into the kitchen, and put water on to boil, staring at it as if to read a fortune in the swirls.

"What are we having for dinner?" Philip asked, looking up from his newspaper.

"Spaghetti," she said, "like my mother makes it."

He sighed, smiled in appreciation, and folded the newspaper.

When the water boiled, Olivia submerged the pasta and stirred the tomato sauce simmering on the stove, six times clockwise, and six times anti-clockwise, thinking of Nino, wondering how she could justify a trip to Italy right now. She looked at Philip, who was now leaning back in the chair, his eyes closed. "Are you okay?" she asked.

He opened his eyes. "Tired," he said. "But no pain right now."

She smiled at him. She had married Philip, just as he had predicted in his wartime letters. Once home, they had begun seeing each other again. Her feelings for Philip were different from those she had for Nino, but no less genuine.

Within the week, Philip was back at work, headaches gone as if they'd never surfaced. Olivia began to hatch plans that would take her to Trieste. Claire was in Italy, and presented the best excuse for a trip there. She had settled with her Italian officer in Bari. Olivia struggled with her decision, not even sure how much to tell Claire. In the end, she phoned Claire from work, and asked for an invitation to visit, swearing to tell her everything when she saw her.

"Are you sure about this?" Claire asked. "Don't you remember what happened? You know Nino can't be trusted. Why would you go to him now?"

Olivia had no answer then, nor did she have one now. Nino was a regret in her life, an unfinished business she was determined to complete.

She mailed Nino a brief letter, thanking him for his, and saying she was planning to be in Italy later in the month, and could take a few days to go north and visit him.

Philip didn't question her sudden decision to visit Claire — rather, he assumed she had been asked to go from the Home Office on business she couldn't discuss, and she didn't tell him otherwise.

As she neared the Trieste Centrale train station, Olivia imagined the Orient Express of the 1800s, the elegant, luxurious compartments. She stared dreamily out the window, at the cerulean sea where it met the sky, its whitecaps like strokes from an artist's brush, thinking of the horizon of her own life defined by war, by the curls and folds and breakers of all that had occurred.

The train slid into the station toward a grand 19th-century building, reminiscent of the Austro-Hungarian empire. She stepped down and headed along the platform to the monumental hall of arches. For a moment, she caught herself reflected in one of the glass walls — tall, slender, with her hair secured in a low ponytail. She didn't recognize her confidence, startled by the glimpse of herself as others might see her. She thought of that young girl falling in love in the Criterion, who had then boarded a ship, anxious and unsure. She flashed through a montage: Massingham, Cairo, Monopoli, Bari, Pescara, Musadino, Germany, London, each place, each experience altering her, until she became this person here, in Trieste, now.

As she crossed the station, she saw Nino leaning against one of the arches. In London three years before, he had looked stricken and resigned. She scanned her memory banks for other times: Italy, recently returned from his mission, looking haggard — a reflection of his difficult time in northern Italy. Violence rose to the surface— *as if in slow motion, the boy's body hovers for a moment before crumpling to the ground, massive blood staining the snow on the path* — as did the poverty and hardship of the locals in Monopoli, children and families outside their houses, hoping for relief. How lucky she had been for the most part, how careless and unafraid, buried in work, when she should have placed more value on the life around her. Her brain settled for a moment in a space she avoided, the emotions too raw: *...the camp, the women shellshocked, tortured, missing limbs, moaning and crying out against invisible attacks...* She wondered how they had all managed to return home to husbands and fathers, who may not have seen fighting, who may not have had to make terrible choices to stay alive.

This Nino looked well, healthier than three years ago. His eyes looked bluer and brighter than she remembered. A surge overcame her, suppressed emotions ready to explode. Nino held out his arms and she stepped into them easily, as if they had not been separated all these years.

"You look well," he said, stepping back and smiling.

"You too," she murmured, wondering how she appeared to him really. "I haven't booked a hotel," she said. "I wasn't sure where we were going or when."

"It's all taken care of." He smiled, lifted her bag, then touched her elbow. "How was the trip?" he asked.

Her heels tapped a steady rhythm on the marble tiles. "I was imagining I was on the Orient Express," she said, trying to hide her excitement. "Minus the luxury."

He laughed. "Unfortunately, the Orient Express never did stop here, but the Simplon Orient Express did."

"*Murder on the Simplon Orient Express* just doesn't ring right."

"Which is why the Simplon was left out," Nino said.

She laughed. How easily they slipped into their old relationship. Breathless, delighted, she followed Nino outside, where he steered her to the left of a large piazza and stopped in front of a jeep. "Here we are." Across from them, several army trucks roared by, then a horse and buggy.

They climbed in, drove slowly along Riva Tre Novembre. The sidewalks teemed with people talking and laughing, going about their daily business; children shrieked happily as they played in front of sombre grey battleships moored in the harbour; in the window of one of the buildings a large sign read: CHOLERA VACCINATIONS HERE. Olivia shuddered. In London, there had been an influenza outbreak, though she hadn't been too concerned about it, because it appeared to kill mainly older or vulnerable people. Cholera would not be so discriminatory. She'd be careful about what she ate or drank. In any case, Nino would guide her in this.

"You look well," Nino said again, turning to look at her. "Are you well?"

She heard the question in those words. She nodded, silent, though more needed to be said, some explanation as to why she'd changed her mind and was here now. "I can only stay a couple of days," she said breathlessly. "I have to get back to work."

He didn't ask any more. Instead, as they drove, he pointed to landmarks: the Castle of San Giusto on the hill; the Grand Canal with its massive church at the end; the Piazza dell'Unità — the largest sea-facing plaza in Europe. For a moment, she fantasized leaving her life behind and moving here with Nino.

"You can ask me whatever you want," she said, to put him at ease.

He shook his head, and smiled at her. They drove beneath a banner hung between two buildings with British flags at either end, and in the middle INGHILTERRA D'OGGI: MOSTRA DEL PROGRESSO SOCIALE (The Britain of today: an exhibition of social progress) and the address of a gallery.

"We're both loved and hated here," he said.

"And who are the 'we'?" she asked.

"The British and we Italians who work with them." He waved his hand, as if to brush away further questions, then took her hand and squeezed it.

Late afternoon, and the streets and piazzas were full; voices and music spilled out of restaurants and outdoor cafés, quite unlike a city in strife, split in two. In a window, a sign read FREE TERRITORY OF TRIESTE. "Do you feel free here?" she asked.

"As free as is possible," Nino said. He stopped in Via Cavana, and they walked along a narrow street to the Hotel James Joyce. "I don't know if it was a hotel when Joyce was here, or whether it was one of the many residences where he lived and deserted when he couldn't pay the rent," Nino said. "But I thought you'd enjoy being here."

"How wonderful," she said, and slipped her arm through his. He had remembered she loved books, and had found her the perfect place.

He left her to check in and said he'd collect her for dinner in a couple of hours.

After she unpacked, she went to Reception and made a long-distance call to Philip, relaying information about her three days with Claire. She told him she and Claire were going to take a little trip together to the north of Italy; she wanted to see her family home in Musadino, and the two of them could catch up on each other's lives. Philip sounded wistful, saying he wished he could have gone with her. She pushed down the guilt and reassured him she'd be home by the weekend.

"I'm working for the Home Office," Olivia told Nino later, over dinner. "In Special Operations, where they can make better use of my skills."

"I hope after all this ends, I'll be stationed in London too. That's my understanding, given all the years I've worked with and for the British."

"You always said you wanted to live in Britain," she said. "You'll like it. It's much better now they've rebuilt everything. Actually, it's miraculous they did it in such a short time." She thought about her parents' house, and for a moment, relived that terrible morning so many years ago, the men's voices, the cart full of stones, the sound of glass breaking.

"What's wrong?" Nino said.

"Nothing. Nothing. I recalled something unpleasant. I can't help it. Memory takes me there emotionally." She took a deep breath. "I'm fine now. Really." She smiled. "Tell me about yourself."

They were sitting at one of the outdoor restaurants in Piazza dell'Unità, from where they could see the port, and the hillside up to the Carso, where lights slowly began to appear as the sky darkened. *Bari, December 2, 1943... In twilight, the harbour shimmers with lights, and the ships are silhouettes of masts and guns and ropes. Couples, singles, officers, soldiers, civilians all walk along, chatting, skirting the port, the soldiers unloading the cargoes... Groups of sailors pass us, their white uniforms stiff and pressed, their laughter echoing in my ears... Nino slides his arm around me, and we sit watching the ships, mired in our own thoughts... tense, confused by Nino's attentions, and even more by my own nervous longing.*

"Are you all right?" Nino said, touching her elbow.

She forced herself back to the present. "Your work here," she said. "Is there much unrest?"

Nino sighed. "Constant ethnic conflicts." Four years earlier, when the Treaty of Peace with Italy came into effect, he told her, this border between two military administrations — the Allies and Yugoslavs — had cut across areas that had once been Italian. As a result, those Italians were unwelcome in Yugoslavia, not allowed to speak Italian, and encouraged to leave. Those who remained were considered "communists" by those who left; and those who left were considered "fascists" or "cowards" by those who stayed. Mirroring this, the Slovenes on the Italian side of Trieste were being encouraged to leave. The result was a massive emigration of people who were dispossessed by the imposed borders. They fled to Australia, Argentina, Canada and the United States. "One of those ships — the *Australia* — left for Melbourne in April," Nino said. "An Italian diaspora." He shook his head.

"How terrible." Olivia thought about all the people who were displaced, whose homes, overnight, had become alien territory. How frightened her mother must have been, deported to Italy and left on her own in Musadino, when her father was conscripted. Wars displaced civilians, cast them into the world to make new lives for better or for worse. Her family had been lucky to own a home they could inhabit. She thought about all the Slovenians and Italians here and around Trieste, who had lived side-by-side for centuries, now forced to become adversaries.

She looked up, frowning, instinctually aware someone was watching them. Young man, round face, wide-set eyes, mole by left temple, familiar. She scanned her memory banks and immediately saw him in the Trieste train station. "Someone is following us," she said quietly.

Nino hardly moved. "Where?"

"Don't turn around. He's sitting in the far corner. He was in the station earlier."

"It's not you he's following, it's me," Nino said, shifting slightly. "Probably an ultranationalist. There are a lot of fascists here, and they view the Civil Police as anti-Italian, because of our British association."

"That must be stressful," Olivia said, glancing at the man, whose black shirt suddenly acquired new meaning.

"Come. Let's get out of here," Nino said, calling for the bill. "We'll see what he does."

They walked leisurely across the piazza to the water's edge. The man remained in the restaurant. A coincidence, Olivia thought. Perhaps he, too, had arrived on the same train and was staying in the same hotel. As she thought this, however, she was not convinced. She was highly trained to spot irregular things and people. In London, one of her main work details was to scan through photographs of terrorists and security risks. Then, she was sent to mingle in demonstrations, protests and crowds, to identify any risks.

"I'm a super recognizer," she said to Nino, explaining this "superpower," as her colleagues called it. She could never forget a face, even if she only saw it fleetingly. "I didn't realize this until I joined SOE." She laughed. "I'd assumed everyone could recall everyone."

"What an amazing skill," Nino said. "I can see how the government would be highly interested in that. We could use your skills here, given the agitators and spies." He paused. "On the surface, Trieste looks lively and calm, but beneath it all..." his voice trailed off, as Olivia pressed his arm.

"He's following us now."

They continued along the shoreline, then turned right at the Grand Canal, a waterway built in the 18th century to provide safe mooring for sea-going ships that extended from the bay inland for about 200 metres. They skirted boats bobbing against the sides. Lampposts were reflected in the water, and the outdoor restaurants were bustling. Olivia glanced back. The man still followed them.

"What does he hope to achieve?" she said.

"Probably just keeping track of me," Nino said.

"But to what end?"

Nino shrugged. They had come now to a splendid domed church, whose grand portico and six Ionic columns reminded Olivia of photographs of the Parthenon. They strolled across its front and followed the canal back to the waterfront on the opposite side. As she walked, she was intensely aware of Nino beside her, his arm brushing against hers. She was catapulted into the same excitement she'd experienced when she first met him — recognition, desire.

"Tell me about your Philip," he said. "Are you happy?"

"I knew Philip before I joined SOE," she said. "He was waiting for me when I got home." She rewound to that time, an eternity away, their reacquaintance, dates, proposal, wedding. She'd been leading a pleasant life with Philip, until that meeting in London upended her. She forced herself to think about Philip dispassionately. They were well suited, both worked, both loved reading, but... "I'm happy enough," she said.

Nino slid his arm around her waist, and drew her to him. His body was warm and inviting. How she had longed for him. She could hardly allow herself to admit it. He turned to face her, and kissed her, long and deeply, and she was back in Bari, smuggled into his room, lying naked in his arms, engulfed in love.

"Let's go to your hotel," Nino whispered, his voice returning her to Trieste on a summer evening, her heart and body open and expectant, despite Claire's niggling warning.

"What about our friend?" Olivia said, motioning to the black-clad man following.

Nino laughed. "Who cares? Let him stay out there as long as he wants."

He held her hand as they walked back to the hotel, up the stairs to her room, where the moment the door was closed, Nino crushed her in his arms. "I'm missed you," he murmured, then held her apart, his hands expertly undressing her, so she was naked and trembling before him. He slid his hands down her back and stopped at the scar.

"Both of us scarred now," he said. He kissed her, undressed, and pressed himself against her.

Olivia felt transported — that's the only way she recalled it later — transported out of herself, back to her first time with him, both shy and passionate. She had not experienced this kind of possession — because that's how it felt — since then and only with Nino, as if she had abandoned her will and submersed herself into his.

Those three days, in which they hardly left her room, she relegated to a cipher in her heart. On that bed, she pressed the watch into his hands. "This kept me safe for a while, then it kept my parents safe," she said. "But now, you need it more than me." She ignored the repeated knocks, and the notes slipped under the door, knowing they'd be from Philip. She thought best not to speak to him while she was in this state.

On the flight to London, she replayed those three days, analyzed them, tried to find a promise in them. Her cheeks burned when she recalled herself whispering, "I love you, I love you," to which he had held her tighter, and repeated the same words. At the train station, they'd said goodbye with no talk of futures. She wondered for a moment what would happen if he turned up in

London. Should she have listened to Claire, and not gone to see Nino? She had been happy enough, settled, and now had been set afloat, entirely unsure of what was coming. She made herself breathe slowly and purposefully.

Philip wasn't at the airport when she landed in London. Her parents met her instead.

"What's wrong? Where's Philip?" she asked.

"He hasn't been well," her mother said, taking her arm. "We tried calling you, but got no answer."

"The headaches?" Olivia asked. *Why didn't I answer the phone?* she thought. She returned to that room, that bed, Nino, the phone ringing incessantly. "He had some before I left, but he said they were gone."

"We'll fill you in on the way home," her mother said, and went on to tell her Philip had had a relapse a couple of days after she left, and they had taken him to the hospital where he had undergone a series of tests, and where he remained.

"I must go to him right now!" Olivia said, her eyes filling with tears.

"There's no need. It's late. The doctor will speak with you tomorrow," her mother said. "I'm sure it'll be all right."

However, it wasn't. The next day, the doctor hemmed and hawed, until he made her understand Philip had a form of brain cancer, and there was little anyone could do.

She took her husband home and nursed him for three months. When he lost his ability to speak, she encouraged him to write her notes, but soon he couldn't make out letters, he couldn't read, until at the end, he couldn't even recognize her.

15

Trieste, 1952-54

"I'm being followed," Nino told Antonio one night, while the two of them sat in a local bar. "It's probably harmless, but I thought you should know." They met a couple of times a week to unwind and strategize, and chose secluded tables at public places, given the animosity against anything British.

"Your follower is being followed too," Antonio said, laughing. "So don't worry."

How could he not worry? The violence in Trieste continued, with daily bombs exploding and injuring civilians of all ilk. It was only a matter of time before Trieste's Zone A would be handed to Italy, while Zone B would go to Yugoslavia, because now that Tito had broken with Moscow, the Americans considered Yugoslavia a cushion between east and west.

"I feel I've been living in a subterfuge," Nino said. "Can one live in a subterfuge?" He imagined dark walls, wails, whispers, everything beyond him.

Antonio laughed again. "We do what we can."

"What do you do exactly?" Bianca's voice said.

Nino turned, startled, then stood up. "Bianca! What brings you to Trieste?" He slid back a chair for her.

"Actually, I've been here for a few months," she said and looked at Antonio.

Nino stared from one to the other, puzzled, wondering if there was something between them. "Are you here with the baron? Or working?"

"No, no baron," she said, her face a rosy flush. "I was hoping to see you." She ordered a drink and smiled at them.

Eight months had passed since Olivia's visit. Seeing Bianca in front of him only heightened his longing for Olivia. Why hadn't he asked her to stay? He'd been unsure. *I'm happy enough*, she'd said of her married life. What constituted *enough* happiness? They had both declared their love, yet here he was alone. He had written her twelve impassioned letters, begging her to come to him, but had received no reply.

Bianca settled in a chair between them, easily contributing to common topics — the resistance, Rowan, her university studies. Nino watched her animated face, marvelled at her beauty once again. She was still the Bianca of memory.

After an hour or so, Antonio finished his drink and stood up. "See you both soon," he said, with a parting wave.

Nino and Bianca sat for a few moments, the silence taut between them.

Then Bianca said, "I heard she came to see you some months back."

He wondered how Bianca knew. "And?" he said.

"Are you getting back together with her?" Bianca leaned forward, her dress exposing the half-moons of her breasts.

"We were never together," Nino said slowly, "not in the way you mean."

"What do I mean?" she asked. She opened her purse and drew out a silver cigarette case, which she placed on the table between them.

"We were at war, Bianca. You, of all people, should know what that means." He pulled out a lighter. "You might have married Lorenzo if I hadn't shown up in Pistoia."

"Oh, you are mean," she said, her eyes filling with tears.

He was remorseful immediately. "I'm sorry," he said. "Let's not hurt each other any more."

She smoked her cigarette, staring at him, her eyes clear and searching. Presently, she stubbed out her cigarette. "I want to come home," she said. "I'm still your wife."

He frowned, thinking of their marriage, the impossible stalemates. He made himself return to their innocent selves, before the war, before Olivia. How simple his life had been, how uncomplicated. He sighed, for a moment imagining himself inside a tent staring out at the machinations of the world, trying to comprehend ways of living.

Bianca stared at him, her head cocked, as if trying to hear the turmoil in his mind.

He wondered why now? What had brought her here? He didn't trust her. Too much time had passed; too many people were now lost to him.

She took out a pen, wrote her phone number on the back of a coaster, and handed it to him. "Call me."

Nino said nothing as he watched her walk away, the thread of memory and shared experiences drawing him to her. She knew who he was before this war. Perhaps he could become that someone again. He pocketed the card, and later, in the barracks, held it up and stared at it. With Olivia beyond him, perhaps he and Bianca had a chance. He called her.

Over the next few months, they reunited, and by October of 1952, Bianca was pregnant. She moved back into the Pozzecco house, which she considered safer than Trieste. In June of 1953, she gave birth to a little girl, named Bella after his beloved aunt. A vague future spread before them.

Nino's final days in Trieste began on November 3, the day before the Italian national celebration of Italy's victory in WWI. Tensions were high, and when Italian nationalists tried to hoist the Italian flag over Town Hall, General Winterton refused to allow it, and sent policemen to confiscate the flag. Rumours abounded that various squads were amassing in preparation for a major fight — Tito's supporters on one side, and Italians made up of various affiliations on the other.

"We have intel of planned disturbances," Antonio said, and went undercover to a nationalist enclave, an Italian flag wrapped around his neck. He carried a forged journalist card for a far-right newspaper, and took photographs — one of which was of a man proudly displaying a home-made bomb — which he then brought back to Nino's office.

Nino spread the photos on his desk, wishing for the umpteenth time that he had Olivia's superpower. How easy it would be to identify all the troublemakers. The faces stared back, rebellious and proud. He shook his head. Why couldn't everyone live together, no matter their ethnicities?

As Antonio had warned, 3,000 people attempted to enter Zone A from Italy in organized parties, but the Allied border police refused them entry. In spite of this, large numbers succeeded and took part in the demonstrations now aimed at the British military police, who were attacked with stones and other projectiles by a large crowd. General Winterton called in Nino's unit who, outnumbered, fought off the crowd as best it could. One of Nino's colleagues was injured and another fired a warning shot in the air when surrounded by a hostile mob, the hatred of the crowd directed at Nino, as if *he* were personally responsible for the decisions being made in foreign countries behind closed doors.

Bianca called, her voice trembling. "Are you all right?"

"Don't worry about me. We're well protected here," he said, though he wasn't certain of this himself.

"I'm scared," she said. "I don't suppose you can come home."

He shook his head though she couldn't see it. She knew he couldn't leave. "Bianca, calm down. Everything is fine. How is little Bella?"

"We're waiting for the hour when you return," Bianca said dramatically.

"Give Bella kisses from me," Nino said.

That night at the barracks, everyone was on edge.

The following day, established members of the neo-Fascist Party organized a student strike, and like the previous day, began pelting stones and other missiles at the police, who again fired warning shots, to no avail. Nino felt he had been thrust into a hand-to-hand combat, until finally, the Zone Commander called out British and American troops to defuse the situation.

From early morning of the third day, the city filled with protesters, who attacked policemen and set fire to their vehicles. A mob crossed the city, assailed and destroyed the headquarters of the Independence Front, then came to Piazza Unità, where they crawled behind barricades, approached police headquarters and threw hand grenades. Shots rang out, but in the dense crowd it was impossible to see who was shooting.

British troops drew a cordon around the building and using loudspeakers, warned the crowd that if they crossed the line, they would be shot. A dead line.

One man crossed and was wounded.

Another detonated a homemade bomb that injured protesters around him, though the bomb-maker blamed the police.

A student disarmed a policeman and tried to shoot him with his own gun before being hit.

The riot ended when Piazza Unità was occupied by US troops, who interposed themselves between the protesters and the police precinct.

Six people were dead and one hundred and sixty two injured, including seventy-nine policemen.

Immediately, rumours circulated: the Italian Intelligence Agency had staged the clashes to force the Allies out; Premier Pella had financed some of the march in the city, though he may not have intended a riot; the Yugoslav secret service had paid members of a gang to create violent clashes; the Ministry of Interior had engaged local agitators, The Circle of Cavana for the Defence of Italianity, to foment the crowd.

Everyone in the Civil Police was in danger, blamed and hunted as if they had fired the shots. Newspaper articles were paper bombs hurled in their direction. It was easy to criticize the police, without recalling the hand grenades and other weapons with which they had been attacked. The ongoing injuries were many: several of Nino's colleagues were wounded, one in critical condition, one paralyzed. Another had his foot blown off. Many had concussions or suffered from anxiety.

A few weeks later, Nino was at his desk when the phone rang. "Inspector," a muffled voice said. "There's a bomb in your car." A click and the line went dead.

Nino sat, frowning, the phone still in his hand.

"What is it?" Bruno, his assistant, asked.

Nino shook his head, unwilling to believe the phone call, yet certain it was not a hoax. "Notify bomb disposal," he said, moving to the window. In the large courtyard, his 124 Spider Fiat was parked in the shade of an oak tree, with its cream convertible top, as if awaiting a seaside vacation. Nino quietly informed Bruno of the phone threat. "Make sure no news of this gets out," he said.

"But Inspector," Bruno began.

"Please. No one must know."

Bruno nodded and called the bomb disposal unit. Nothing happened immediately. Nino lingered at his desk; the sun continued to shine; the car remained under the shade of the oak tree. The only difference was the policeman stationed nearby, watching.

Later, Bruno told Nino he'd had the call traced, and it had come from their own switchboard. "Whoever warned you was in this building," he said.

Nino sighed and sat back down at his desk, not knowing in these fractured times where people stood. Antifascists, communists, neo-Nazis, Slovenes, Italians — everyone against everyone else.

Only a week before, he had had to step in when a cortège of 2,000 people filled the centre, provoking and attacking Slovene citizens, chanting anti-Slav slogans. Two workers were stabbed, and Nino quickly arrested one of the demonstrators who was pulling out a revolver. All this made him anti-Italian to the remaining Fascists, some of whom, he now realized, must be within his own unit.

Under cloak of darkness, finally the bomb disposal experts arrived, and carefully towed the car away.

"They've found it," Bruno said the following day, when the car was returned to its position in the shade. "Under the hood. It would have gone off if you'd turned on the ignition."

"How many know about this?" Nino asked.

"The bomb disposal unit, Antonio, three or four others… maximum ten. But don't worry. No one will say anything."

Nino raised his eyebrows. Ten. As well as whoever had warned him and whoever had planted the bomb, there would be others who knew. It was unnerving to think one of his own men had tried to assassinate him.

"Post a guard around the car," he told Bruno. Whenever he left the barracks from then on, he was accompanied by a security detail, and when he returned, he was driven in private, unofficial cars for his own safety. All agents had orders to move about in pairs, armed, and to avoid certain streets.

He took two weeks off and went to Pozzecco, where Bianca and Bella were overjoyed to see him. They spent happy days exploring the countryside together. Bella was almost three, fascinated with paper and books, asking questions one after the other, questions that often began with "Why…" Nino spent hours sitting on the floor in her room, reading to her, trying to explain why the sky was blue, the grass green, where water was before it came out of a faucet, why pigs made that strange oink sound, why they couldn't live in the house together forever and ever.

"We'll be leaving Trieste soon," Nino told her. "And going to Britain. You'll have to learn English," he said and smiled.

"What's English?" Bella asked.

"Like Italian only different," Nino said.

"England!" Bianca said. "But what about my family?"

"I don't want to live in this country any more," he said. He didn't tell her about the assassination attempt, or that fascists and ultra-nationalists were a constant threat.

"I'll have to speak to my father," she said. "He'll be devastated."

"It's not so far away," Nino reasoned. "You'll be able to visit them, and they you." He counted the days when he could go to England as promised by the British.

As the time grew nearer to October 26, 1954, when Italian troops would sail into the Trieste harbour, and the AMG would leave Trieste, political and ethnic tensions escalated, and now economic ones too: Triestinos felt their livelihoods threatened by the influx of Italian refugees from the communities to be ceded to the Yugoslavs.

Two weeks before the changeover, Nino and eleven others were secretly extracted and taken to Britain, where Nino expected he would be given citizenship and intelligence work, as he had been doing since he first joined SOE.

He called Bianca, and told her he was in Britain now. He'd let her know when she could join him. Nino had always wanted to live in London, and now finally, he felt he'd earned it with his dozen years of loyalty to the British. He kept apprised of news of Trieste, and heard a mass emigration was in progress: thousands of Triestinos had bought passage and sailed to Australia. One of these ships, the *Toscana*, hung out a banner which read: *"E arrivata la madre e i figli partono"* — "The mother has arrived, and her children are leaving." *Such bitterness*, Nino thought, happy to be away from it all.

However, his optimism waned as he languished in a London hotel for month after month, while paperwork was shuffled to and fro, and nothing happened. He knew no one in London now. His uncle Claudio had died in the war, and his cousins had moved to northern towns. Olivia had forsaken him. He roamed the city, often returning to the route he and Olivia had taken twelve years before, as if fate could reunite them. He didn't know where she lived, and he made no effort to find out, focusing on Bianca and little Bella. Sometimes he thought he spied Olivia standing in a shop, or seated at a park bench. A mirage of the past, a refraction of light. He waited and waited. Some of the other agents extracted with him returned to Italy disillusioned, wondering if they'd been used as pawns in this international chess game.

He persevered, wrote letters to his superiors, and finally, after six months, received a response advising him to choose relocation to Australia, America, or Canada, where he could work with that country's security agency.

At first, he wrote back to remind them of their promise to relocate him to Britain. However, he received vague responses, citing unemployment rates, and encouraging him to take up the offer of another country. They would facilitate immigration.

He held out for a while, and often at night, found himself standing in front of the Criterion as if he expected Olivia to come out, her small gloved hands reaching for him in the icy air. Swirls of steam rose here and there, the city breathing, its secrets safe, the damage hidden under new concrete, new optimism. He saw himself unanchored, rootless, like others scattered by war across cities, countries, continents. For a moment, he wondered what his life might have been without Mussolini, without the *squadristi*, without the loss of his parents, and now the loss of his country. Historical atrocities, he thought, are like inheritances passed down one generation to the next, leaving everyone wavering in the midst of everywhere and nowhere.

Eventually, despondent that things hadn't worked out, he decided to go to Canada. He wrote to Bianca to tell her his decision. He would call for her and Bella when he was settled.

The disappointments continued there too — the promised job didn't materialize.

From Canada, he contacted London once more, telling them of his unhappiness, asking to be relocated to Britain as promised.

He never heard back.

INTERMISSION

Pozzecco, Italy, 2023

In that year before my father died, I sat by his bedside day after day, night after night, while he disclosed his story, which ended here. I tried to coax more out of him, but he shook his head. The rest, he said, you know.

What I know is tainted now by all I didn't know.

Two months ago, a phone call: I have a half-sister, Nina, in the UK.

I've been at the airport café in Trieste for over an hour, waiting nervously for her. We spoke briefly on the phone, both of us perplexed by each other's existence. Although in his last days, my father spoke to me of his wartime experiences and of his unceasing love for Olivia, he never mentioned a child. And Nina, too, has stories of her mother, but none that mention me. Until now.

Finally her flight lands. Passengers emerge — businessmen and women, tourists in shorts and sandals, small children and babies in airline buggies, young men and women travelling alone or together — necks craning for loved ones or taxi drivers or whoever is meeting them. I spot her immediately and step forward.

"I'm Bella," I say. For a moment, we scrutinize each other, then we form an awkward hug. On my wrist, my father's watch keeps me safe.

"This is super odd and stressful," Nina says, and laughs as we walk to the baggage carousel. She is an attractive, tall, slender woman with clear hazel eyes. I imagine her to be similar to the Olivia my father loved.

Nina takes her suitcase off the conveyor belt, and carries it to the car. She is also like me, a year older, with the same pale complexion, the same wavy hair. The resemblance is remarkable.

We drive to Pozzecco, to the family home I still keep, though I haven't returned since 2010, not since my father's fall. In Canada, he'd say, "Aunt Isabella was right. I will die in a foreign land." He made me promise to bury his ashes in the family plot in Pozzecco.

He died a year later.

As well as my father's ashes, I've brought letters and photos from his boxes, and Nina, too, has brought a packet of letters and other memorabilia.

All week, we spend bittersweet hours, recounting each other's lives — marriages, divorces, fleeting relationships — trying to make up for the lost years, recounting what we know of our father's life, Olivia's life and Bianca's. I listen, transfixed by Olivia's story. She died earlier this year.

On Nina's last day, armed with a small trowel and my father's ashes, we walk past the last house, then onto a snippet of highway cutting through fields of alfalfa, the fresh air infused with the scent of freshly cut greens. At the edge of a field we stop at the cemetery and count twenty-nine inscriptions of my surname — Fabris — in the tombstones, dating back two centuries, some displaying glass oval photos of the dead. How beautiful these ancensors look, photos taken in their early twenties. How beautiful youth is, I think, wishing I had returned years before, when I could have asked my father questions. Nina is quiet beside me.

"These are your ancestors too," I say, and she nods.

We take turns with the trowel and dig two holes: one between my grandparents' graves, and the other on Aunt Isabella's. From my backpack, I withdraw the plastic bag.

Nina reaches for it, and buries her hand in our father's ashes, takes out a handful and kisses it, before carefully dropping it into the holes. "This is the closest I'll ever be to my father," she says, wiping the ash from her lips.

"But surely your mother spoke of him," I say.

"As a singular enchantment that lasted a lifetime, a lost love."

"My father pined for her his entire life," I say, recalling my mother's words at the end of her life. *Olivia was a spectre who haunted all our married life.*

We distribute the ashes evenly, then refill the holes with earth. *Dust to dust,* I think. *Ashes to ashes. Phoenix rising.*

"I'll ask about a headstone, or an inscription on one of the others," I say, as we walk back to the house.

"I don't think it matters really," Nina says, "unless you're thinking of family continuity. Do you intend to be buried here?"

"I've never thought about it," I say. "I don't think so. My home is in Canada." I have no children and neither does Nina. "He's the last Fabris. His name should be there."

Back at the house, we settle in to continue to examine each other's memorabilia.

"I never knew Philip, who I thought was my father," Nina says. "He died before I was born, and my mother never remarried." She reaches into her carryon bag, pulls out a manila envelope, and out spill my father's love letters. We read them together. *Olivia, my only treasure, How much I love you. If you could only imagine the happiness I feel when I hold you in my arms... You own my heart, my blood...You are ardent, beloved... Let's hope the war will end soon, so we can be united forever.... . I burn with desire for you, to hold you... I'm yours...I'm yours... I'm yours.* I'm overwhelmed by his passionate words, his powerful emotions, so unlike the reclusive, elusive father of my youth. I open my envelope of Olivia's letters, and we read these too, each of us trying to understand this intense love between them — a love that transcended life itself.

"Why were they not together?" I ask. "Why did my father marry my mother, when he was in love with someone else?"

Nina slowly draws out the last letter. "I didn't know whether to show you this or not," she says, handing it to me. "I opened it after my mother's death."

The envelope is stamped November 1952, and addressed to my father. Scrawled across it in my mother's handwriting is the word DECEASED. My breath catches in my throat.

I slide the letter out of the envelope, and hear Olivia's young voice.

Dear Nino,
I'm writing after all this time to give you some news.
Our brief time in Trieste produced turmoil in the depth of my being. I felt shipwrecked, so deep inside a quicksand, I could not

struggle out. I can't describe my unhappiness and guilt. I berated myself because I'd betrayed Philip, who died soon after my return. What saved me in the end is the birth of our daughter, Nina. You see, I'm including the announcement and her photo.

. You'll understand that I couldn't answer your letters, not in that state. Yet you were and are always in my thoughts. My warlike spirit sleeps, though yet within me roars. Is it too late for us? Or are we destined to run along parallel tracks?

I await your reply, and remain as always,
Your Olivia

I keep staring at the letter, a lump in my throat, my mother's words circling in my head: *Everyone, she said, will betray you.*

"How could she do such a thing?" I say, my loyalties fluctuating, thankful my father never knew of this unforgivable betrayal.

"They could have been together," Nina says.

I nod, thinking about my father's and Olivia's enduring love, despite distance, absence, loss.

For a moment I glimpse another dimension in which they are here in this old house, children around them, a flawless family, hearts united in perfect happiness. Only the ridges of their scars remain, those totems of survival. I want to hold on to this picture, even as it dissolves into the present, then they are gone.

Yet here I am, returned to this house, hundreds of years old, filled with the memories of a lifetime, and along with them, the embers of those consumed in the flames.

At the airport, Nina and I hold each other tight, promising to call, email, and travel to each other when possible.

Since then, I've flown to the UK, time and time again, searching for my father in libraries and books and declassified documents that slowly exposed their secrets.

Last year, in London, at The National Archives, I found my father's secret service file. Imagine how bittersweet it was to see this last letter he sent, the hopeful words, his firm belief that when his commanding officer read of his unhappiness in Canada, he would authorize my father's return to Britain, to the rightful work he had been promised.

No such thing happened, of course, but attached to his letter, I found a memo from the Home Office, which stated that if Mr. Fabris writes again, we will call him back to Britain.

How easily our lives revolve around accidental things: a gesture in the desert, a ship in the wrong sea, a train boarded at dusk, a car in the shade of an oak, a letter not sent, a letter not received.

AFTERWORD

In 2012, forty years after my father's death in 1972, my mother was moving and, in the process of downsizing, she produced some of my father's personal items. Two of these were both mysterious and interesting. The first was an "Attestato Di Benemerenza" or "Certificate of Merit" issued by Hewitt Lt. Col. Comb. No. 1 Special Force C.M.F. in Siena, on September 30, 1945. The certificate states:

From the 8th of September 1943 until June 25th, 1945, Mr. Leo Donati [my father] has collaborated with this Allied Command. During this time he served as an interpreter and radiotelegraph instructor in Special Operations training schools. Mr. Donati has always proven to be excellent in his work, and has made a valued contribution to the common Cause of Freedom.

The second was a "Certificato al Patriota" or "Certificate to the Patriot" also signed by Hewitt, and states:

In the name of the governments and peoples of the United Nations, we thank Donati Leo for having fought the enemy on the battlefields, militating in the ranks of patriots, among men who bore arms for the triumph of freedom, carrying out offensive operations, acts of sabotage, providing military intelligence.

With their courage and dedication, the Italian patriots have made a valid contribution to the liberation of Italy and to the great cause of all free men. In this new Italy, holders of this certificate will be hailed as patriots who fought for honor and freedom.

My brother Leo and I were intrigued. What was this No.1 Special Force? We knew nothing about my father's war experience, and my mother knew only that he had come to Italy with the British. She had originally believed he was Maltese. My brother and I embarked on an extensive search both in the UK and in Italy, to try to figure out what it all meant.

Although the UK National Archives began releasing Special Operations Executive related files to the public in 1998, our search was made difficult partly because in 1973, a fire had destroyed some 16 to 18 million official military personnel records, and partly because many files were continuing to be protected until after the death of individuals named in them.

What we discovered in the end is that my father had been recruited into Churchill's Secret Army, the Special Operations Executive (SOE) to fight a clandestine, guerilla war against the German Nazis and Italian Fascists.

Sadly, though we followed the traces of SOE into Italy, and read books and files in which my father was named, few of his personal experiences or movements are documented, beyond some locations and activities — he was recruited in Kenya, served in Cairo and Algiers before going to Sicily and Salerno; we know he set up a wireless station in Ischia; trained agents in wireless and cipher in La Selva, joined 291 FSS (Field Security Service) in Rutigliano, then moved to SOE headquarters in Siena in 1945. What we don't know are what his activities entailed, and how he felt about it all. My father was sworn to secrecy and he took those secrets to the grave. "We had been trained to forget," one of his colleagues said.

The Nino created here is a composite of many SOE agents whose missions are documented. My fascination with SOE grew as I read files, listened to first-person accounts in the Imperial War Museum Archive, and discovered the many young men and women who were willing to sacrifice themselves in the fight for freedom. And so, I began to create a story, imagining Nino — a young Italian man — and Olivia, a young British woman, both recruited into SOE and soon coming together.

The watch story at the beginning of this novel was inspired by a chatline post I read from a man in Italy, who was trying to identify a watch his father had received from a soldier whose life he'd spared. From the inscription on the back, several UK veterans identified the watch as one belonging to an RAF pilot.

Since that discovery in 2012, I have spent many months over different years in the Rome, Udine and Trieste archives, and the Regional Institute for the History of the Liberation Movement of Friuli Venezia Giulia (IRSML-FVG). My brother Leo spent a comparable time in the UK National Archives and The Imperial War Museum. Some of that research made it into the novel.

ACKNOWLEDGEMENTS

This book has been years in the making, and I owe thanks to many people along the way. First of all to my father, Leo Donati, for the inspiration of this novel, to my mother, Verbena Donati, for the letters between her and my father, and to my brother Leo, who went on this journey with me. Also Frank Hook, Diane Watson, Caterina Edwards and Leo Donati for first reading and thoughtful comments. To Marilyn Biderman and Laurie Grassi for editing and pointing me to the core of this novel. To all the wonderful friends I made in Italy, I thank you and value your friendships. Instrumental in their knowledge and historical experience are Silvano Subani, Pietro Petruzzi, Roberto Spazzali, Vittorio Leschi, and Marco Simic in Trieste. Thank you to Roderick Bailey for supplying a timeline of my father's SOE locations, Mario Catamo and Anna Pia De Luca for joining in the research, Rosalba Petruzzi for the extended interviews, Ornella Petruzzi and family for their friendship, to my cousins Maria-Antonietta Catamo, Patrizia Giachin, Rosalba and Giuliana Catamo, for their hospitality and affection. Many thanks to Karen Haughian for her insightful editing, love of language, and friendship. I am grateful also to Access Copyright for the research grant that allowed me time to travel to the archives and to my husband Frank for his unwavering support, love and everything else.

PERMISSIONS AND NOTES

The Massimo Salvadori quote at the beginning of the book is from Massimo Salvadori Papers, Smith College Archives, CA-MS-00118, Smith College Special Collections, Northampton, Massachusetts. https://findingaids.smith.edu/repositories/4/resources/22 Accessed November 04, 2022. Permission granted to use by his son, Clemente Salvadori.

Chapter 4: The Dante Alighieri quote "The image of her when she starts to smile dissolves within the mind and melts away, a miracle too rich and strange to hold" is from *Dante's Vita Nuova, New Edition: a Translation and an Essay*, translated by Mark Musaby.

"Rail Charge" is from *Descriptive Catalogue of Special Devices and Supplies*, The National Archives (TNA) HS 7/28

Chapter 7: Roderick Bailey quote *"Italy was an enemy country, not an enemy-occupied one, and anti-Fascist Italians who volunteered to return as secret agents faced a traitor's fate if caught. The courage of those Italians who were prepared to face the firing squads deserves recognition, and stands as an effective counter to enduring images of Italy's fighting abilities"* is from The Imperial War Museum blog, 25 June 2012. Permission granted by Roderick Bailey, February 14, 2024

Chapter 7: The poem except is from the sonnet "Alla Sera" by Ugo Foscolo (1778-1827). In public domain.

The SOE agent instructions "Security Talk," "How to Defend Yourself Against Surveillance," "Points to be Considered Your Disguise," and "Security Standing Orders" come from *Special Operations Executive Manual: How to be an Agent in Occupied Europe*. The National Archives HS 7/55 and HS 7/56. Permissions under Open Government Licence https://www.nationalarchives.gov.uk/doc/open-government-licence/version/3/

"Night & Fog Decree," was a secret order issued by Adolf Hitler on December 7, 1941, under which "persons endangering German security" in the German-occupied territories of western Europe were to be arrested and either shot or spirited away under cover of "night and fog" (that is, clandestinely) to concentration camps. (https://www.britannica.com/topic/Night-and-Fog-Decree)

The National Archives in the UK were essential to the writing of this book. My thanks to both my brother Leo and Steven Kippax who searched, scanned and sent me particular files from the archives. Invaluable also was the Imperial War Museum archive of private papers and audio interviews with former SOE agents. Along the way, I consulted many online sources, including L'archivio dei diari http://archiviodiari.org, which contains first-person accounts and diaries cataloguing experiences of Italians in WWII; *Lo Sguardo Lontano: L'Italia della Seconda Guerra mondiale nella memoria dei prigionieri di Guerra* by Erika Lorenzon https://edizionicafoscari. unive.it/media/pdf/books/978-88-6969-268-0/978-88-6969-268-0_2kJ9dXK.pdf gave me a glimpse into the mind and memories of Italian POWs; *The Labour and the Wounds* by M. Salvadori helped me piece together the Salerno landing. A variety of books and audio about SOE that mentioned my father include: Margaret Pawley's *An Obedience to Instructions: FANY with the SOE in the Mediterranean*, David Strafford's *Mission Accomplished SOE and Italy 1943–45, Goodbye Trieste* by Vladimiro Lisiani, Christopher Woods in his lecture on SOE in Italy and Harry Hargreaves in the Imperial War Museum Oral Archive. Roderick Bailey's *Target Italy: The Secret War Against Mussolini, 1940–1943* furnished colourful, first-person accounts of SOE agents in Italy, which helped me construct composite characters.

The "Question of Trieste" still lives on in the collective memory. Although the Free Territory of Trieste was divided between Yugoslavia and Italy in 1954, it wasn't until November 10, 1975 that the division became official with the signing of the Treaty of Osimo. The bitterness is ongoing, especially because Triestini feel the Italian government has abandoned the port of Trieste, favouring the one in Venice. Depending on who I spoke to, the sentiments where clear: "Trieste was returned to Italy" — a claiming of ownership, although other than the years between WWI and WWII Trieste had belonged to the Austrian-Hungarian Empire for 500 years —

or "Italy came to Trieste," implying a colonization. It makes for interesting dynamics. In Trieste, I interviewed remaining members of the AMG police force and historians including Pietro Petruzzi, Silvano Subani, Vittorio Leschi, Roberto Spazzali, and Marco Simic. Subani's *The Trieste Police from 1945 to 1954* furnished the inner workings of the AMG force. I returned to Trieste countless times, and consulted the Archivio di Stato di Trieste, as well as the Istituto regionale per la storia del movimento di liberazione nel Friuli-Venezia Giulia. A very interesting Paper, "Cold War Trieste on Screen: Memory, Identity and Mystique of a City in the Shadow of the Iron Curtain" By Katia Pizzi shed light on how film perpetuates a national collective amnesia when dealing with difficult historical events. I continue to be fascinated by my birth city and its complex autobiography.

ABOUT THE AUTHOR

Genni Gunn, author, musician and translator, has published thirteen previous books: three novels – *Solitaria, Tracing Iris* (which was made into the film *The Riverbank)* and *Thrice Upon a Time*; three story collections — *Permanent Tourists, Hungers* and *On the Road*; three poetry collections — *Faceless, Mating in Captivity* and *Accidents*; a collection of personal essays — *Tracks: Journeys in Time and Place*; the opera libretto *Alternate Visions;* and three translations. Her books have been translated into Dutch and Italian, and have been finalists for major awards: *Solitaria* for the Giller Prize; *Thrice Upon a Time* for the Commonwealth Writers' Prize; *Mating in Captivity* for the Gerald Lampert Poetry Award; *Devour Me Too* for the John Glassco Translation Prize; and *Traveling in the Gait of a Fox* for the Premio Internazionale Diego Valeri for Literary Translation. Before she turned to writing full-time, Genni toured Canada extensively with a variety of bands. She currently lives in Vancouver.